Ael Ran Through the Corridors of the *Enterprise*

into one of the cargo Transporter Rooms, pulled out her phaser and leapt up onto the platform, with a great group of her own people and Kirk's. The young man behind the Transporter console set the delay, headed for the platform himself, and they all dissolved in shimmer together.

It must have been something different about the Federation Transporters, something unsettling in their engineering—or maybe just Ael's own suppressed fear, crying out in her mind—that made her think she heard, as she dematerialized, the sound of phaser fire outside the Transporter Room, and a scream . . .

Look for STAR TREK Fiction from Pocket Books

MY ENEMY, MY ALLY

DIANE DUANE

A STAR TREK® NOVEL

POCKET BOOKS

New York   London   Toronto   Sydney   Tokyo

An *Original* Publication of POCKET BOOKS

POCKET BOOKS, a division of Simon & Schuster Inc.
1230 Avenue of the Americas, New York, NY 10020

This book is published by Pocket Books, a division of
Simon & Schuster Inc., under exclusive license from
Paramount Pictures Corporation.

ISBN: 0-671-65866-2

First Pocket Books printing July 1984

12   11   10   9   8   7

POCKET and colophon are trademarks of
Simon & Schuster Inc.

Printed in the U.S.A.

To Ael's godmother—

"—cara mihi ante alias;
    neque enim novus iste Dianae
venit amor, subitaque
    animum dulcedine movit—"

    —arma eraeque canō!

ACKNOWLEDGMENTS

Sometimes people can be of incredible assistance to you without saying a word. This is the place to acknowledge one such contributor, whose simple existence made writing this book easier: the stately, sharp-minded, wonderful Dorothy Fontana (or "D.C." Fontana, as some of you may know her). Dorothy has in the past done me many amazing and undeserved kindnesses—but the one most in my mind at this writing is one she did for you too (if you love *Star Trek*) during her stint as the series' story editor, and as writer of some of its best stories.

Dorothy knows Vulcans and Romulans better than anyone else, having been intimately involved with their creation. Much of her vision of those enigmatic and delightful species—as creatures as complex as any other hominid, not mere logic-boxes or disposable hostiles to be shot up and forgotten about—informs this work, and I delight to add that influence to the list of my glad debts to her. When we think of the power that Leonard Nimoy and Mark Lenard have brought to the Vulcans and Romulans they've played, let's not leave D.C. out of the reckoning. Without her, Spock and Sarek and both the original Romulan Commanders would have been very different people. My own feeling (and even Vulcans these days seem to admit that feelings have value) is that the Vulcans and Romulans are as marvelous as they are partly because they take after Dorothy. So—to the Lady Who *Knows*—great thanks and love.

Also:

Inside the Franklin Institute in Philadelphia (to the right of the statue of the Great God Franklin, and three flights up) is the Fels Planetarium. Hidden away in the Planetarium is a door with a very odd doorbell attached to it. And working behind that door are Don Cooke, the Director of the planetarium, and his staff—a group of people very sanely devoted to that study of the Earth's backyard that we call "astronomy."

These people share with the author the conviction that "Thataway" is not an appropriate set of course determination coordinates for the flagship of the Terran branch of Starfleet. The Fels group's eager (though sometimes bemused) assistance with some thorny astronomical questions ("George! *B* minus *V?*" "Yes, what about it? . . .") made it possible to plot not only the positions of major stars for several thousand light-years from Sol, but also the real positions and shapes of the Galactic Arms, in enough detail so that the structure of the Galaxy itself made it obvious where the Romulans and Klingons lived. To Don and all his happy people, and to their doorbell (a never-ending source of merriment), affectionate thanks, still air, and good seeing.

. . . Then none was for a party;
   Then all were for the state;
Then the great man helped the poor
   And the poor man loved the great;
Then lands were fairly portioned;
   Then spoils were fairly sold:
The Romans were like brothers
   In the brave days of old.

Now Roman is to Roman
   More hateful than a foe,
And the Tribunes beard the high,
   And the Fathers grind the low.
As we wax hot in faction,
   In battle we wax cold;
Wherefore men fight not as they fought
   In the brave days of old. . . .

                                        —Macaulay

Daisemi'in rhhaensuriuu
    meillunsiateve
        rh'e Mnhei'sahe yie ahr'en:

Mnahe afw'ein qiuu;
    rh'e hweithnaef
        mrht Heis'he ehl'ein qiuu.

(Of the chief Parts of the Ruling Passion, only this can be
truly said: Hate has a reason for everything. But love is
unreasonable.)

                    —V. Raiuhes Ahaefvthe [of Romulus
                    II], *Taer'thaiemenh*, book xviii,
                    par. 886: J. Kerasus, translator

One

Her name, to which various people had recently been appending curses, was Ael i-Mhiessan t'Rllaillieu. Her rank, in the common tongue, was *khre'Riov*: commander-general. Her serial number was a string of sixteen characters that by now she knew as well as she knew her fourth name, though they meant infinitely less to her. And considering these matters in such a fashion was at least marginally appropriate just now, for she was in a trap.

How long she would remain there, however, remained to be seen.

At the moment her patience was mostly intact, but her spirit had moved her to rattle the bars of the cage a bit. Ael propped her elbow on her desk, rested her chin on her hand, and said to her cabin's wall screen, "Hwaveyiir. Erein tr'Khaell."

The screen flicked on, and there was the Bridge, and poor Ante-centurion tr'Khaell just as he had been twenty minutes ago, still hunched over and pretending to fiddle with his communications boards. At the sight of Ael he straightened quickly and said, *"Ie, khre-'Riov?"*

Don't play the innocent with me, child, thought Ael. *You should have had that dispatch decoded and translated ten minutes ago . . . as well you know.* "Erein, eliukh hwio' 'ssuy llas-mene arredhaud'eitroi?"

She said it politely enough, but the still, low-lidded look she gave him was evidently making it plain to tr'Khaell that if Ael had to ask him again about what was holding up the dispatch's deciphering, it would go hard with him. Sweat broke out on tr'Khaell's forehead. *"Ie, khre'Riov, sed ri-thlaha nei' yhreill-ien ssuriu mnerev dhaarhiin-emenorriul—"*

Oh indeed! I know how fast that computer runs; I was building them with my own hands before you knew which end to hold a sword by. Of course, you can't just come out and tell me that the Security Officer ordered you to let her read the dispatch before I saw it, now can you? "Rhi siuren, Erein."

Poor tr'Khaell's face gave Ael the impression that t'Liun was going to take rather longer than "five minutes" to read the dispatch. Tr'Khaell looked panic-stricken. *"Khre'Riov—"* he started to say. But "Ta-'khoi," Ael said to the screen, and it flicked off.

Pitiable, Ael thought. *Truly I could feel sorry for him. But if he chooses to sell his loyalty to two commanders at once, who am I to deprive him of the joy of being caught between them? Perhaps he'll learn better.* And after a second she laughed once, softly, as much at herself as at tr'Khaell. *Perhaps the Galaxy will stop rotating.*

She pushed away from the desk and leaned back in her comfortable chair, considering with calm irony how little her surroundings looked like the cage they actually were. *They truly think they've deceived me,* she thought, amused and contemptuous, looking around at the spare luxury of her command cabin. *Pad the kennel with velvets, they say to each other; feed the old thrai on fat flesh and blood wine, put her in command of a fleet, and she won't notice that the only ones who pay any attention to her orders are the ones stuck inside the bars with her.* Ael's lips curled slightly upward at the thought. *"Susse-thrai"* had been the name bestowed upon her, half in anger, half in affection, by her old crew on *Bloodwing;* the keen-nosed, cranky, wily old she-beast, never less dangerous than when you thought her defenseless, and always growing new teeth far back in her throat to replace the old ones broken in biting out the last foe's heart. You might cage a thrai, you might poke it through the bars and laugh; but it would find a way to be avenged for the insult. It would break out and tear off your leg and eat it before your face—or run away and wait till you had died of old age, then come back and excrete on your grave.

Then Ael frowned at herself, annoyed. "Crude," she said to the room, eyes flicking up to the ceiling-corner by the bed as she wondered whether t'Liun had managed to bug the place already since last week. "I grow crude, as they do." *Chew on that, you vacuum-headed creature, and wonder what it means,* thought Ael, getting up to pace her cage.

The most annoying part was that it was true. That courtesy, honor, noble behavior should be cast aside by the young, perceived as a useless hindrance to expediency, was bad enough. But that she should begin to sink to their level herself, descending into brute-beast metaphors and savagery instead of the straightforward dealing that had been tradition for four thousand years

3

of civilization—that was galling. *I will not fight them with their own methods,* Ael thought. *That is the surest way to become them. I will come by my victories honestly. And as for Sunseed—*

She stopped in front of another of her cabin's luxuries, one better than private 'fresher or sleeping silks or key lighting. Beyond the wide port, space yawned black, with stars burning in it—stars that at *Cuirass*'s present sublight speed hung quite still, apparently going nowhere. *As I am,* she thought, but the thought was reflex, and untrue. Ael grimaced again and leaned her forehead against the cool clearsteel.

In one way, she had no one to blame for where she was right now but herself. When she had heard about the Sunseed project based at Levaeri V, and had begun to realize what it could do to Rihannsu civilization if fully implemented, shock and horror had stung her into swift action. She had taken leave from *Bloodwing* and gone home to ch'Rihan to lobby against the project—openly speaking out against it in the Senate, and privately making the rounds of her old political cronies, all those old warrior-Senators and those few comrades in the Praetorate who owed her favors. However, Ael had not realized the extent to which the old warriors were being outweighed, or in some cases subverted or cowed, by the young ones—the hot-blooded children who wanted everything right now, who wanted the easy, swift victories that the completion of Sunseed would bring them. Honorless victories, against helpless foes; but the fierce young voices now rising in the Senate cared nothing about that. They wanted safety, security, a world without threats, a universe in which they could swoop down on defenseless ships or planets and take what they wanted.

Thieves, Ael thought. *They have no desire to be*

warriors, fighting worthy foes for what they want, and winning or losing according to their merits. They want to be robbers, like our accursed allies the Klingons. Raiders, who stab in the back and loot men's corpses, or worlds. And as for those of us who remember an older way, a better way, they wait for us to die. Or in some cases, they hurry us along. . . .

She pushed herself away from the cool metal of the port, breathed out once. Somewhere among those stars, out in that blackness, ch'Ríhan and ch'Havran hung, circling one another majestically in the year's slow dance around amber Eisn; two green-golden gems, cloud-streaked, seagirt, burning fair. But she would probably never walk under those clouds again, or beside those seas, as a result of that last visit to the sigil-hung halls of the Senate. The young powers in the High Command, suspicious of Ael from the first, now knew for sure that she was opposed to them, and their reaction to her opposition had been swift and thorough. They dared not exile her or murder her, not openly; she was after all a war hero many times over, guilty of no real crime. Instead they had "honored" her, having Ael sent out on a long tour of duty, into what was ostensibly a post of high command and great peril. Command she wielded, but with eyes watching her, spies of various younger Senators and Praetors. And as for peril . . . it came rarely, but fatally, here in the Outmarches—the deadly peaceful space that the power surrounding most of it called the Romulan Neutral Zone.

Names, Ael thought with mild irony, *names . . . How little they have to do with the truth, sometimes.* The great cordon of space arbitrarily thrown about Eisn was hardly neutral. At best it was a vast dark hiding-place into which ships of both sides occasionally dodged,

5

preparing for intelligence-gathering forays on the un-friendly neighbor. As for "Romulan"—After first hearing the word in Federation Basic, rather than by universal translator, Ael had become curious to understand the name the Empire's old foes had given her world, and had done some research into it. She had been distastefully fascinated to find the word's meaning rooted in some weird Terran story of twin brothers abandoned in the wild, and there discovered and given suck by a brute beast rather like a thrai. It would take a Terran to think of something so bizarre.

But whether one called Eisn's paired worlds ch'Rí-han and ch'Havran or Romulus and Remus, Ael knew she was unlikely to ever walk either of them again. *Never again to walk through Airissuin's purple meads,* she thought, gazing out at the starry darkness. *Never to see that some loved one had hung up the name-flag for me; never to climb Eilairiv and look down on the land my mothers and fathers worked for a thousand years, the lands we held with the plowshare and the sword . . .* For the angry young voices in the Senate, Mrian and Hei and Llaaseil and the rest, had put her safely out of their way; and here, while they held power, she would stay. They would wait and let time do what their lack of courage or some poor tattered rag of honor forbade them.

Accidents happened in the Neutral Zone, after all. Ships far from maintenance suddenly came to grief. That was likely enough, in this poor secondhand War-bird with which they'd saddled her, this flying break-down looking for a place to happen. Crews rebelled against discipline, mutinied, on long hauls . . . and that was likely too, considering the reprehensible lot of rejects and incompetents with whom she was trapped here. Ael thought longingly of her own crew of *Bloodwing;* fierce, dogged folk tried in a hundred battles and faithful to her . . . but that faithfulness was why her enemies in the High Command had had her transferred from *Bloodwing* in the first place. A crew that could not be bought, the taste of the old loyalty, made them nervous. It was a question how long even Tafv, so far innocent of the Senate's suspicion, would be able to hold on to them. And it was no use thinking about them in any case. She was stuck with the ship's complement of *Cuirass,* half of them in the pay of the other half or of her enemies in Command, nearly all of them hating nearly all the others, and all of them definitely hating *her;* they knew perfectly well why they'd been cut orders for so long a tour.

And if those problems failed to wear her down to suicide, or kill her outright, there were others that surely would. Those problems had names like *Intrepid* . . . *Inaieu* . . . *Constellation.* If Ael survived too long, she knew she would be ordered into the path of one of them. Honor would require her to obey her orders; and since *Cuirass* was alone and far, far from support, honor would eventually be the death of her. Her unfriends in the Senate would find the irony delightful.

Well, Ael thought. *We shall see.* She shifted her eyes again to the desk screen and reread the letter coolly burning there, blue against the black.

FROM THE COMMANDER TAFV EI-LEINARRH TR'RLLAILLIEU, SET IN AUTHORITY OVER IMPERIAL VESSEL *BLOODWING,* TO THE RIGHT NOBLE COMMANDER-GENERAL AEL T'RLLAILLIEU, SET IN AUTHORITY OVER IMPERIAL CRUISER *CUIRASS,* RESPECTFUL GREETING. IF MATTERS ARE WELL WITH YOU, THEN THEY ARE WELL WITH ME ALSO. HONORED MOTHER, I HEAR WITH SOME

MY ENEMY, MY ALLY

REGRET OF YOUR RECENT ASSIGNMENT TO THE OUTMARCHES, IN THAT I SHALL FOR SOME TIME BE DENIED THE PRIVILEGE OF PRESENTING MY DUTY TO YOU IN PERSON. BUT WE MUST ALL BOW WILLINGLY TO THOSE DUTIES EVEN HIGHER THAN FAMILY TIES WHICH THE IMPERIUM REQUIRES OF US; AS I KNOW YOU DO.

PATROLS IN THIS AREA REMAIN QUIET, AS MIGHT BE EXPECTED, OUR PRESENTLY-ASSIGNED CORRIDOR BEING SO FAR FROM ANY ENEMY (OR COME TO THINK OF IT, ANY FRIENDLY) ACTIVITY. HIGH COMMAND TELLS US LITTLE OR NOTHING ABOUT HAPPENINGS IN THE OUTMARCH QUADRANTS WHICH YOU ARE PATROLLING—SECURITY UNDERSTANDABLY BEING WHAT IT IS—BUT I CAN ONLY HOPE THAT THIS FINDS YOU SAFE, OR BETTER STILL, VICTORIOUS IN SOME SKIRMISH WHICH HAS LEFT OUR ENEMIES SMARTING.

MASTER ENGINEER TR'KEIRIANH HAS FINALLY MANAGED TO DISCOVER THE SOURCE OF THAT PECULIARITY IN THE WARP DRIVE THAT KEPT TROUBLING US DURING *BLOODWING'S* LAST TOUR OF THE MARCHES NEAR THE HA-SUIWEN STARS. EVIDENTLY ONE OF THE MULTISTATE EQUIVOCATOR CRYSTALS WAS AT FAULT, THE CRYSTAL HAVING DEVELOPED A FLUID-STRESS FAULT THAT MALFUNCTIONED ONLY DURING MEGA-GAUSS MAGNETIC FIELD VARIATIONS OF THE KIND THAT OCCUR DURING HIGH WARP SPEEDS—AND NEVER IN THE TESTING CYCLE, WHICH IS WHY WE COULD NOT FIND THE SOURCE OF THE PROBLEM BEFORE. I HAVE RECOMMENDED TR'KEIRIANH FOR A MINOR COMMENDATION. MEANWHILE, OTHER MATTERS ABOARD SHIP REMAIN SO UNREMARKABLE AND SO MUCH THE SAME AS WHEN I LAST WROTE YOU THAT THERE IS LITTLE USE IN CONTINUING THIS. I WILL CLOSE SAYING THAT VARIOUS OF *BLOODWING'S* CREW HAVE ASKED ME TO OFFER THEIR OLD COM-

MANDER THEIR RESPECTS, WHICH NOW I DO, ALONG WITH MY OWN. THE POWERS LOOK ON YOU WITH FAVOR. THIS BY MY HAND, THE ONE HUNDRED EIGHTEENTH SHIP'S DAY SINCE *BLOODWING'S* DEPARTURE FROM CH'RÍHAN, THE EIGHTY-NINTH DAY OF MY COMMAND. TR'RLLAILLIEU. LIFE TO THE IMPERIUM.

Ael smiled at the letter, a smile it was well that none of *Cuirass*'s crew could see. Such a bland and uncommunicative missive was hardly in Tafv's style. But it indicated that he knew as well as Ael what would happen to the letter when Ael's ship received it. It would be read by tr'Khaell in Communications, passed on to Security Officer t'Liun, who had tr'Khaell so firmly under her thumb, and avidly read for any possible sign of secret messages or disaffection—then put through cryptanalysis as well by t'Liun's tool tr'Iawaain down in Data Processing. Much good it would do them; Tafv was not fool enough to put what he had to say in any code they would be able to break.

Oh, t'Liun would find *something* in cryptanalysis, to be sure. A stiff and elegant multiple-variable code, just complex enough to be realistic and careless enough to be breakable after a goodly period of head-beating. She would find a message that said, PLAN FAILED, APPEALS TO PRAETORATE UNSUCCESSFUL; FURTHER ATTEMPTS REFUSED. Which, being exactly what t'Liun (and the High Command people who paid her) wanted to hear, would quiet them for a little while. Until it was too late, at least.

Ael leaned back and stretched. Tafv's mention of repairs to the warp drive told her that he and Giellun tr'Keirianh, Powers bless both their twisty minds, had finally succeeded in attaching those stealthily-acquired

Klingon gunnery augmentation circuits to *Bloodwing*'s phasers—an addition that would give the valiant old ship three times a Warbird's usual firepower. Ael did not care for the Klingon ships that the Empire had been buying lately; their graceless design was offensive to her, and their workmanship was usually hasty and shoddy. But though Klingons might be abysmal ship-wrights, they did know how to build guns. And though the adaptation to *Bloodwing*'s phasers had bid fair to take forever, it had also been absolutely necessary for the success of their plan.

As for the rest of the letter, Tafv had made it plain to Ael that he was close, and ready, and waiting on her word. He had also told her plainly, by saying nothing, that his communications were being monitored too; that Command had refused to allow him details on Ael's present location, which he evidently knew only by virtue of the few family spies still buried in Command Communications; that there was some expectation of the enemy in the quadrant to which Ael had been sent; and that her old crew was willing and ready to enact the plan which she and Tafv had been quietly concocting since the "honor guard" had come to escort Ael off *Bloodwing* to her new command on *Cuirass*.

Ael was quite satisfied. There was only one more thing she lacked, one element missing. She had spent a good deal of money during that last trip to ch'Ríhan, attempting to encourage its presence. Now she had merely to wait, and keep good hope, until time or Federation policy produced it. And once it did . . .

The screen chimed quietly. "Ta'rhae," she said, turning toward it from the port.

Tr'Khaell appeared on the screen again, his sweat still in evidence. *"Khre'Riov, na-hwi reh eliu arred-hau'ven—"*

Four and a half minutes, Ael thought, amused. *T'Liun's reading speed is improving. Or tr'Khaell's shouting is.* "Hnafiv 'rau, Erein."

The man had no control of his face at all; the flicker of his eyes told Ael that there was something worth hearing in this message indeed, something he had been hoping she would order him to read aloud. *"Hilain na nfaaistur ll' efwrohin galae—"*

"Ie, ie," Ael said, sitting down at her desk again, and waving a hand at him to go on. News of the rather belated arrival in this quadrant of her fleet, such as it was, interested her hardly at all. *Wretched used Klingon ships that they are, they should only have been eaten by a black hole on the way in.* "Hre va?"

"Lai hra'galae na hilain, khre'Riov. Mrei kha rhaau-khir Lloannen'galae . . . te ssiun bhveinu hir' Enter-prise *khina."*

Ael carefully did not stir in her chair and kept most strict guard over her face . . . slowly permitting one eyebrow to go up, no more. "Rhe've," she said, nodding casually and calmly as if this news was some-thing she might have expected—as if her whole mind was not one great blaze of angry, frightened delight. *So soon! So soon!* "Rhe'. Khru va, Erein?"

"Au'e, khre'Riov. Irh' hvannen nio essaea Lloann-'mrahel virrir—"

She waved the hand at tr'Khaell again; the details and the names of the other ships in the new Federation patrol group could wait for her in the computer until her "morning" shift. "Lhiu hrao na awaenndraevha, Erein. Ta'khoi." And the screen went out.

Then, only then, did Ael allow herself to rock back in the chair, and take a good long breath, and let it out again . . . and smile once more, a small tight smile that would have disquieted anyone who saw it. *So soon,* she thought. *But I'm glad. . . . O my enemy, see how well the Powers have dealt with both of us. For here at last may be an opportunity for us to settle an old, old score. . . .*

Ael sat up straight and pulled the keypad of her terminal toward her. She got rid of Tafv's letter, then said the several passwords that separated her small cabin computer from the ship's large one for independent work, and started calling up various private files—maps of this quadrant, and neighboring ones. "Ie rha," she said as she set to work—speaking aloud in sheer angry relish, and (for the moment) with utter disregard to what t'Liun might hear. "Rha'siu hlun vr'*Enterprise*, irrhaimehn rha'sien Kirk. . . ."

12

Two

"Captain's personal log, stardate 0304.6:

"Nothing to report but still more hydrogen ion-flux measurements in the phi Trianguli corridor. Entirely too many ion-flux measurements, according to Mr. Chekov, who has declared to the Bridge at large that his mother didn't raise him to compile weather reports. (Must remember to ask him why not, since meteorology has to have been invented in Russia, like everything else.)

"Mr. Spock is 'fascinated' (so what else is new?) by the gradual increase in the number and severity of ion storms in this part of the Galaxy. He will lecture comprehensively and at a moment's notice on the importance of our findings as they relate to the problem—the implications of a shift in the stellar wind for the sector's interstellar 'ecology,' the potentially disastrous effects of such a shift on interplanetary shipping and on the economies of worlds situated along the shipping lanes, etc., etc., etc. However, even Spock has admitted to me privately that he looks forward to solving this problem and moving on to something a little more challenging. His Captain agrees with him. His Captain is bored stiff. My mother didn't raise *me* to compile weather reports, either.

"However, it's an ill wind that blows nobody good . . . or however that goes. At least things have been quiet around here.

"Now why is it that, when I say that, my hands begin to sweat? . . . "

"Jim?"

"Not now, Bones."

"Medical matter, Captain."

James T. Kirk looked up from the 4D chesscube at his Chief Surgeon. "What is it?"

"If you make that move," said Dr. McCoy, "you'll live to regret it."

"Doctor," said the calm voice from across the chesscubic, "kibitzing is as annoying to the victims in chess as it is in medicine . . . which is doubtless why you practice it so assiduously."

"Oh, stick it in your ear, Spock," said McCoy, peering over Jim's shoulder to get a better view of the cubic. "No, I take that back: in your case it would only make matters worse."

"Doctor—"

"No, Spock, it's all right," Jim said. "This'll be a lesson to me, Bones. Look at this mess."

Bones looked, and Jim took the opportunity to stretch and gaze around the great Recreation deck of the *Enterprise*. The place was lively as usual with crewpeople eating and drinking and talking and playing games and socializing and generally goofing off. There was a merrily homicidal game of water polo taking place in the main pool: amphibians against drylanders, Jim judged, as he saw Amekentra from Dietary break surface in a glittering, green-scaled arc, tackle poor Ensign London amidships, and drag Robbie under with her in a flash and splash of water. Closer to Jim, in the middle of the room, a quieter but equally deadly game of contract bridge was going on: a Terran-looking male and a short round Tellarite lady sat frowning at their cards, while the broad-shouldered Elaasian member of the foursome peered at his hand, and his partner, a gossamer-haired Andorian, watched him with cool interest and waited for him to bid. Nearest to Jim, some forty or fifty yards away, a Sulamid crewman leaned against the baby grand, with a drink held coiled in one violet tentacle, and most of his other tendrils and tentacles draped gracefully over the Steinway. Various of those tentacles wreathed gently, keeping time, and the Sulamid's eight stalked eyes gazed off into various distances, as the pianist—someone in Fleet nursing whites—wove her way through the sweetly melancholy complexities of a Chopin nocturne. That was appropriate enough, for it was "evening" for Jim, and for about a fourth of the *Enterprise*'s crew; delta shift was about to go on duty, alpha shift's day was drawing to a quiet close, and all was right with the world.

Except here, Jim thought, glancing at the chesscubic again, and then, with wry resignation, back up at Spock. The Vulcan sat in his characteristic chess-pose, leaning on his elbows, hands folded, the first two fingers steepled—gazing back at Jim with an expression of carefully veiled compassion, and with what Jim's

15

practiced eye identified as the slightest trace of mischievous enjoyment.

Jim became aware of another presence at his side, to the left. He looked up and found Harb Tanzer, the Chief of Recreation, standing there—a short, stocky, silver-haired man with eyes that usually crinkled at the corners with laughter . . . as, at the sight of the chess-cubic, they were beginning to do now. Jim was not amused. "Mister," he said to Harb, "you are in deep trouble."

"Why, Captain? Something wrong with the cube?"

With some difficulty Jim restrained himself from groaning out loud, for the whole thing was his own fault. He had mentioned to Harb some time back that 3D chess, much as he loved it, had been getting a little boring. Harb had gone quietly away to talk to Moira, the master Games computer, and shortly thereafter had presented the ship's company with something new—4D chess. Spock had objected mildly to the name, for hyperspace, not time, was the true fourth dimension. But the Vulcan's objections were swiftly lost in fascination with the new variant.

Harb had completely done away with the form of the old triple-level chessboard, replacing it with a hologram-style stack of force-field cubes, eight on a side, in which the pieces were "embedded" during play. The cubic was fully rotatable in yaw, pitch and roll; if desired, parts of it could be enlarged for closer examination, or for tournament play. The pieces themselves (the only physical element of the set) were handled by an exquisitely precise transporter system, with a set of controls on each player's side of the gametable. This innovation effectively eliminated "you-touched-it, you-have-to-move-it" arguments, illegal "behind-the-back" moving, and other such minor excitements. Not that either of the *Enterprise*'s premier chess players would ever have had recourse to cheating. But the new design opened up possibilities as well as removing them: and it was one of these newer variations that Spock was presently inflicting on the Captain.

Harb had programmed the table's games computer so that a player could vanish desired pieces from the cubic, for a period of his own determination, and have them reappear later—if desired, in any other spot made possible by a legal move. Pieces "timed out" in this fashion could appear behind the other player's lines and wreak havoc there. But this innovation had not merely expanded the usual course of play. It had also completely changed the paradigm in which chess was usually played. Suddenly the game was no longer about anticipating the opponent's moves and thwarting them —or not merely about that. It was now also a matter of anticipating a whole strategy from the very start: a matter of estimating with great accuracy where an opponent would be in fifteen or twenty moves, and getting one's pieces there to ambush him—while also fooling the opponent as to where one's own weak and strong areas would be at that time.

As a result, Jim now found himself playing with a deadly seriousness he hadn't been able to bring to the game in a long while . . . for everything was changed. All the strategies he had laboriously worked out over the years for play against Spock—strategies that had finally begun working—were now suddenly useless. And worse than that, Spock was still walking all over Jim in the game—which said uncomfortable things to the Captain of the *Enterprise* about his ability to tell what his First Officer was thinking. Once again Jim found himself wondering whether Spock's dual heritage was giving him an unfair advantage . . . whether the

Vulcan half of him, so coolly analytical, was better at understanding his own human half, and thereby, the actions of the full humans around him.

Though Jim remembered McCoy, some time back, warning him against such generalizations: "As if you could chop a mind in half like an apple," Bones had said, derisive and amused. "He's one whole being—a *Spock*—and the sooner you armchair shrinks get that through your heads, the better you'll be able to deal with him." *Still* . . . Jim thought. But it was late for theorizing, and at any rate no amount of it was going to get him out of this one. He tilted his head back to look at Harb Tanzer. "Couldn't you have stuck to shuffleboard?" he said.

"I can see where it might have been wiser," said Harb, looking down at the cubic.

Regretfully, Jim had to agree with him. He had tried one of his favorite offenses from 3D chess—an all-out, "scream-and-leap" offensive opening that in the past had occasionally succeeded in rattling Spock slightly with its sheer bloody-minded enthusiasm. Unfortunately, mere howling aggressiveness was of no use in this game, not even briefly. Spock had merely sat in calm interest, watching Jim's game unfold, responding calmly to Jim's screams and leaps. Spock had moved rather conservatively, moving first one queen and then his second into mildly threatening mid-level positions, counterbalancing Jim's double-queen pin on the king's level (four, at the time) from levels three and eight. Jim had run merrily amok for a while, inexorably pushing Spock into what looked like a wholly defensive position in the center-cubic upper levels, then timing out both his rooks, one of his knights, and several pawns in rapid succession, in what was meant to be a nettling display of security.

That was when Spock had lifted his head from a long scowl at the board, and very, very slowly put that one eyebrow up. Jim had stared back at Spock, entirely cheerful, not saying anything but mentally daring him to do his worst.

He had. Jim's half of the cubic now looked like the Klingon half of the Battle of Organia at the end of the fourth quarter . . . not that his pieces even held as much as half the cubic anymore. Spock had not even needed to wait for his own timed-out pieces to return. Not that there were many of them; Jim now suspected that Spock had purposely restrained himself there, to keep Jim from feeling too bad—or perhaps to keep the win from looking too much like mindreading. Jim, looking in great annoyance at his poor king penned up in the upper levels with queens above and below him—in Spock's silent demonstration of his own brand of poetic justice—considered that he would have preferred mindreading to the implication that Spock could anticipate him this completely *without* it. The situation elsewhere was no better. Spock's king was redoubtably fenced around by knights and rooks; his bishops were so perfectly positioned in the center cubic that they controlled it practically by themselves. And Jim had nothing available with which to attack them even if they had been more poorly positioned. Both his queens were gone now, and almost everything else was timed out in preparation for what was supposed to have been the closing of a cunning and totally unpredictable trap. . . .

When will I learn, Jim thought. He looked up over his shoulder. "What do you think?" he said to Harb.

"Sir," said the Chief of Recreation, "I think you've got a problem."

"Thank you very much, Mr. Tanzer. *I* think that as

19

soon as I finish this, you're being transferred to Hydroponics. Head first. Bones?"

McCoy looked down at the cubic. "As it stands now, mate in six."

"Five," Spock said, in that cool dry voice in which no one was meant to hear arrogance, or kindness either.

Jim stared calmly into the cubic, trying to look deeply thoughtful. He was actually hoping for a broken glass somewhere in the room, a call from the Bridge, a red alert—any distraction that would get him out of this mess before it proceeded to its inevitable conclusion. But nothing happened. Finally he sighed, and looked up at Spock with as much good grace as he could muster, reaching for the "resign" touchpad. "I have to admit, Mr. Spock—"

Bones laid a hand on Jim's arm, stopping his gesture. "Wait a minute, Jim. Would you mind if I played this one out for practice? Would you, Spock?"

Jim looked up at McCoy in mild surprise, then across at his First Officer. Spock's eyes widened in carefully simulated concern. "I would think," he said to Jim, "that such a sudden impulse toward masochism would be the symptom of some deeper disorder—"

"Oh, come on, Spock. Just to keep my hand in."

"Doctor," Spock said almost pityingly, having caught Jim's slight nod, "you could hardly keep your hand in the cubic unless you had first *put* it in—and despite our many past differences, I must say I cannot recommend such a course of action."

"I take it that means yes." Bones slipped into Jim's seat as the Captain stood, smiling, and got out of it.

"I believe the appropriate phrase is 'Be my guest,'" said Spock, leaning forward to study the cubic with renewed interest.

McCoy settled down and gazed into the cubic too. "All right, where's the damn memory on this—Oh," he said as Harb reached down over his shoulder to touch the retrieval control, bringing up the small shielded "status" hologram with its readouts of locations of timed-out pieces and their schedules for reappearance.

"You understand, Doctor," Spock said politely, glancing up, "that for each piece whose status you now alter, you must forfeit a real-time move."

"Mmmhmm," McCoy said, not looking up. Spock lifted one eyebrow and went back to his own examination of the cubic. Jim exchanged a bemused glance, over McCoy's head, with Harb, then became aware of movement off to the right of him, and glanced that way. The pianist, finished with her Chopin, was making her way toward them. It was Lia Burke, one of the newer additions to McCoy's staff; a whip-slender woman with dark curly hair, a cheerful grin, and the devil in her eyes. "You still here, Commander?" Jim said, bantering, as she joined him and Harb beside McCoy. "You were recalled from leave for that last mission of ours; I thought you were going to go pick up your vacation where you left off. . . ."

She shrugged, a quick amused gesture. "Sir, I thought so too. Problem is, I find that working on the *Enterprise* is more fun than taking a vacation anywhere else." That made Jim grin back at her appreciatively; he felt the same way. "Besides, Dr. McCoy says he can use another nurse on staff for a while. Chris Chapel has her hands full with her doctoral dissertation right now . . . so an extra pair of hands is a help. And even for two nurses, there's still plenty to do down there." She peered over McCoy's shoulder at the cubic. "Looks like there's shortly going to be more to do than usual, though. He always gives us more work when he's upset. . . ."

"Lia," McCoy said, delicately touching one cubic-control surface after another and still not looking up, "hush up before I put r-levosulamine in your coffee and give you cerebral hemorrhoids." Lia hushed, though not without a look of tolerant merriment at Jim and Harb. ". . . Spock? Ready for you." McCoy looked across at the Vulcan. "Three moves."

"Very well," Spock said, and touched several controls one after another, taking his three permitted moves in rapid succession. First one of his bishops, then the second, moved out of their positions in the center cubic—not entirely relinquishing control of it, but drawing the noose around Jim's king just a bit tighter; and the third piece, a knight, came in and sat on the one spot on the seventh level that Jim had been praying Spock would overlook. "Check," Spock said calmly, tilting his head just a bit and gazing into the cubic as if to celebrate the lovely knight fork.

Jim groaned softly. Without a word Spock was commenting on what happened to people who set traps for their opponents and then purposely waved the fact in their opponents' faces. "Your move, Doctor," Spock said to Bones, with the same mostly-hidden sympathy he had shown Jim.

McCoy scowled at the control pad, touched one section. One of Jim's few remaining useful pieces, a knight, slipped up from the second level where it had been protecting several pawns on a diagonal from Spock's white-cube bishop. It took the secondary knight option, three levels straight up and one cube over, blocking the check and threatening one of Spock's queens.

"A valiant choice, Doctor," Spock said. "But I would not have expected you to make a move that would so prolong the game's suffering." He reached out a hand to his pad. "The response is obvious, though unfortunately rather crude. Queen to level eight queen's-rook three, resuming the pin and now threatening your knight on the vertical diagonal."

Spock rested his head on his folded hands again. "Your move," he said calmly—

—and all hell broke loose in the cubic. One of Jim's rooks appeared in the cube occupied by Spock's white-cube bishop, sacrificing itself in their mutual annihilation. The other rook appeared in the cube to which Spock's first queen had moved, and took her out too.

Both Spock's eyebrows went straight up. "'Kamikaze' chess, Doctor?" he said, sounding—to Jim's ears—as if he were fighting down astonishment very hard. "Marginally effective. But inelegant—"

"Mr. Spock," Bones said, gazing into the cubic, "generally I prefer to work with protoplasers and light-scalpels. But for some things—knives are still the best."

A pawn timed back in and blew up Spock's second queen, the only piece on the board left in a really threatening position. And two other pawns timed in—one in the unprotected eighth file of Spock's ground level, one in the eighth file of his eighth level—then both sizzled with transporter effect, and with charming simultaneity turned into queens.

Very slowly, Spock reached out and touched a control on his side of the cubic. Black's king fell over onto its side, fizzed briefly bright with transporter effect, and vanished.

Jim and Harb and Lia all stared.

Spock's absolute expressionlessness was more eloquent than any words. McCoy gazed into the cubic, lifted his arms to stretch, and as he did so, said very softly, as if to himself, "So. One whole being . . ." He stood up. "Thank you, Mr. Spock," he said, nodding gravely at the Vulcan. Then McCoy turned away and grinned at Jim, leaning slightly toward him. "You really must stop underestimating yourself," Bones said in Jim's ear. And the Chief Surgeon straightened, and strolled off toward the Rec Deck doors, whistling.

The intercom whistled as he went, a note a third higher than McCoy's. *"Bridge to Captain Kirk,"* said Uhura's voice out of the air.

Jim simply looked at Harb Tanzer for a moment before answering. Harb shook his head at Jim and went off across the Rec deck to find something to tend to. Lia Burke, staring in astonished delight after McCoy, realized what she was doing, excused herself, and strode off in the Doctor's wake. "Yes, Uhura?" Jim said.

"Sir, we have a dispatch in from Starfleet that needs your command ciphers for decoding. Do you want it in your quarters?"

"No, that's all right. I'll be up on the Bridge in a few minutes."

"Yes, Captain. Bridge out."

Jim just looked down at the cubic for a moment, then across at Spock. The Vulcan, somewhat recovered, quirked one eyebrow at his Captain. "Jim," Spock said, "perhaps you will wish to make a note of the date and time. I admit to astonishment."

"I admit to a damn sight more," Jim said softly. "Spock, did I miss something?"

The soul of tact as always, Spock hesitated. "Various

opportunities—yes. Yet the winner of a game does so no less than the loser. And where one mind may find a way out of a position, another may see no plain way—yet be no worse a player for it. The motivations and patterns within a living mind, the endless diversity of the ways those patterns deal with new occurrences—and one's success at understanding those patterns, or not—those are what make play delightful. Not expertise alone. One of your Terran artists said it: 'There is hope in honest error—none in the icy perfection of the mere stylist.'"

Jim heard the message, and smiled, knowing better than to thank Spock openly for it. "True. But I made enough 'honest errors' in that game to last me a month; and specifically, I never even saw the possibility of McCoy's whole final scenario. I *should* have seen it. Was the table recording? I want to take that endgame apart later, with you looking over my shoulder and pointing out my mistakes."

"Certainly, Captain. The analysis will be beneficial to your play."

Jim nodded. "At this point, I suspect anything would be an improvement." And he smiled again, this time at catching the amused flicker of eyes that said Spock appreciated not having any such statement made about *his* own game. "Come on, Mr. Spock—let's see what miracle Fleet wants us to pull off today."

"The question is," said Uhura, gazing down at the communications station's screen, "what's really going on out there? You don't send such a collection of firepower—along with a destroyer, no less—all out together on a routine patrol. Who does Fleet think it's fooling?"

Those were fair questions, for which Jim had no answer. He shook his head and looked down at the dispatch burning on Uhura's screen. To James T. Kirk, commanding NCC 1701 *Enterprise,* blah, blah, blah . . .

. . . YOU ARE ORDERED TO ABORT PRESENT MISSION (REF: DISPATCH SFCC/T 121440309 DATED SD 0112.0) AND PROCEED WITH ALL DUE HASTE TO GALLONG 177D 48.210M/ GALLAT +6D 14.335M/DISTARBGALCORE 24015 L.Y. FOR RENDEZVOUS IN PHI TRIANGULI OUTER PATROL CORRIDOR WITH SHIPS OF TASK FORCE ENUMERATED BELOW. ONCE ASSEMBLED YOU WILL TAKE COMMAND OF THE TASK FORCE AND PROCEED IN GOOD ORDER TO THE SECTOR DEFINED BY A HUNDRED-PARSEC SPHERI-CAL RADIUS SURROUNDING Σ285 TRIANGULI/NR 551744, THERE TO PERFORM STANDARD PATROL MANEUVERS OF STRIN-GENCY AND SECURITY LEVELS CONSONANT WITH THE STRATE-GIC CLASSIFICATION OF SURROUNDING SPACES. FOR THE DURATION OF THIS OPERATION YOU ARE GRANTED "UNUSUAL BREADTH OF DISCRETION" AS DESCRIBED IN STARFLEET REGULA-TIONS VOL 12444 SECTION 39.0 FF. OPERATION TO CONTINUE UNTIL FURTHER NOTICE. (SIGNED) WILLSON, K., ADMIRAL, SFC DENEB.

(CC: WALSH, M., CPT, CMDR NCC 1017 CONSTELLATION: RI-HAUL, NHS., CPT, CMDR NCC 2003 INAIEU: SUVUK, CPT, CMDR NCC 1631 INTREPID: MALCOR, K., ADMRL, SFC SOL III/TERRA: T'KAIEN, ADMRL, SFC 40 ERI IV/VULCAN)

Uhura frowned down at the dispatch, then glanced up at Kirk, looking wry. "It reveals a lot more by what it doesn't say than by what it does, Captain. I haven't seen such a roundabout way of referring to the Neutral

Zone since we were last at war with the Romulans. Do you suppose Fleet's afraid someone's cracked our command ciphers?"

"Maybe. Though that's supposed to be impossible. . . ." Jim looked up from the message. "But you're quite right, Uhura. There's not so much as a hint about whatever's going on out there."

"Romulan trouble, certainly," Uhura said. "And what exactly is 'unusual breadth of discretion' supposed to mean?"

Spock glanced up at the Bridge ceiling, a resigned gesture, and for a Vulcan, an exasperated one. Jim shook his head. "It doesn't mean anything *exactly*," he said, "and that's the problem. The section is a catchall reg for use in unstable situations. It means that if I need to go into this situation and break one or more Prime Directives, and if by doing so I keep the situation from blowing up, and Fleet likes the way I handled things, they'll probably give me a medal. It also means that if they *don't* like the way I handle the situation, they'll probably court-martial me . . . whether I solve the problem or not."

Uhura sighed. "Thus saving their own precious reputations, as usual."

"Yes," Spock said. "And thereby indicating that there is something afoot from which the higher echelons of Fleet feel their reputations must be saved. The situation must be grave indeed."

"Speculating without data, Spock?" Jim said. "That's a surprise."

Spock made the gentle you-must-be-joking expression that Jim knew so well. "Sir, I am the *Enterprise*'s science officer. And politics is a science . . . no matter how clumsy, crude and emotion-riddled a science I may find it. There is not much data, but enough to indicate this at least—that there is trouble of some kind occurring, or about to occur, in the Neutral Zone."

"And that Starfleet wants its resident experts in things Romulan on the scene to deal with the problem," Uhura said. "Meaning the *Enterprise* . . . and you two."

Jim made a face. Having officers so sharp made for pleasant work much of the time, but it also meant that unpleasant truths came right out into the open. "Unfortunately, I have to agree with you both. But—that business aside—Spock, I can't help being annoyed that, just as you're starting to get some results, we have to break off our researches here, without even the courtesy of being given a good reason why, and go warping off on some fleet maneuver two thousand light-years away. . . ."

"One thousand nine hundred sixty-eight point four five light-years," Spock said. "Eight point three three days at warp eight."

"Right. Dammit, just for once I'd like to start a mission, and take it right through to the end, and then stop, without being called away to do something else. . . ."

"It is true," the Vulcan said soberly, looking down at the dispatch, "that the data were finally beginning to correlate. But I am sure they will continue to do so in our absence."

"Certainly . . . if some other ship continues the research. Heaven only knows if Fleet will bother to assign another. And besides, if what you've found so far is any indication, this isn't just some dull little research that can be dropped and then come back to. If the stellar ecology in this part of space is really changing, the effects will be much more far-reaching than we even suspect now. *This* is the time to do something about it—not a month or a year from now, when it might be too late."

Spock looked at Jim with an expression of ironic resignation. "Sir, we are entirely in agreement. But Starfleet, as we have noticed many times before, has its own priorities. And we have our duty."

"Yes. I just wish their priorities and ours coincided more often. However, entropy is running, and things are the way they are. . . ." Jim tapped a finger on Uhura's console, thinking. "Well. Uhura, have the computer pull out the last several months' Fleet dispatches and abstract everything that might be relevant to this business: intelligence reports, logs from ships on Neutral Zone patrol, what have you. Routine and classified information, both. Send it all through to my terminal and I'll look at it before I go to bed."

"Those data have been in your computer for the last twenty minutes," said Uhura with a slow, mischievous grin, "and since you gave me your command ciphers, the classified materials have been there for about five."

Jim smiled down at her. "Uhura, are you bucking for a raise?"

The smile she gave him back was amused, but weary. "Captain, gamma shift on this run has not exactly been Wrigley's Pleasure Planet, if you catch my drift. I've been over my board from translator circuits to logic solids about a hundred times, out of sheer boredom." She stretched a bit, cracking her knuckles. "Not a bad thing, actually; I've stuffed this station's comm circuitry so full of neoduotronic upgrades that the main board can probably hear other ships *think*. But having something else to do is a delight. Which reminds me—" She turned back to the board. "Here's something that came in just before that dispatch did. It should be done transcribing now." She reached out to one of the comm board's recording slots, pulled a slim cassette out of it, and handed the cassette to Spock.

"Mail?" Jim said.

Spock turned the cassette over, reading the label-strip that burned bright at his touch, then faded slowly. "Not precisely, Captain. This appears to be some additional data I requested from the Federation Inter-stellar Commercial Transport Authority—a master list of all ship losses in known space over the past several years. It should be most helpful in ascertaining whether some trends I have been detecting in the data we've previously amassed are in fact real trends, or statistical artifact."

The Vulcan was already moving to sit down at the library computer, his eyes alive with that old familiar look of interest. *There goes the endgame analysis for tonight,* Jim thought with amused regret. *Oh well . . .* "Very well, Mr. Spock. Let me know how it works out. In the meantime, Uhura, have your computer give the rendezvous coordinates to the helm. Mr. Chekov, get a move on and plot us a course. We're not getting any closer to phi Trianguli just sitting here. . . ."

"Begging the Captain's pardon," said Chekov, straight-faced, as he touched various controls on the helm and passed Uhura's coordinates on to the naviga-tions computer for a course. "But both local star-streaming and galactic rotation are carrying us roughly toward the phi Trianguli patrol corridor at a velocity of some eighteen kilometers per second. . . ."

Greatly amused, Jim looked from Chekov over to Spock. "Mr. Spock," Jim said with mock severity, "you are corrupting this man."

"Indeed not, sir," said Spock, glancing up from his

science station and speaking as innocently as Chekov had. "I have merely been encouraging Mr. Chekov's already promising tendency toward logic. A characteristic, might I mention, that is entirely too rare in Terrans . . ."

"Yes, Mr. Spock," Kirk said, unable to resist. "So I noticed earlier this evening. . . ."

All over the Bridge, faces turned away in every possible direction, and hands covered mouths, to spare Spock the sight of much smiling. Jim took no official notice of this, while once more noticing the truth of the old saying that the only thing faster than light in otherspace was starship gossip. Spock merely gazed across the Bridge at Jim, one more look of tolerant acceptance in a series of thousands. Very quietly, Chekov said, "Course plotted and laid in, sir."

"Very good, Mr. Chekov. Get us going—warp eight: Fleet seems to be in a hurry. Uhura, if you would be so kind, log me off the Bridge. Thank you for a pleasant game, Mr. Spock, and a good night to you. Good night, everyone."

"Sir," Spock said, and various "'Night, sir"'s and "Good night, Captain"'s came from about the Bridge as Jim stepped into the lift wall and let out a tremendous yawn.

"Please repeat," the lift's computer said sweetly. "That didn't make sense."

Jim laughed. "Oh, yes, it did, dear! Deck five." He yawned again, thinking for the moment less about the vagaries of Fleet than about his bed.

Much later in the evening he was still yawning, but the thoughts behind the yawns were very different. Jim sat as he had been sitting for nearly an hour now, with the twelfth page of Uhura's report burning on the screen in front of him. An annoying document, this; like the dispatch from Starfleet, what it did say was less revealing than what it didn't.

The first part of it concerned civilian and military shipping, and was utterly unilluminating. Fleet ship movements in the sectors bounding the Neutral Zone, and in the sectors farther away, were routine and undisturbed. And business was progressing as usual in the Neutral Zone, as far as long-range sensors based in the Zone inspection stations could tell. . . .

Those few agents whom the Federation had managed to insinuate into the Empire knew that their chief value lay in staying alive and unnoticed; so they dared do nothing that would attract attention to themselves— such as pry too closely into areas of real interest, including the seats of government and the counsels of the great. As a result, their reports tended to be brief and scanty of detail. But in the reports for the last three months, Jim found more than enough to interest him.

He had long been fascinated by the "modified tri-cameral" or three-house legislative-executive branch of this Emperorless Empire. The Tricameron was comprised of a "Senate"—evenly divided against itself into a half that proposed and passed legislation, and a half that vetoed it—and a "Praetorate," a sort of quadruple troika or duodecimvirate: twelve men and women who implemented the Senate's decrees, declared war or peace, and (it seemed to Jim) spent most of the time squabbling amongst themselves for power. That was partially due to the nature of their office, since a Praetor could be "made," by election or manipulation of influence. But a Senator could only be born—the senatorial office was hereditary, passed from father or mother to eldest sister's-son or -daughter: and the only thing that could remove a Senator from office was death.

That was what interested Jim right now. For over the past few months, it seemed several Senators had lost their posts in just that fashion. Considered by itself, this fact was unremarkable. Often enough, some Senator or Praetor would antagonize another one possessing more influential alliances, and pay the price by being publicly executed, or ordered to commit suicide, by a majority of the Twelve. But four different senators, from both the proposing and vetoing sides of the Noble House, had died recently . . . of what were reported as natural causes.

Jim sat there thinking that an inability to live after being poisoned was natural enough. Yet at the same time he was disturbed, for as he understood it, assassination was not the Romulan style. It was supposed to be disdained as a dishonorable act, a sign of barbarity and weakness in the person who hired the assassin: the type of "irresponsible" behavior that made the Romulans despise the Klingons. One more thing that made no sense.

Irrational. Illogical. And the Romulans are still culturally close enough to their parent Vulcan race not to have given up logic entirely. . . .

Four deaths are hardly enough to allow me to deduce logically that all hell is about to break loose over there. But the Romulans are so . . . so consistent . . . that the irrationality seems huge.

Damn Fleet! They won't give me even a hint of what's going on. Postulating worst case . . . always a wise course of action, where Starfleet's concerned . . . how am I supposed to prevent a war, or at worst win one, if they won't tell me how they expect it to start?

Unless . . . Unless what? Some piece of information

hand-carried to Fleet, not yet disseminated? Some highest-level intelligence too sensitive to declassify or openly transmit? What could be that sensitive?

Or . . . unless they don't know what's going on either . . . and want us to find out . . . Jim breathed out, thinking of old stories of how the great cats were once hunted on Earth; with "beaters" who would run into the brush where the tigers were hiding. There the beaters would hoot and shout and hit around them with sticks, banging on pots or on shields, so that the noise would panic the tigers and make them break cover, revealing themselves. Or else make the tigers, in understandable annoyance, attack the beaters. *And there we'll be, three starships and a destroyer, parading up and down outside the borders of the Neutral Zone, shouting and beating on pots. . . .*

The sudden, bizarre image of Spock banging with straight-faced efficiency on a saucepan abruptly made Jim realize how very late it must be getting. He leaned forward, elbows on the desk, and rubbed his eyes—then rested his chin against his folded hands and stared once more at the screen. Page twelve of the report stared back at him, burning there golden and still. Jim had read Uhura's careful compendium backward and forward several times now, but page twelve kept pulling him back. On page twelve were listed the Romulan vessels patrolling the far side of the Neutral Zone, and their schedules. The ships were maintaining those schedules to the minute, as usual. Jim would have been very surprised indeed if they hadn't; Romulans were always punctual as clockwork, in peace as in war. And there on the list were the old familiar names—*Courser, Arien, Javelin, Rea's Helm, Cuirass, Eisn, Wildfire. Enterprise* and her crew knew those names well from many brushes in the Neutral Zone, many skirmishes, many long dull patrols spent pacing one another on either side of the Line. Jim leaned slowly forward, propping his chin on one fist, and stared at the screen.

The usual names . . . in the usual places.

All the names but one.

Where the hell is Bloodwing?

Unnoticed by its owner, the fist clenched.

Three

"Khre'Riov?"

Ael stretched in her center-chair in the Bridge, and turned her head just enough to show she was paying attention to Centurion t'Liun, without actually having to look at her. "Ie?"

"Nniehv idh ra iy'tassiudh nnearh."

What you mean, of course, is that my gig is allowed to be "ready" because your security people have checked it and failed to find anything that would confirm your suspicions of me. Fool! Do you think you're dealing with someone who works on your level? Aloud, all Ael said was "Khnai'ra rhissiuy, Enarrain"; and if the thanks was rather warmly phrased, so much the better. It would confuse t'Liun into a standstill.

Ael got up from her hard seat and headed for the lift, and sure enough, t'Liun was standing there at her post when she could have been sitting, and gazing at Ael with what t'Liun doubtless thought was perfectly faked

36

respect. *How I detest you!* Ael thought as she went past the narrow, dark, cold-faced little woman. *You would sell your sisters'-sons and -daughters to Orion slavers for a quarter-chain of cash if the deed would buy you power. No matter, though; you and yours will be rid of me soon enough.* Ael stepped into the lift. "Ri'lae-fv'htaiell, Enarrain," she said, and waved the lift doors shut.

T'Liun headed down toward the center seat as ordered, but rather hurriedly. That was the last thing Ael saw as the doors closed on her; and it made her laugh. How she wishes I would leave her that seat forever! And she laughed softly about it all the way down to Engineering, where her gig was kept.

It was a pretty little ship—a one-man scout, actually, very sleek and lean, with a high-absorption black coating and warpdrive capacity. It was many years newer than *Cuirass* or any of her sorry equipment; and this was because it was Ael's own, brought with her from *Bloodwing*—the one thing she had insisted on taking. Privately she called it *Hsaaja,* after the first *fvai* she had demanded to ride as a child—a cranky, delicate, annoyed and annoying beast that was eternally hungry. This Hsaaja, like the first, was a glutton where fuel consumption was involved. But also like the first, nothing of his size could match him for speed . . . and neither could some larger craft: *Cuirass,* for example. *Hsaaja*'s presence made t'Liun acutely nervous. That suited Ael very well.

The ship stood with his forward cockpit open. She went up the ladder, settled and sealed herself in, then called the upper Engineering deck and told tr'Ake-idhad to go ahead and exhaust the smaller, lower deck where *Hsaaja* stood. His instrumentation came on and the power came up at the sound of her voice; air hissed out of the deck, the sound of the pumps becoming inaudible. The doors rolled away, and the lights went down, leaving Ael in starlight and the flashes of the landing beacons set in the floor. She took *Hsaaja* out on chemical jets, and once well clear of the ship, cut in the ion-drivers and headed for her fleet.

They were all at the prescribed distance for fleet maneuvers, about a hundredth of a light-second from each other and from *Cuirass*—well out of visual range. Ael considered kicking in just a touch of warpdrive, then decided against it. Not from any concern about panicking t'Liun, who was certainly monitoring her course—that would in fact have been a minor pleasure. But she saw too little of realspace these days; and the otherspace in which ships moved while in warp was a wavering, uneasy vista, not pleasant to look at at all. She sat back, handling the controls at her leisure, and took her own good time.

Hsaaja's computer already was displaying the three new ships' ID signals—strings of numbers and the code for their class type. Klingon ships, all right. *I do wish Command would stop buying those flying middens,* Ael thought. But then Command couldn't, as Ael well knew. The Rihannsu had entered into a trade agreement with the Klingons: an agreement that was nothing but a fair scabbard over a sharp sword—the threat of war if the Rihannsu should fail to buy a certain number of ships every year. It was the old story, the old saying: "Buy a murderer once and you will get lifetime service." And the Klingons, with their present economical problems, would like nothing better than the excuse of a broken treaty to justify raiding the Rihannsu outworlds. So ch'Ríhan fulfilled its half of the agreement, more out of fear than integrity. And the Fleet was now about half a collection of poor old Warbirds falling into ill repair, because spare parts for them were no longer being made, and half Klingon ships which could be repaired—with spare parts sold at extortionate prices— but which immediately malfunctioned again anyway.

Planned obsolescence, Ael thought bitterly, as her ship coasted closer to the nearest of her fleet. *Or maybe it's true what they say, that the Klingon government contracts for its ships to be built by the lowest bidder. . . .*

Still, her curiosity got the better of her. She tapped her console for more information from the ID signals. Names came up along with the numbers: *Arakkab, Kenek, Ykir.* Ael stared at her datascreen; but there the names hung in black and blue, with no alternate Rihannsu naming, no extra information. *Klingon names?* she thought, in some bemusement. *Maybe they simply haven't had time to assign them decent names yet?* But that seemed ridiculous. No Rihannsu ship was allowed into service without being properly named; it would be terribly unlucky, not to mention an insult to the Elements and to the ship itself—one that the ship would surely avenge on its crew at some point.

Ael's unease did not show on her face: it never did. But it was down in her stomach already, clenching there like a fist. On an uncomfortable hunch she told her ship's computer to scan behind her, read the ID of the ship she had just left.

KL *Ehhak,* said her datascreen.

And it was all suddenly and horribly plain. Ael did not need to go any nearer to the other ships, though she did, for completeness' sake and to prevent anyone from becoming suspicious. She found, on final approach to the first ship, exactly what she knew she would: a brand new *K'tinga*-class warship, with Klingon markings on the exterior. Before she had even set foot out of *Hsaaja* onto its hangar deck, she knew exactly what was going to happen to her and this fleet in the next few weeks. She was going to be ordered to lead them across the Neutral Zone and into Federation space, there to start a "Klingon" war with the Federation. She and her fleet would, of course, not survive the experience; she would be permanently out of the Senate's way. And while the Klingons and the Federation were busy blowing one another to plasma, for months—years it might be—the Rihannsu would be off doing other things.

What? Ael thought, while the obsequious, annoying commander of *"Arakkab"* welcomed her and escorted her around his ship; while her body did all the proper things, smiled, or laughed in a reassuring fashion at nervous jokes, or made appreciative remarks about new (and ill-made) equipment. *What will they do? Raid both sides, most likely. Do something about our sorry economy in the most direct and dishonorable way possible. Pillage those worlds where the war has passed, scavenge about behind Klingons and Federation like a* sseikea *skulking behind a* thrai, *picking up scraps. They will take advantage of the disorganization and mistrust of such times, use them to expand, to enlarge the Empire at the cost of both sets of enemies. And when one of the great powers has reduced the second to slavery or powerlessness, then the new voices in the Senate will cry out for war. "Hit the winner now, while he is weak," they'll say. More war, more death. Perhaps even victory —but, O, dishonorable, vile—*

The tension of the fist clenching her insides got no less as time went on, as she beamed over to *Ykir* with some of the officers from *Arakkab*, and was greeted in turn by another commander, whose thick-featured face she later thought of with grim pleasure—for these people and these ships deserved one another. *O Fire above us and Earth below,* she thought. *Convicts, failures, the castoffs of Command. No doubt very proud of being given new ships, and a mission. How far will that get them?* For *Intrepid* was out there waiting, along with *Constellation,* and worse still, the destroyer *Inaieu;* and worst of them all, *Enterprise.* Even with *Bloodwing,* with a crew both skilled and utterly loyal to her, she had survived her encounters with *Enterprise* with the greatest difficulty. And some of her own relatives had not been so lucky. What would happen to *this* poor lot?—newly assigned, from the look of them, and incompetents all, in ships falsely named? And what would happen to *her,* for that matter—in a ship full of paid help, already busy with treachery to her, a ship itself wearing an alias? Not all her skill could save her from a ship whose name had been taken from it. There was no tampering with names.

She went right through *Ykir,* and then through *Kenek,* extrapolating at furious speed, while the bland or confused or malicious faces around her never noticed a thing. *Forget staying on* Cuirass *and surviving,* she thought. *And even if I should—what then? Capture by* Enterprise *or one of the other ships. Processing, and release—back to the Empire. A shameful death, and a protracted one, while the Senate laughs. No indeed; I shall die before it comes to that.*

Yet my young friends would like that, would they not? They think they have me netted. Honorable suicide would suit them nicely. My death in battle would suit them too, or my execution in disgrace back home. Perhaps they even think I might suicide rather than carry out my dishonorable orders to cross the Zone in the first place. Surely the question of honor would come up— should I receive those orders. And Ael smiled just once at a moment she did not need to, while looking up some ugly conduit full of circuitry in *Kenek*'s engine room. She silently blessed the bureaucracy, just this once, for getting her orders stuck in itself. She resolved that when she got back to *Cuirass,* she would help those orders stay stuck for a while.

"Hra'vae?" she said in apparent wonderment, while some underofficer explained to her (inaccurately) some detail about the marvelous new Klingon gunnery conduits. She was thinking of *Bloodwing*'s new equipment, and her anger was turning humorous—her most dangerous mood, as Ael knew well. She made no attempt to abate it. She would need to be dangerous for the next few days. *Treachery,* she thought. *I cannot abide treachery.—As they shall come to know. . . .*

Eventually the tour was done. Ael beamed back to *Arakkab,* and bade its commander a very cheerful farewell—strongly intending that the two of them should not meet again until they had both passed out of this place where the Elements were physical. She got back into *Hsaaja* and took off for *Cuirass* again, noting as she approached how very worn the bird-of-prey shadows along its underbelly were, in what bad shape the ship appeared to be. At one time, this would have scandalized her. Now she did not worry. It would shortly be none of her concern.

One thing she did, before she came about where *Cuirass* could scan her. In the shadow of *Kenek*'s deflector screens, up at minimal power, she hit a control in *Hsaaja,* and felt the slight bound of the ship as explosive bolts knocked something out of a concealed hatch. She could not see the object—it was covered with the same nondetectable coating as *Hsaaja* was—but her datascreen came alive as it went, reading out the readiness of the little probe's engines, the status of its tiny computer. In an hour or so it would have maneuvered its way around behind *Kenek* on shielded impulse drive. In the nightwatch of the four ships, it would burn out its little primary pod in a single one-second warp eight burst. Tafv would find it, and its message, before the ship's night was over.

Then it would all begin.

Ael went back to *Cuirass* to get ready.

Four

The space around sigma-285 Trianguli was, to put it baldly, dull. Not one of the stars in the area had a name; and hardly any of them seemed worth naming anyway. They were, generally speaking, a weary association of cooling red dwarfs—little Jupiter-sized stars of types N and R, and here and there a sputtering S-type "carbon" star with water-vapor in its atmosphere. ("Running out of steam," Uhura remarked, looking over Spock's shoulder at the data-breakdown on one of them.) Some of the stars had planets, but those were dull too—bare rocks, where life might have been, millennia ago, but certainly wasn't now. There was nothing on those worlds that anyone wanted. Which was just as well; right next door to the border with the Neutral Zone would have been an uncomfortable place to live.

It was dark space to fly in—a bad place for seeing

who was getting close to you, but a good spot for a quiet rendezvous with people whose looks you already knew. So *Enterprise* found it when she came out of warp and coasted down into 285's feeble little gravity well, settling into a long elliptical orbit around the star. Other shapes, barely illuminated, broke their orbits and gathered slowly in around her. Two of them kept to the usual five-kilometer traffic limit: *Constellation* and *Intrepid*, ships of *Enterprise*'s own class. The third ship held itself ten kilometers away, but for all the extra distance, it looked the same size as *Intrepid* and *Constellation* did. This was even more of an illusion than the dim space alone could have caused, for the third ship was *Inaieu*.

Inaieu, as one of the destroyer-class starships, had been built large; built to carry a lot of people on very long hauls, and built to carry more power and more armament than any three starships—just in case. Her upper-hull disk was three times the size of *Enterprise*'s; her engine nacelles twice as long, and there were four of them—one above, two on the sides, one below. Her central engineering hull was a quarter-mile in diameter, and a mile long. Having been built at the Starfleet shipyards at Deneb, she flew under Denebian registry, and had been named for the old High King of Deneb V who, as the song said, "rose up and smote her enemies." Jim watched her now on the Bridge screen—massive, menacing and graceful, a great, glowing, blood-red shape in 285's simmering light—and felt glad to have her along on this business, in case some heavy-duty smiting should be necessary.

"How long, Mr. Spock?" he said.

Spock glanced up from his station. "The meeting is not scheduled to begin for another twenty-five point six minutes, sir. Captain Rihaul is obviously already aboard *Inaieu;* Captain Walsh is in transit via shuttlecraft; Captain Suvuk has not yet beamed over."

McCoy, standing behind the helm and watching everything as usual, looked surprised. "Shuttlecraft? Why doesn't Captain Walsh just beam over like everybody else?"

Jim looked with wry amusement at McCoy. "That's right, you don't know Mike Walsh, do you? You two are going to get along just fine. Mike hates the transporter. Remind him to tell you about the time on Earth when he was heading for the Sydney Opera House and wound up instead in Baltimore Harbor. Or on second thought, don't remind him. He'll tell you anyway."

McCoy humphed. "Two sensible men in this crazy Fleet, anyway—Jim, do I have to go to this silliness? This is supposedly a strategy and tactics meeting. Why should I scramble up my stomach and my brainwaves in that thing to sit and listen to—"

"Sorry, Bones. All the section chiefs have to be there. Regulations."

"—bloody battle plans on one side and a whole horde of overlogical Vulcans on the other—"

Jim started to laugh. "Oh, Bones! The truth will out, I see. . . ."

"Indeed," Spock said, without looking up from his work. "The thought of a whole starship full of Vulcans, all doing perfectly well without one single human to leaven the deadly weight of their logic, intellection and sobriety, obviously has shocked the good Doctor into the unwelcome thought that he might possibly not be necessary—"

"Careful, Spock," McCoy grumbled. "You're up for a physical in a couple weeks. . . ."

Spock merely raised an amused eyebrow at McCoy,

letting the expression say what he thought of such a déclassé retort. Jim sat back, looking past *Inaieu* on the screen to where *Intrepid* hung, glowing like a coal. It was a couple of years now since the first *Intrepid* had run afoul of the spacegoing amoebalike creature that *Enterprise,* with a lot of help from Spock, had managed to destroy. The Vulcans had naturally gone into the expected restrained mourning for their many dead; but the monument that they found most fitting was another Vulcan starship.

She was built along the usual heavy-cruiser design, but with details of construction so much improved that Fleet had decided to use the Vulcans' design, later, to refit all the heavy cruisers. Jim had looked at the plans and pictures of *Intrepid,* and had found the design surprisingly pleasant—not only more logical than the original starship design, but very often more pleasant to look at, and sometimes downright beautiful. McCoy had looked over the plans mostly in silence, only commenting at the end of his perusal that the Vulcans had at least made the bathrooms larger. But Jim had noticed that all through, McCoy had been making the "hmp" noises that meant he approved even if he didn't want to admit it. At any rate, there hung *Intrepid* herself, and whether it was logical or not, Jim was glad to see her. Her new captain, Suvuk, was a briefly retired admiral whom Jim was looking forward to meeting—a veteran of decades of cruises, and the kind of man Terrans would call a hero, though the Vulcans insisted that he was just doing his job.

"Pretty ship," he said. "Look how they've trimmed her nacelles down. . . . Spock, did they sacrifice any power for the weight they dropped there?"

"They improved power generation fifty-three percent before they made the alteration," Spock said; "so

47

those engines run at a hundred thirty-three percent of the best level the *Enterprise* could manage. I fear Mr. Scott is probably deep in that ugliest of emotions, envy. . . ."

McCoy groaned softly. "Can we get on with this?" he said under his breath. "I've got a Sickbay to tend to."

"Momentarily, Doctor," Spock said. "I am waiting for a final piece of data for this research of mine. While we are off on *Inaieu*, the computer will process it and provide us with a solution—"

"That ion-storm business?"

"Affirmative."

The Bridge doors hissed open, and Ensign Naraht shuffled in with a sound like someone dragging concrete blocks over the carpet. Jim smiled. He always smiled when he saw Naraht; he couldn't help it.

Naraht was one of the thirty thousand children born of the last hatching of the Horta, that now-famous silicon-based creature native to Janus VI. The *Enterprise*, early in her five-year mission, had been called to Janus VI to exterminate a "monster," and instead had wound up first injuring, then saving, the single surviving Horta who was about to become the "mother" of her whole eggbound race. Once out of the egg, the hatchlings grew with the usual speed; they were tunneling rock within minutes of their birth, and all the thirty thousand who hatched reached latency, and high intelligence, within standard days.

Any race so strange, and yet so adaptable to "bizarre" creatures like hominids, was naturally of immediate interest to the Federated Worlds. And the Hortas—curious creatures that they were—returned the interest with interest. Nothing could have kept them out of the Federation; and as for the political formalities, a creature used to moving easily through solid rock will be only slightly slowed down by red tape. It took no more (and in some cases much less) than the three years in which a Starfleet Academy class graduates for Hortas to start appearing on starships.

Naraht had come to the *Enterprise* highly qualified, with an Academy standing in the top tenth of his class. ("He" was an approximation; his official Fleet "arbitrary gender designation" was "orthomale type B-4A," which McCoy usually described as "close enough for jazz.") The Horta had chosen to specialize in biomaths, that peculiar science claimed by both psychiatry and interactional mesophysics. This put him, at least nominally, in McCoy's department. But Engineering and Analytical Chemistry both wanted to get their hands, fins or tentacles on him; not surprising, since Hortas eat rock, deriving both nutrition and flavor from the metallic elements and silicates found in it. Naraht could take a bite of any metal or mineral you pleased, and seconds later give you a readout of its constituent elements, with the expert precision of a gourmet reporting on the ingredients and balance of a wine sauce.

Jim had watched the intradepartmental squabbling over Naraht with amusement, and hadn't allowed himself to be swayed by it; the *Enterprise* was made for the entities who rode in her, not the other way around. He left Naraht happy in biomaths, and simply kept an eye on his progress. Meantime, Spock apparently found it illogical to waste his talents, and had been calling him up to the Bridge for consultations now and then. Jim didn't mind this at all; he had long since confessed to himself that he never got tired of being earnestly "Yes, Captain"ed by someone who looked like a giant pan pizza (sausage, extra cheese).

"I have the data you wanted on the meteoric debris, sir," Naraht said to Spock, drawing himself up to his full height in an approximation of "attention." Behind him, Jim heard McCoy most carefully preventing his own laughter; Naraht was basically a horizontal creature, and his "full height" was about half a meter at best.

"Report, Mr. Naraht," Spock said, beginning to key data into his library computer.

"Yes, sir. In order of greatest concentration—iron-55 forty-five point eight zero percent, nickel-58 twelve point six one percent, lead-82 nine point eight eight percent, mercury-201 nine point four six percent, gallium-69 nine point three zero percent, gold-198 eight point one one percent, samarium-151 three point one zero percent, rhodium-101 one point two three percent, palladium-106 zero point two zero percent, iridium-193 zero point three zero, and trace amounts of neodymium, yttrium, strontium and tantalum making up zero point zero one percent."

Spock was staring at his station with great interest. "Mr. Naraht," he said, "are you quite certain of that figure for the iridium?"

"To six decimal places, sir! Zero point three zero four one four one two two."

"That is *eight* decimal places, Ensign," Spock said; but he said it so mildly that McCoy looked at him very oddly indeed.

"Oh," Naraht said. "I'm sorry, sir! I thought you might like some more."

" 'Liking' is one of the humanities' emotions to which Vulcans are not generally prone," Spock said, in that same mild voice. Jim held his own smile out of sight, particularly noticing that Spock hadn't said at all that *he* might not occasionally like something. "Nevertheless I am inclined to overlook the error—just this once."

McCoy looked down at Jim, who had swiveled his chair around to look at the screen—and to have something to do besides laugh. Bones's look said, very plainly, *Is it just me, or is Spock teasing that boy!* Jim shrugged and took Bones's clipboard away from him, pretending to study it while the lecture went on behind him. "Enthusiasm about science is to be commended," Spock was saying, "but enthusiasm *in* science is to be avoided at all costs; it biases the judgment and may blind one to valuable observations. Guard against it."

"I'll remember, sir," said Naraht. "Will there be anything else?"

"Not at the moment, Ensign. You may go."

Naraht went shuffling off toward the Bridge doors. "Mr. Naraht," Spock said, just as Jim thought it might be safe to turn around again. Behind him he heard Naraht pause.

"Sir?"

"That was well done, Mr. Naraht. Keep working and we will make a scientist of you yet."

"Sir!"

"You are dismissed."

Off went Naraht, rumbling and shuffling, into the lift. Spock went back to his work at his station, ignoring Uhura's quizzical look at him, as well as Jim's and McCoy's. Bones couldn't stand it. "Mr. Spock," he said, deadpan, and somehow sounding only slightly interested, "did I hear you compliment that lad?"

Spock was still touching pads and switches on his library computer, so that he didn't look up. "I accurately assessed his performance, Doctor. Feedback is most important for continuation of optimum performance, as even you must know."

"I take it then," Jim said, equally nonchalant, "that you find his performance generally satisfactory?"

"Oh, quite satisfactory, Captain. In fact, he exhibits many of the most positive traits of a young member of *your* branch of humanity—being by turns, or all at once, cheerful, conscientious, obedient almost to a fault, courteous, enthusiastic, respectful of superiors—"

"And he's probably thrifty, brave, clean and reverent, too," McCoy said. "In other words, Mr. Spock, we've got a genuine 'space cadet' on our hands."

"Bless 'em all," Jim said. "Where would Fleet be without them?"

"But the point is, Jim, that Spock approves of him! Can I stand the strain!"

"Doubtful," Spock said with a sigh, turning away from his work. "Doctor, Mr. Naraht has an eminently logical mind—unsurprising: so did his mother. If his emotional tendencies—"

"Aha! The truth *will* out!" McCoy said jubilantly. "That's it! You like that boy because you knew his mother the Horta—*and she liked your ears!*"

Spock simply looked at McCoy. Jim started to whoop with laughter. Unfortunately, Uhura's board chose that moment to let out one of its more strident whistles. She put her transdator back in her ear, looked off into space for a moment, then said, "Captain, it's *Inaieu*. They're ready for you."

Jim got up out of the helm, still shaking with laughter. "Tell them we're on our way. Gentlemen, the defense against the charge of nepotism-by-association will have to wait till this is over with. Uhura, call the Transporter Room."

"No shuttlecraft?" McCoy said, a little sorrowfully.

"Sorry, Bones, we're late."

"One of these days," McCoy growled as the three of them stepped into the lift, "that damn Transporter'll glitch, and we really *will* be."

Inaieu was if possible even huger than it looked. Jim at first wondered if some slippage in protocol, or confusion on the part of his own transporter chief, had sent him to the cargo transporters instead of the one for staff and crew; for the room they beamed into seemed almost the size of a small hangar deck. But the Eyrene transporter officer on this side reminded Jim forcibly that not only ships, but people, came in rather different sizes.

Deneb was a large star with more than one planet. The Klaha, the first Denebian race that Fleet had made contact with, lived on Deneb V; it was that species which Federation nomenclature meant when it referred to "Denebians." But the peoples of the other worlds, the Eyren and the !'hew and the Deirr, were Denebians too—not simply because of sharing a star. The worlds of this huge blue primary were all big, and dense, and had heavy gravity, for which their various versions of the humanities were equipped. So the *Inaieu* had been built to accomodate the primarily "Denebian" crew who would be handling her—such as the Eyrene transporter officer. She was typical of her people, looking very much like an eight-legged, circular-bodied elephant with no head and four trunks—a squat, golden-skinned, powerful person, and one (with her six-foot diameter) rather too large for any merely hominid-sized transporter platform.

When they were all materialized she came out from behind her console and bowed by way of respectful greeting—a Denebian bow, more of a deep knee bend. "Captain, gentlemen," she said, "you're expected in Main Briefing. Will you follow me, please?"

"Certainly, Lieutenant," Jim said, noting the stripes on one of the four sleeves; noting also, with mild amusement, that all there was to the uniform was those sleeves. The Lieutenant led the way out into the hall, moving very quickly and lightly—and understandably so; the common areas of the ship were apparently kept at light gravity for the convenience of a multispecies crew. "Hi-grav personal quarters?" Jim said to McCoy.

"So I hear. They had to do quite a bit of juggling with the power-consumption curves to make it work out. But this ship's got power to burn."

"That's no joke, lad," Scotty said, peering in an opening door as they went past one of *Inaieu's* six engine rooms. "That one warpdrive assembly in there is by itself half again the size of the *Enterprise's.*"

Jim glanced at Scotty, who was now nearly walking backward, and looking hungrily back the way they'd come. "Later, Scotty," he said. "I think we can spare you time for a tour. We have to do a routine exchange of ships' libraries anyway; you might as well stop in to see the Chief Engineer and exchange pleasantries."

"And equations," McCoy said.

Scotty smiled, looking slightly sheepish, as the group entered a turbolift about the size of a shuttlecraft, and their Eyrene escort said, "Deck eighteen. Low-grav." The lift went off sideways, then up, at a sedate enough pace; but even so Jim had to smile to himself. All the Denebian races, it seemed, loved the high accelerations and speeds they were so well built to handle; and the thought of the speeds the lifts in this ship probably did when there were only Denebians aboard them made

54

Jim shudder slightly. But that was part of their mindset, too; no Denebian would ever walk anywhere it could run, or do warp three if it could make warp eight. Life was too interesting, they said, to take it slowly; and certainly too short—if you have only six hundred years, you must make the most of them! So they plunged around through space, putting their noses (those of them who had noses) into everything, and thoroughly enjoying themselves; the Galaxy's biggest, merriest overachievers, and a definite asset to the Federation. Jim was very fond of them.

"Here we are. This way, gentlemen," said the Eyrene lieutenant, and hurried out of the lift. The four of them went out after her, hurrying only slightly, and were relieved to see her turn leftward and gesture toward an open door. "Main Briefing, gentlemen."

"My thanks, Lieutenant," Jim said, and led his officers in.

Main Briefing, as he suspected, was about the size of a tennis court. The table was of that very sensible design that the Denebian races used when dealing with other species; a large round empty space in the middle, where Klaha and Eyren and !'hew would stand—they never sat—and chairs or racks scattered around the outside of the table for hominids, along with bowl-chairs for the Deirr. This way everyone, whether they had hominid stereoscopic vision or multiple eyes or heat sensors, could see everyone else; and of course everyone was wearing intradermal translators, so that understanding was no problem. At least, no more so than usual . . .

The company seated at that table rose, or bowed, to greet Jim and his party as they entered. One of them got up out of her bowl chair with the sucking sound that

Jim remembered so well; and he started to grin. "Nhauris," he said, holding out his hands, "you haven't changed a bit."

"Neither have you, flatterer," said the Captain of *Inaieu,* flowing toward him and reaching out a tentacle to wind in a comradely grip around one of his wrists. Nhauris Rihaul was a Deirr, from Deneb IV; half a ton of what looked like wet brown leather, all wrinkles and pouches and sags, shaped more or less like a slug that had half mastered the art of standing upright—but a slug eight feet long and five feet across the barrel. One long multipupiled eyeslit ran across what would have been a forehead, if she had properly had a head. Under the eyeslit was a long vertical slash of a mouth, lipless and apparently toothless, though Jim knew better. From beneath the mouth sprang the cluster of handling tentacles, ranging from tiny ones to huge thick cables. It was one of the smaller ones that was holding him, pumping his arm up and down in Nhauris's old mocking approximation of a handshake. "Jim, how are you?"

"Fine, Captain," Jim said—the old answer—"as soon as you stop that!"

She did, though not without bubbling briefly with Deirra laughter, a sound like an impending gastric disturbance. "Well enough. Captain, I have to apologize for asking you to hold this meeting here; properly it should have been on *Enterprise,* since she's flagship for this operation. But I think we might have crowded your briefing room a bit."

"I think you're right," he said, looking at the two Klaha, three Eyren and one !'hew standing at the center of the table, each one of them nearly the size of half a shuttlecraft. "In any case, let's get introductions over with so that we can get down to business. Captain Rihaul, may I present my first officer and Science

Officer, Mr. Spock"—Spock bowed slightly—"my Chief Engineer, Montgomery Scott; my Chief Surgeon, Leonard McCoy."

"Honored, gentlemen, most honored," Captain Rihaul said, taking them each by the hand, though foregoing the jump-start motion she had used on Jim. "Welcome aboard *Inaieu*." She led them toward the table. "I present to you my officers: first officer and Chief of Science Araun Yihoun; Chief of Surgery Lahiyn Roharrn; Chief Engineer Lellyn UUriul. And our guests; outside the table, from *Constellation*—"

"Jim and I have met, Nhauris," said Mike Walsh, reaching out to grip Jim's hand warmly. "Academy— then posts together on *Excalibur,* ages back. When did we last see each other? That M-5 business, wasn't it? Horrible mess, machine getting out of hand . . ."

Out of the corner of his eye Jim could see McCoy getting very interested indeed. "This meeting's a lot better than that one," he said, looking Mike up and down. Long ago, Jim and his classmates had used to tease Mike that it was a good thing Starfleet didn't have the old space agencies' maximum height requirement; otherwise Walsh would never have made it past atmosphere. He was six foot six, a slim man with sandy blond hair, a long, loose-limbed lope, and a look of eternal, friendly calculation, as if he were doing odds in his head. Probably he was; Mike had a reputation among his friends for being the biggest gambler in Starfleet. It might have been a problem, if he didn't always win. Nobody played poker with Mike Walsh—at least, not twice—but people fought to get aboard *Constellation*. Her command record since Mike took her was almost the equal of *Enterprise's* for danger, daring, and success not only snatched from the jaws of failure, but afterward used to beat failure over the head. It was easy enough for Jim to understand. Mike Walsh hated to lose as much as Jim did; and he had carefully surrounded himself with people who felt the same way. It was a good way to stay alive in a dangerous galaxy.

Mike waved at his officers—a Terran Oriental, and two handsome, intense-looking women, one a Tellarite. "My First, Raela hr'Sassish; my Chief Surgeon, Aline MacDougall; my Chief Engineer, Iwao Sasaoka."

"And here is the Captain of *Intrepid*," Rihaul said from one side. "Captain Kirk, may I present Captain Suvuk."

"Sir," Jim said, bowing slightly—not just because Vulcans were not handshaking types. This was, after all, the man who had saved nearly thirty other ships and the lives of thousands of Starfleet personnel by willingly delivering himself into the hands of the Klingons during their last brief war with the Federation. That war had been won on another front, at Organia. But Suvuk, even after being physically tortured, and then subjected to the Klingon mind-sifter, had still, in rapid succession, broken free of his captors on the Klingon flagship *Hakask* at Regulus; disabled the ship's warp-drive and melted down its impulse engines, strewing unconscious, injured, and occasionally dead Klingons liberally along the way as he went; made solid-logic copies of everything of interest in the Klingons' library computers, then dumped the computers themselves; and had finally made it back aboard the newly-built *Intrepid* in a stolen Klingon shuttlecraft, well before the Organians' ban fell and both Klingons and Federation suddenly found their weapons too hot to handle. The Federation had later given Suvuk the Pentares Peace Commendation, with the extra cluster for conspicuous heroism.

But it did not take decorations to make it obvious that this was a man to be reckoned with. Suvuk was much shorter than Spock, and slighter; that Jim had known from holos he'd seen, and had wondered at, hearing the reports of what he did on *Hakask*. Now Jim didn't wonder. What the holos didn't adequately express was the sheer force of the personality living inside that rather ordinary-looking body. This was someone Jim had suspected might exist, without ever having seen confirmation of it—a full Vulcan so powerfully certain of himself that he had no need to be bound any more than he desired to be by the conventions of his homeworld. The face was sharp, set and cool, like that of almost every Vulcan Jim had ever seen. But it was also still, from within, in some way that most younger Vulcan faces only imitated. There was slight wrinkling around the eyes and mouth, an almost lazy droop to the eyes; a look of ease and relaxation, though the body held itself erect and alert, its power ready, but leashed. *This is what Spock might look like in sixty years or so,* Jim thought. *I hope I live to see it. . . .*

"Captain," Suvuk said. Jim was surprised again; who would have thought such a powerful voice would come out of such a small person? He held up one hand in the Vulcan parted-hand salute. "I greet you, for my world as well as for myself. We have had cause to acknowledge your contributions to us before this; nor would it be speculation to state that we doubtless will again." He turned to Spock and Scott and McCoy. "Long life and prosperity to you, Spock," he said, and Spock lifted a hand and returned the salute and the greeting. "To you also, Mr. Scott, and Dr. McCoy. Doctor," Suvuk said, letting his hand fall, "I read your recent paper on conjoint enzyme adjustment and cryotherapy as applied to the traumatized Vulcan simulpericardium. May I compliment you on it? It is precise, comprehensive, and conclusive."

McCoy's face was so still that Jim knew he was concealing absolute astonishment under it, saving it for later. "Captain," he said, "I'm gratified to hear you say so. All I need to know now is whether the technique will work as well in the field as it did on paper and in the lab."

"Oh, as to that, you may make your mind easy," Suvuk said, "for the T'Saien Clinic at the Vulcan Science Academy is already using it on their patients. I should know; I was one of them, some months back." McCoy's eyebrow went up; that was all he allowed himself for the moment, though Jim strongly suspected the Saurian brandy would be flowing in Sickbay when they got back. "But we may discuss that later," Suvuk said. "My Chief Surgeon will also desire to hear what more you may have to say; the syndrome is a problem for us. My Chief Surgeon, Sobek; my Chief Engineer, T'Leiar; my First Officer, Sehlk." One after another his officers nodded in acknowledgement—the slightly stout doctor, Sobek; the willowy, blue-eyed T'Leiar, with her long black hair; and Sehlk, a man much like Suvuk, but younger—small, darker skinned than the others, and with a keen, ready, intense look about him, all very much controlled. "Captains, gentlebeings all, shall we sit? Captain Kirk no doubt has a great deal to discuss."

Everyone found his, her or its place. Jim heard Rihaul sit down with the usual bizarre noise in her bowl chair, and had to repress a laugh again. Deirr weren't really wet—their smooth, slick skin just looked that way, and in contact with some surfaces, acted that way. Rihaul had been complaining since the long-ago days at the Academy, where Jim was her math tutor, that the

Fleet-issue plastic bowl-chairs were the bane of her existence; sitting down in one invariably produced noises that almost every species considered embarrassing, and getting up against the resultant suction required mechanical assistance, or a lot of friends. Nowadays Nhauris and Jim had a running joke that the only reason she had become a Captain was to have a command bowl-chair that was upholstered in cloth.

"I think the first matter before us," Jim said, "is to briefly discuss the strategic situation. Tactics will follow." Spock handed him a tape; Jim slipped it into the table and activated it. The four small holoprojection units around the table came alive, each one constructing a three-dimensional map of the Galaxy, burning with the bright pinpoints of stars. The map rotated until one seemed to be looking straight "down" through the Galactic disk, and the focus tightened on the Sagittarius Arm—the irregular spiral-arm structure, thirty thousand light-years long and half as wide, that the Federation, the Romulans and the Klingons all shared. From this perspective, the Sag Arm (at least to Jim) looked rather like the North American continent; though it was North America missing most of Canada, and the United States as far west as the Rockies and as far south as Oklahoma. Sol sat on the shore of that great starry lacuna, about where Oklahoma City would have been.

"Here's where we stand," Jim said. The bright "continent" swelled in the map-cube, till the whole cubic was full of the area that would have been southwestern North America, Mexico and the Californias. "Federation, Romulan and Klingon territories are all marked according to the map key." Three sets of very lumpy, irregular shapes, like a group of wrestling amoebas, flashed into color in the starfield: red for the

Klingons, gold for the Romulans, blue for the Federation. There was very little regularity about their boundaries with one another, except for one abnormally smooth curvature, almost a section of an egg shape, where the blue space nested with and partly surrounded the gold. "Disputed territories are in orange." There was a lot of orange, both where blue met red and where red met gold; though rather more of the latter. "These schematics include the latest intelligence we have from both Romulans and Klingons. You can see that there are some problems in progress out there. The alliance between the Klingons and the Romulans is either running into some kind of trouble, or is not defined the way we usually define alliances. This gives us our first hint as to why we're out here, gentlebeings —unless Fleet was more open with one of you than it was with me."

Suvuk shook his head slightly; Walsh rolled his eyes at the ceiling. "I've rarely seen them so obtuse," Rihaul said. "Surely something particularly messy is coming up."

"Indeed," Jim said. "Which is why we will be needing to keep in very close touch with one another. Any piece of data, any midnight thought, may give us the clue to figuring out what's going to happen. My staff has done some research involving recent Romulan intelligence reports; I'll be passing that data on to you for your study and comment. Anything, any idea you may come up with, don't hesitate to call me. My intention is to keep this operation very free-form, at least until something happens. For something *will* happen."

"I wholly agree, Captain," Suvuk said. "Our mission here is as surely provocatory as it is investigatory. One does not waste a destroyer on empty space, or space one expects to stay empty. We are expected to force the Romulans' hand, as Captain Walsh would say."

Jim looked with carefully concealed surprise at Suvuk, who had flashed a quick mild glance at Walsh. *Is it just me?* he thought. *But, no, Vulcans don't make jokes. Certainly this one wouldn't*—"Yes, sir," Jim said. "With that in mind, here's our patrol pattern as I envision it; please make any suggestions you find apt."

The map's field changed again, becoming more detailed. The long curved ellipsoid boundary between the two spaces swelled to dominate the cubic; stars in the field became few. "Here we are," Jim said. "Sigma-285 and its environs. I suggest that we spread ourselves out as thinly as we can—not so far as to be out of easy communication with one another, but far enough apart to cover as much territory as possible with any given pattern."

"The ships would be a couple of hundred light-years or so apart," Walsh said.

"That's about right; the boundaries I was considering for the whole patrol area, at least to start with, would be defined by 218 Persei to the Galactic north, 780 Arietis to the south, and the 'east-west' distance along the lines from 56 Arietis to iota Andromedae; about half a Galactic degree. This way, any ship in need of assistance can have it within from a day to an hour, depending on what the situation is."

"*Inaieu* should at all times be at the heart of that pattern," Rihaul said, "so that she will have minimum response time for the other ships."

"That's right," Jim said. "That was my intention. I don't propose to hold *Enterprise* at flag position, out of the way, during the operation; firstly because she'll better serve us running patrol like everyone else, and secondly because she has something of a name among the Romulans. While out by herself, she may draw their attention, draw them out and give them an opportunity to let slip what's going on, on the other side of the Zone; either by communication among themselves, or with us. We have experts in Romulan codes and the Romulan common language aboard, awaiting such an opportunity. And should there be an engagement, all steps are to be taken to preserve and question survivors . . . if any Romulans allow themselves to survive."

"Noted," Suvuk said. "Captain, have you yet assigned patrol programs?"

"They're in the table for your perusal. Positions in the task force rotate."

"I see that *Enterprise* is flying point for our first run down the length of the Zone," Rihaul said, with a merry look at Jim, after she had studied the screen on the table before her. "Well, we could hardly grudge you that, could we? Your campaign, Captain. But do leave us something to do. We, too, get these sudden urges to save all Civilization."

"Captain," Jim said to her, grinning, "I have a nasty feeling that this operation will provide every one of us with ample opportunity to indulge those urges. Meanwhile I will give your request all the attention it deserves. . . . Anything else, gentlebeings? Comment? Suggestions?"

"Only that it would be logical to implement patrol immediately," Suvuk said.

"So ordered, sir." Jim got up; the others rose with him. "Everyone is dismissed to their commanders— would the Captains remain? Bones," he said to McCoy over the bustle in the room, mostly caused by Denebians running out as if to a fire, "no need for you to hang around if you don't want to—"

"Jim, are you kidding?" McCoy was obviously far gone in self-congratulation. "Did you hear what that man said about my—"

"Oh. Well, as long as you feel that way about it—" Suvuk came up to them at that point, along with the Vulcan medical officer, Sobek. "Captain," Suvuk said, "you wished to see me?"

"Only to deliver McCoy into your company, sir. He is so retiring that if I didn't order him to, he would certainly never allow himself the vanity of discussing one of his papers at any length. In fact, I'm sure he'd love to see your Sickbay—in detail. Please accompany Captain Suvuk, Bones. Don't worry about us: we won't wait up for you."

Jim watched in amusement as the Vulcans led McCoy away, politely talking medical terminology at him at a great rate. Bones had no time for more than one I'll-get-you-for-this look over his shoulder before they had him out of the room. "Spock," Jim said softly to the Vulcan, who had been solemnly watching the whole process from behind him, "I haven't had time to read it. Was the paper really that good?"

Spock looked at him sidelong. "After the spelling had been corrected," he said, "indeed it was."

Mike Walsh came over to Jim with that old calculating look on his face. "How about it, Jim? Got a few free hours for poker this evening?"

"No," Jim said firmly. "But I have twenty credits that say you can't beat our ship's chess champ with a queen handicap."

"Oh really? You're on. When do we start?"

Jim looked at Spock, eyed the door, put an eyebrow up. Spock looked thoughtful, nodded fractionally, and headed out for the lift and the transporters. "Right now," Jim said. "Come on, let's get Nhauris up."

"You two get out of here!"

"Dangerous business, coming between a Captain and her ship. Obviously this chair isn't doing too well at it. . . . Why, Captain, I do believe you've put on a bit of weight!"

Five

According to a widely-held Rihannsu military tradition, the best commanders were also often cranky ones. Normally Ael avoided such behavior. The showy, towering rages she had seen some of her own commanders periodically throw at their crews had only convinced Ael that she never wanted to serve under such a person in a crisis. Pretended excitability could too easily turn into the real thing.

Now, however, she saw a chance to turn that old tradition to good advantage. She came back from her tour of her fleet not positively angry, but looking rather discommoded and out of sorts when she reentered her Bridge. T'Liun noticed it instantly, and became most solicitous of Ael, asking her what sort of condition the other ships were in. Ael—hearing perfectly well t'Liun's intention to find out the cause of the mood and exploit it somehow—told t'Liun what she thought of the other ships, and the Klingons who had built them, and the Rihannsu crews who were mishandling them, at great length. It was a most satisfying tirade, giving Ael the opportunity to make a great deal of noise and relieve some of her own tension, while leaving t'Liun suspecting her of doing exactly that—though for all the wrong reasons.

Then off Ael stormed, and went on a cold-voiced rampage through the ship, upbraiding the junior officers for the poor repair of equipment that was generally in good condition. Late into the ship's night she prowled the corridors, terrorizing the offshift, peering into everything. The effect produced was perfect. Slitted eyes gazed after her in bitter annoyance, and in eavesdropping on ship's 'com, after she had theoretically retired for the night, Ael heard many suggestions made about her ancestry and habits that revised slightly upward her opinion of her crew's inventiveness. Ael felt much amused, and much relieved by the discharge of energy. But far more important, no one had noticed or thought anything in particular of a small interval she spent peering up a circuitry-conduit—an inspection from which she had come away frowning on the outside, but inside quite pleased. Ael fell asleep late, her cabin dark to everything but starlight—thanking her ancestors that the most immediate of them, her father, had once made her spend almost three months taking his own old Warbird apart, system by system, and putting it back together again.

In the morning she took things a step further. She called together t'Liun and tr'Khaell and the other senior officers and instructed them that they were to begin a complete check of all ship's systems. Her officers, not caring for the prospect of trying to do several weeks' work in the several days she was ordering, did their best to reassure Ael that the systems were in perfect working condition. Ael allowed herself, very briefly, to be mollified—thus setting up for a rage that even her worst old commanders would have approved of, when a message came in from Command later that day, and t'Liun's communications board overloaded and blew up.

Ael had been restraining herself the day before. Now she let loose, resurrecting some of the savagely elegant old idioms for incompetence that her father had used on her the day she forgot to fasten one of the gates of the farm, and three hundred of the *hlai* got out into the croplands. She raged, she flushed dark green-bronze (an inadvertent effect; she still blushed at the memory of that long-ago scolding, but the effect was fortuitous —it made the rage look better). She ordered the whole lot of them into the brig, then changed her mind: that was too good for them. They would all work their own shifts, as well as extra shifts doing the system analysis she had ordered in the first place. But none of them would touch the Elements-be-blessed communications board, which had probably been utterly destroyed by t'Liun's fumblings. Who knew what orders Command had had for them, and must they now send messages back saying, "Sorry, we missed that one"? She would let t'Liun have that dubious pleasure, and served her right; but in the meantime someone had best bring her a toolkit, and the rest of them had best stay out of her sight and make themselves busy lest she space them all in their underwear, *now get out!*

Afterward, when the Bridge was quiet except for one poor Antecenturion too cowed to look up or speak a word, Ael lay on her back under the overhang of the comm station and called silently on her father's fourth name, laughing inside like a madwoman. *Possibly I am mad, trying to make this work*, she thought, first killing all power to the board so that none of the circuit-monitoring devices t'Liun had installed in it would work. *But how then—should I lie here and do nothing? No, the thrai has a few bites left in her yet.* . . . Ael gently teased one particular logic solid out of its crystal-grip, holding it as lovingly as a jewel. The equipment she had been brought naturally included a portable power source; this she attached both to the solid and to the board, bringing up only its programming functions.

Reprogramming the logic solid, which held the ship's ID, was delicate work, but not too difficult; and she thought kindly of her father all through it. *Ael,* he had said again, *times will come when you won't have time to run the program and see if it works. It must be right the first time, or lives will be lost, and the responsibility will be on your head when you face the Elements at last—probably long before that, too. Do it again. Get it right the first time. Or it's the stables for you tomorrow.* . . .

She sat up with the little keypad in her lap, touching numbers and words into it, and thinking about responsibility . . . of lives not merely lost, but about to be thrown away. *Bitter, it is bitter. I am no killer.* . . . *Yet Command sent me here to be a prisoner; to rot, or preferably to die. What duty do I owe these fools? They've pledged me no loyalty; nor would they ever. They are my jailers, not my crew. Surely there's nothing wrong in escaping from jail.*

Yet I swore the Oath, once upon a time, by the Elements and my honor, to be good mistress to my crews, and to lead them safely and well. Does that mean I must keep faith with them even if they do me villainy? . . .

The thought of the Elements brought Ael no clear counsel. There was little surprise in that, out here in the cold of space, where earth was far away, and water and air both frozen as hard as any stone. The only Element she commonly dealt with was fire—in starfire and the matter-antimatter conflagration of her ship's engines. Ael had always found that peculiarly agreeable, for she knew her own Element to be fire's companion, air, and her realm what pierced it: weapons, words, wings. But even the thought of that old reassuring symmetry did nothing for her now. *Loyalty, the best part of the ruling Passion, that's of fire: if any spark of that fire were alive in them, I would serve it gladly. I would save them if I could. But there is none.*

Besides . . . there's a larger question. She sat still on the floor of her Bridge for a moment, seeing beyond it. There was the matter of the many lives that would be lost, both in the Empire and outside it, should the horrible thing a-birthing at Levaeri V research station come to term. Thousands of lives, millions; rebellion and war and devastation lashing through the Empire itself, then out among the Federation and the Klingons as well. For the Klingons she cared little; for the Federation she cared less—though that might be a function of having been at armed truce with them for all these years. Still—theirs were lives too.

And beyond mere war and horror lay an issue even deeper. When honor dies—when trust is a useless thing—what use is life? And that was what threatened the spaces around, and the Empire itself, where honor had once been a virtue . . . but would be no more. Tasting the lack of it for herself, here and now, in this place where no one could be trusted or respected, Ael knew the bitterness of such a lack right down to its dregs. Even the knowledge of faith kept elsewhere, of Tafv on his way and her old crew coming for her, could not assuage it. She had led a sheltered life until now, despite wounds and desperate battles; this desolate tour of duty had dealt her a wound from which she would never recover. She could only make sure that others did not have to suffer it.

She could only do so by sacrificing the crew of *Cuirass* to her stratagem. There was too much chance that they would somehow get word back to Command of what was toward, if she left them alive. But by killing them, Ael would make herself guilty of the same treachery she so despised in them; and with far less excuse (if excuse existed), for she knew the old way of life, knew honor and upright dealing. There was no justifying the spilling of all her crew's lives, despite their treachery to her. Ael would bear the weight of murder, and sooner or later pay their bloodprice in the most intimate possible coinage: her own pain. That was the way things worked, in the Elements' world; fire well used, warmed; ill used, burned. All that remained was the question of whether she would accept the blame for their deaths willingly, or reject it, blind herself to her responsibility, and prolong the Elements' retaliation.

She remembered her father, standing unhappily over one of the hlai that Ael had not been able to catch. It had gotten into the woods, and there it lay on the leafmold, limp and torn; a hnoiyika had gotten it, torn its breast out and left the hlai there to bleed out its life, as hnoiyikar will. Ael had stared at the hlai in mixed fascination and horror as it lay there with insects crawling in and out of the torn places, out of mouth and eyes. She had never seen a dead thing before. "This is why one must be careful with life," her father had said, in very controlled wrath. "Death is the most hateful thing. Don't allow the destruction of what you can never restore." And he had made her bury the hlai.

She looked up and sighed, thinking what strange

words those had seemed, coming from a warrior of her father's stature. Now, at this late date, they started to make sense . . . and she laughed again, at herself this time, a silent, bitter breath. Standing on the threshold of many murders, she was finally beginning to understand. . . .

Evidently I am already beginning to pay the price, she thought. *Very well. I accept the burden.* And she turned her mind back to her work, burying her wretched crew in her heart while instructing the logic solid in its own treachery. First, she pulled another logic solid out of her pocket, connected to the first one and then to the little powerpack. It was a second's work to copy the first solid's contents onto the blank. Then, after the duplicate was pocketed again, some more work on the original solid. A touch here, a touch there, a program that would loop back on itself in this spot, refuse to respond in that one, do several different things at once over here, when *Cuirass*'s screens perceived the appropriate stimulus. And finally the whole adjustment locked away under a coded retrieval signal, so that t'Liun would notice nothing amiss, and analysis (if attempted) would reveal nothing.

Done. She went back under the panel again, locked the logic solid back into its grip, and closed up the panel again, tidying up after herself with a light heart. No further orders would reach this panel from Command. It would receive them, automatically acknowledge them, and then dump them, without alerting the Communications Officer. It would do other things too—as her crew would discover, to its ruin.

Ael got up and left the toolkit lying where it was for someone else to clean up—that would be in character for her present role, though it went against her instincts for tidiness. She swung on the poor terrified Antecenturion minding the center seat, and instructed him to call t'Liun to the Bridge; she herself was going to her quarters, and was not to be disturbed on peril of her extreme displeasure. Then out Ael stalked, making her way to her cabin. In the halls, the crewpeople she met avoided her eyes. Ael did not mind that at all.

She settled down to wait.

She did not have to wait long. She had rather been hoping that Tafv would for once discard honor and attack by ship's night. But it was broad afternoon, the middle of dayshift, when her personal computer with the copied logic-solid attached to it began to read out a ship's ID, over and over. She ripped the solid free of the computer and pocketed it, glanced once around her bare dark cabin. There was nothing here she needed. Slowly, not hurrying, she headed in the general direction of Engineering. The engine room itself had the usual duty personnel, no more; she waved an uncaring salute at them and went on through to where *Hsaaja* stood. As the doors of the secondary deck closed behind her, the alarm sirens began their terrible screeching; someone on the Bridge had visual contact with a ship in the area. Calmly, without looking back, Ael got into *Hsaaja,* sealed him up, brought up the power. It would be about now that they realized, up in the Bridge, that their own screens were not working.

"Khre'Riov t'Rllaillieu urru Oira!" the ship's annunciator system cried in t'Liun's voice, again and again. But Ael would never set foot on *Cuirass*'s Bridge again; and the cry grew fainter and fainter, vanishing at last with the last of the landing bay's exhausted air. Ael lifted *Hsaaja* up on his underjets, nudged him toward the opening doors of the bay, the doors that no Bridge override could affect now. Then out into space, hard

downward and to the rear, where an unmodified War-bird could not fire. *Cuirass* shuddered above Ael to light phaser fire against which the ship could not protect herself. Space writhed and rippled around *Cuirass*; she submerged into otherspace, went into warp, fled away.

Ael looked up with angry joy at the second Warbird homing in on her, its landing bay open for her. She kicked *Hsaaja's* ion-drivers in, arrowing toward home, and security, and war.

Six

"How's the focus, Jerry?"

"Mmm—can't see any difference. Here, change places with me."

They were the first words Jim heard that morning as he passed through Recreation in search of a cup of coffee and Harb Tanzer, the Rec Chief; but Jim forgot the search for a moment and paused in the middle of the room. The place was as busy as always—the gamma workshift had gone off duty some six hours before, but was still playing hard; and delta shift would start trickling in shortly, as soon as alpha relieved them. Jim was alpha shift right now, all the department heads of the various ships in the task force having gone over to that schedule to make meetings and communications easier. That was why he was slightly surprised to find Uhura, apparently long awake and sprightly, stretched out more or less under the control console for the holography stage and tinkering with its innards. Standing over the console was Lieutenant Freeman from Life Sciences, making swift adjustments and scowling at the results.

"How's that?"

"Uh-uh. Come on, Nyota, let me do it."

"Heading up to the Bridge?" said a voice by his shoulder. Jim turned around. There was Harb Tanzer, holding two cups of coffee, one of which he offered to Jim.

"Do you read minds?" Jim said, taking a careful sip.

"No, I leave that to Spock." Harb grinned. "Vulcans might think it was an infringement on their prerogatives. Or I'd probably get in trouble with their unions or something. Do Vulcans have unions?"

"Only by mail," Jim said, and took another drink of coffee, watching with satisfaction as Harb spluttered into his. "What're these two up to?"

"I was about to come find out myself; they've been in here since the middle of delta. Uhura's up early, and it has to be the middle of the night for Freeman. . . ."

"It can wait. I was looking for you. You're up early, too, now that I think of it."

"Talking to the computer, that's all. Checking out the crew efficiency levels."

"You *do* read minds."

"No, just my job description."

"How are they?"

Harb actually shrugged. "They're fine, Captain. Reaction time to orders is excellent—very crisp. The crew as a whole is calm, assured—very unworried. They trust you to bring them through this without any major problems."

"I wish I had their confidence in me."

"You should."

"So McCoy tells me . . ."

"Yes, I saw that game. Jim, the computer's analysis shows no department aboard this ship exhibiting signs of an anxiety level higher than plus-one. It's the unknown that frightens people. This is just Romulans."

" 'Just . . .' " Jim gazed over at Freeman, who was now lying under the console, and Uhura, who was adjusting the controls on top. "Oh, well. How are the other ships?"

"*Constellation*'s fine. Randy Cross, the Rec officer over there, tells me they're about on a par with us—plus-ones and an occasional plus-one point five. By the way, why do they call Captain Walsh 'Mike the Greek'? I thought he was Irish or something."

"Reference to an old Earth legend, I think. The Greek either invented democracy or handicapping, I can't remember which." Harb snorted into his coffee again. "But do a little discreet snooping for me and see if there's a betting pool going on over there."

"Certainly, Captain. Want a little action?"

"Mr. Tanzer! Are you accusing me of being a gambler?"

"Oh, *never*, sir."

"Good—I think. What about the Vulcans?"

"Well, *Intrepid* doesn't have a Recreation department per se, though they have the same sort of rec room as we have. Recreation's handled out of Medicine, and gets prescribed if someone needs it. But Sobek tells me that no one does. They're all running the usual Vulcan equivalency levels, plus-point five or so. *Inaieu*, though—"

"I bet they're having a good time over there. They love trouble."

"Plus-point fives and point sevens, right across the board."

Jim glanced at Harb in concern. "That's *too* good a time."

"Not for Denebians. The Deirr are the most nervous, generally. But they're not very worried either."

Jim gave silent thanks that Rihaul was a Deirr; nervous Captains tended to be better at keeping their crews alive. "Something should be done to harness levels like those, nevertheless. I'll talk to Rihaul. Anyway, you've answered all the questions I had for you." Jim glanced up at the wall chrono. "About ten minutes, yet. No harm in being early . . ." He trailed off. "What *are* they doing?"

"Okay, try it now," Freeman's voice said, slightly muffled since his head and shoulders were up inside the console. "That first tape."

Uhura picked a tape up from the console, inserted it and hit one of the console's controls. Immediately the holography stage lit up with the figure of a seated man, with another man beside him. They both looked bitter. "I coulda *been* somebody!" the first man said angrily. "I coulda been a con*tenda!*"

"No, the other one," Freeman's voice said from inside the machinery. Uhura pulled the tape, and the two men vanished.

Realization dawned. "Harb," Jim said, "*this* is the crewman who's been rechanneling all that archival stuff and showing it on ship's channels in the evenings? I thought he was in Life Sciences."

"Xenobiology," Harb said. "This is his hobby, though. It's useful enough. The data have been digitized and available for flat display for years, but no one's cared enough about a lot of this material to rechannel it for 3-D and ambient sound. Freeman, though, loves everything as long as it was made before 2200. It took him about three months to get the image-processing program running right, but since it's been up he's enlarged the entertainment-holo library by about ten percent. He mentioned to me yesterday that he wanted to do some fine-tuning on the program so he could rechannel some of the old Vulcan dramas and send them over to *Intrepid*."

Jim stepped closer to the console, followed by Harb, and stood there watching the proceedings along with several other curious crewpeople. "Captain," one of them said to him, knotting several tentacles in a gesture of respect. "Well rested?"

"Very well, Mr. Athendë," Jim said absently. "How's Lieutenant Sjveda's music appreciation seminar coming along?"

"Classical period still, sir. Beethoven, Stravinsky, Vaughan Williams, Barber, Lennon, Devo. Head hurts."

"Bet it does," Jim said, wondering where the Sulamid, who seemed to be nothing but a tangle of tentacles and a sheaf of stalked eyes, might consider his head to be. "Not overdo it, Mr. Athendë. Take in small doses."

"Here we are," Uhura said, and dropped another tape in the read slot, hit the control. For a second nothing seemed to be happening on the stage. Then a peculiar grinding, wheezing sound began to fill the air. On the platform there slowly faded into existence a tall blue rectangular structure with doors in it, and a flashing white light on top, and what appeared to be the Anglish words POLICE PUBLIC CALL BOX blazoned on the front panel above the doors. There was a pause, during which the noise and the flashing light both stopped.

Then one of the box's doors opened. To Jim's mild amusement, a hominid, quite Terran-looking, peered out and gazed around him in great interest; a curly-haired person in a burgundy jacket, with a floppy hat, a striped scarf of truly excessive length, and sharp bright eyes above a dazzling smile, ingenuous as a child's. "I beg your pardon," the man said merrily in a British-accented voice, apparently looking right at Jim, "but is this Heathrow?"

Brother, have you ever taken a wrong turn! was Jim's first thought. "Harb," he said, "is that man happy in Xeno?"

"Very."

"Pity. With a talent like this, we could use him in Communications."

"Uhura thinks so too."

"Speaking of which—" But Uhura had been watching the chrono. She reached down and thumped on the side of the console. "Jerry, I'm on duty in a few minutes." She glanced up, caught sight of Jim and Harb standing there, and grinned a little. "Keep up the good work," she said. "I'll see you later."

She left him there with his head still inside the console, and crossed to Jim and Harb. "You really must be bored if you're getting up early to watch old sterries, Uhura," Jim said. "Maybe I should find you some more work to do. . . ."

She chuckled at him. "Harb," she said, "I think we've got the last bugs worked out of it. Mr. Freeman wanted to be very sure—he knows how picky Vulcans are. Once he's done with that last batch for *Intrepid*, though, he's ready for requests."

"Good enough. Thanks, Lieutenant."

"My pleasure. Coming, Captain?"

"After you."

They headed for the Bridge lift together. "Are you taking up this hobby too, Uhura?"

"Oh, no, sir. Bridge," she said to the lift as the doors closed. "This is professional interest. Mr. Freeman has some novel ideas in image and signal processing, computer techniques that a communications specialist might not think to try. He's been doing some specialty programs for the Xeno labs that might actually be of some use in cleaning up subspace communication. Interstellar ionization is always a problem, it mangles the highest and lowest bandwidths and slows down transmission speed. The sub-ether carrier wavicles—"

The doors opened onto the Bridge. "Uhura," Jim said, "I'm still working on my coffee. . . ."

She smiled wryly at him. "Noted," she said. "I'll write you a report."

"Do that. And log me in, please."

"Yes, sir."

"And a good morning to you, Mr. Spock," Jim said, stepping down to the center seat as Spock stood up from it. "Report, please."

"Your initial patrol pattern is running without incident," Spock said, "and the Neutral Zone appears quiet. *Intrepid* is at 'point' position at this time, two hundred eighty-four light-years ahead of us on bearing one eighty mark plus six, in the vicinity of 2450 Trianguli. We have dropped back to pace *Inaieu*, which is at two-seventy mark zero, one hundred fifteen light-years away; and *Constellation* is flying rearguard at zero mark minus three, two hundred ninety-two light-years behind. The whole task force is maintaining an average speed of warp four point four five."

"Very good. How's the weather?"

Spock looked grave. "Generally unremarkable so

far. However, Captain, the computer has presented me with some very unusual figures regarding the ion-flux research we were pursuing before this operation."

Jim nodded at Spock to continue. The Vulcan looked down at the clipboard he was carrying with an expression that suggested there was something distasteful about the data on it. "You remember the analysis of a meteoric debris sample that Mr. Naraht carried out at my request."

"You were interested in the figure for the iridium, weren't you?"

"Affirmative. The amount of the isotope—for it was not "normal" iridium—was abnormally high, indicating that the piece of matter in question had been bombarded with extremely high levels of hard radiation in the recent past. That sample was taken from one of the areas we passed through on the way to maneuvers, an area on which I had other data and desired a fresh sample. The peculiar thing is that other samples from approximately the same area, older ones, do not reflect the same bombardment. And there has been ion-storm activity in that area since."

"Any conclusion?"

Spock looked as unhappy as he ever allowed himself to in public. "None as yet, Captain. It would be possible to indulge in all kinds of flights of speculation—"

"But you are refraining."

"With difficulty," Spock said, quietly enough for only Jim to hear him. "The situation is most abnormal. Mr. Naraht is running further studies for me."

"Yes. How *is* my favorite pan pizza doing?"

"Sir?"

"Sorry, I couldn't resist. How is he?"

Jim never found out, for at that moment Uhura's

board beeped for attention. She put a hand up to the transdator in her ear, listened briefly, then said, "Captain, it's the *Intrepid*, if you want to talk to them."

"Put them on."

Uhura flicked a switch. The main screen's starfield blinked out—to be replaced by a screen full of static.

"Bloody," Uhura said under her breath. "Sorry, sir, I can't raise them now. The *Intrepid*'s comm officer was reporting the bow-shock edge of an ion storm—force four, he said, and it looked to be worsening."

"Were they all right?"

"Oh, yes, he said it wasn't anything they couldn't ride out. It was just their routine hourly report."

"Very well. Pass the information along to the other ships and have them take precautions." Jim sighed in very mild annoyance, then looked up at Spock and saw him still wearing that uncomfortable look. "Well," Jim said, "here it comes. It's not as if you didn't warn Fleet that the climate around here is changing in a hurry. Looks like our operation's going to get caught right in the middle of it."

"So it appears," Spock said. "Though, truly, Captain, I am uncertain what we could do about the problem even if Starfleet Command decided to dedicate all of Fleet to the problem. Relocating entire populations is hardly desirable, or feasible. And there is still something. . . ." He trailed off.

"What?"

"Unknown. I am missing data, Captain. Though I find it most interesting that the subject of our research extends eighteen hundred light-years past the area of the Galaxy where we were studying it."

"*Intrepid* again, Captain," Uhura said, working hard over her board to hold the signal. "Their comm officer managed to get a squirt through between storm wavefronts. It's up to force six, but they predict it'll stabilize at that force and then break somewhere in the neighborhood of 766 Trianguli. They'll leave further reports with the unmanned Zone monitoring stations as they pass them—that way they won't have to waste time trying to punch through the interference. Their status is otherwise normal; the area's clear."

"Eminently logical," Jim said.

—and the ship abruptly went on automatic red alert, lights flashing and sirens whooping. All over the Bridge, people jumped for battle stations. "Ship in the area, Captain!" Uhura said. "Not Federation traffic."

"Identify it!"

"No ID yet. Power consumption reading, nothing more—"

"Warship, Captain," Spock said, back at his post and looking down his hooded viewer. "An extravagant power-consumption curve. Approaching from out of the Neutral Zone at warp eight."

Bingo, Jim thought. *At last it's beginning.* "Course?"

"Not an intercept. I would say it has been unaware of us until now."

"ID now, Captain," Uhura said, looking both excited and puzzled. "It's a Klingon ship!"

"The Klingons have been selling the Romulans ships for a long time now—"

"Noted, sir. But the ID is unmistakably Klingon code and symbology. KL 77 *Ehhak*."

It was a name Jim recognized from accounts of the Battle of Organia: one of the ships that had invested the planet. "What the hell are they doing here? Mr. Chekov, arm photon torpedoes, prepare to lock phasers on for firing. Mr. Sulu, prepare evasive action but do not execute."

"Aye, sir."

"Phasers locked on, sir."

"Excellent. Hold your fire until my express order, Mr. Chekov."

"Aye, sir."

"Intruder's range—"

"Not a Klingon ship," Spock said abruptly. "ID is in fact Klingon. But the power-consumption curve is inconsistent with either the old *Akif*-class or new *K'tinga*-class warships. Range now six hundred eighty light-years and closing. Course is still not an intersect. If this continues they will pass far above and ahead of the task force—"

"Another contact!" Uhura said. "Romulan this time. ChR 63 *Bloodwing*—"

Jim's fist clenched, hard. "Course?"

"Following the first ship," Spock said. "Closing on it at warp nine."

"Uhura, messages to *Inaieu* and *Constellation*. All screens up, and battle stations. But if either ship comes within range, do *not* fire unless fired upon! Let them pass."

"Yes, Captain."

"We'll see what they're up to," Jim said. "I am willing to be forgiving of an accidental intrusion into Federation space—always supposing the intruders tell me why they've come without calling first."

"Indications are that the first ship will shortly be unable to tell you anything, Captain," said Spock. "The ship with the *Bloodwing* ID is closing on it very—More data; the ship ID'ing as *Ehhak* is actually a ship of the old Romulan Warbird class. Cloaking device in place but not functioning. *Ehhak* is beginning evasive maneuvers, but they are proving ineffectual. *Bloodwing* continues to close."

"Range—"

"Two hundred fifteen light-years. Two hundred—Better readings on *Bloodwing*, now. Its power-consumption curve too is atypical. Warp engines have been boosted, and other alterations are indicated—One hundred fifty light-years—"

"Time till they cross the Neutral Zone—"

"At this speed, four seconds." Spock watched in silence. "*Ehhak* has crossed. Now *Bloodwing*. Visual contact—"

The screen leapt to life with their images—two Romulan Warbirds, both screened, screaming out of the Neutral Zone high above the plane of the *Enterprise*'s travel. The pursued ship veered suddenly, trying to shake its pursuer; to no avail. *Bloodwing* would not be shaken. "Still closing," Spock said. "One hundred light-years from us. Seventy-five. They will pass within twenty-two point six three light-years of the *Enterprise* at closest. *Bloodwing* continues to close on *Ehhak*. Within firing range. Firing."

"Gently, Mr. Chekov," Jim said, noticing his navigator's twitch. "They're not shooting at us, not yet."

"Noted, sir."

"Good man. Result of fire, Mr. Spock—"

"None as yet. *Ehhak* is turning again. Toward *Bloodwing*, this time. Firing now—No effect. Standoff. Firing again—"

The blast of blinding light that suddenly filled the screen lit the whole Bridge like lightning. When it faded Spock said quietly. "Evidently some of the alterations installed in *Bloodwing* have been to its phaser systems. Their intent was apparently to draw *Ehhak* into range for quick and certain destruction. Obviously they succeeded."

"Noted," Jim said softly. "*Bloodwing*'s location and course, Mr. Spock."

"Its old course took it somewhat past us, Captain. Turning now: fifty-three light-years away on bearing one-ninety-nine mark plus-eighteen. Approaching us."

"Status," Jim said, beginning to twitch a little himself.

"Slowing," Spock said. "Screens up, but no sign of further belligerence. Down to warp six now; warp five; holding at warp five exactly, and coasting in toward us. If the Romulan continues along this course, *Bloodwing* will be paralleling our course at a distance of one light-second from us."

"Neighborly," Jim said. "Hold the screens as they are. We'll wait and see what they do."

And they waited, the Bridge becoming very still indeed. Closer and closer *Bloodwing* glided to them. After about a minute she had no motion relative to *Enterprise*, but was soaring along beside her in neat formation, a hundred and eighty-six thousand miles away.

Ten seconds passed, and three hundred sixty million kilometers of empty space, and several breaths' worth of silence.

Uhura's board beeped.

She listened to her transdator, then said, "They're hailing us, Captain."

"Answer the hail. Offer them an open channel if they want it."

Uhura spoke softly to her board. The screen shimmered.

They found themselves looking, as they had looked once before, at the cramped Bridge of a Warbird-class Romulan vessel. A man in the usual Romulan uniform —dark-glittering tunic and breeches, with a scarflike scarlet half-cloak fastened front and back over one shoulder—stood facing the Bridge pickup. He was of medium height, dark skinned for a Romulan, with even features and a slightly hooked nose; young and well built, with auburn hair cropped short in a style reminiscent of the Vulcan fashion, and light, narrow, noticing eyes. He spoke in Romulan, which the translator in Uhura's board handled with the usual disconcerting nonsynchronization of mouth movements. "Enterprise," the Romulan said, *"I am Subcommander Tafv tr'Rllaillieu, second in command of the Romulan warship* Bloodwing. *Do I address Captain James Kirk?"*

Jim stood up, feeling an odd urge to match the young man's courteous tone, even if there might be a trick behind it. "You do," he said. Then he paused a moment. "Sir—may I ask if by chance you are related to a Commander by the name of *Ael* t'Rllaillieu?" He said it the best he could, hoping the translator would straighten out his mangled pronunciation.

The Subcommander smiled very slightly. *"You may, Captain. I am the Commander's son."*

"Thank you. May I also ask what brings you into our space under such—unusual—circumstances?"

"Again, you may. The Commander's business brings us here. I am directed to express to you Commander t'Rllaillieu's desire to meet with you and any members of your staff you find appropriate, to discuss with you a matter which will be as much to your advantage as to ours."

"What matter, Subcommander?"

"I regret that I may not say, Captain. This is an unshielded channel, and the business is urgent and confidential in the extreme."

"What conditions for the meeting?"

"The Commander is willing to beam over to your

vessel, unescorted. As I have said, the matter is urgent, and the Commander has no desire to stand on ceremony at the moment."

"May I consider briefly?"

"Certainly." The young man bowed slightly, and the screen went dark, showing stars again, and *Bloodwing* hanging there, silent.

Jim sat down in the helm for a moment, swung it around to face Spock. "Well, well. What now? Recommendations, ladies and gentlemen?"

Spock stood up from a last look down his viewer and folded his arms, looking very thoughtful indeed. "This is a vessel we know, Captain."

"No kidding," Jim said. "She's singed our tail a few times. Of course we've singed hers too. . . ."

"However," Spock said, "while we have often been at enmity with *Bloodwing*, the ship has never acted in a treacherous fashion toward us. In fact, often very much the contrary. Ael t'Rllaillieu, whoever she may be, has dealt honorably enough with us, though we have never seen her."

"True enough," Jim said. He remembered the shock after their first engagement, over by 415 Arietis it had been—on fighting a whole week's fight-and-run battle with *Bloodwing* and finding out afterward that the "t'" prefix on the house-name denoted a woman. *Oh God, not another one,* he had thought at the time. But he had changed his mind since, after a few victories, and a couple of defeats. He wanted to meet this old fox, very much indeed.

And now he had the chance.

"Well, Mr. Spock," he said, "we came all this way to gather information about the Romulans, and now it seems they've got some for us. Let's see what the Commander wants. Uhura?"

She nodded. The screen came back on again; Jim rose. "Subcommander," he said, "if you will be good enough to come within transporter range, and provide my communications officer with the Commander's co-ordinates, we will be delighted to receive her. Beaming in three hundred seconds precisely. Uhura, give the Subcommander a five-second tick for his reference."

"Thank you, Captain," said Tafv, *"we have that information. I will confer with your officer.* Bloodwing out."

Jim turned his back on the star-filled screen. "Uhura," he said, "when you've finished that, page Dr. McCoy and have him report to the Transporter Room. Come on, Spock. We mustn't keep the lady waiting."

Seven

Five minutes later, Jim said to the transporter chief, "Energize, Mr. Kyle."

Light danced and dazzled on the platform, settling into a woman's silhouette. The silhouette grew three-dimensional, darkened, solidified. The dazzle faded away.

Jim stood very still for a second or so, simply regarding her. She was little. Somehow he had always thought of her as being tall, lean and ascetic; or else tall, muscular and athletic. He was not prepared for this tiny woman, smaller even than the other female Romulan Commander he and Spock had dealt with. If she was five foot one, that was granting her an inch or so; if she weighed as much as a hundred and ten pounds, that was on a dense planet. She was wearing her hair braided and coiled at the nape of her neck; exposing the upswept and pointed Vulcanoid ears; there was gray in those neat, tight braids. The woman's build and facial structure were so delicate that she looked as if she could be broken between one's hands—but knowing Romulans, Jim knew much better. She had great dark eyes and a mouth with much smiling behind it, to judge by the few wrinkles that showed there; and looking at her, Jim could see where Subcommander Tafv had come by that proud nose. But probably the most striking thing about her was her age, and the way she bore it. Jim had never thought to see a woman with such an aura of power, or one who seemed to take that power so much for granted. She carried herself like a banner, or a weapon: like something proud and dangerous, but momentarily at rest. Jim found himself wondering whether he would look that good when he was—how old was she? Romulans were of Vulcan stock, after all. She could be well up in her hundreds—

"Permission to come aboard," the Commander said.

"Permission granted." Jim stepped around from behind the transporter console, Spock pacing him. "And welcome."

She stood there quite relaxed, looking Jim up and down, then favoring Spock with the same calm, unthreatening examination. Jim used the moment to continue his own. "They've changed the uniform," he said.

The Commander glanced down at her tunic and breeches and boots, then smiled; a wry expression. "It was well changed," she said. "The kilt on the old uniform was a drafty bit of tailoring, and difficult to work in." She stepped down from the Transporter platform, looking around her with curiosity. "Is my translator functioning adequately?" she said. "It was a hasty business, reprogramming it for Federation Basic."

"So far it seems to be doing well enough," Jim said.

"If you like, though, Dr. McCoy here will help equip you with one of our intradermal models."

"I would appreciate that," said the Commander. "We have talking to do, and there must be no chance of imprecision or error; too much rests on it."

She looked at Jim with such perfect ease that for a moment he was envious. *Would I be so calm after I had delivered myself into the hands of the enemy? What cards is she holding?* "So here at last," she said, "is my old friend Captain Kiurrk." Doubtless some flicker of reaction got out despite Jim's best intentions, for she smiled again. "Perhaps I will just call you Captain; for it does not do to mishandle names." She turned to Spock. "Yours, though, I think I can say, estranged though our languages are. And yours," she said, glancing toward Bones, "might almost be Romulan. But 'Doctor' is an honorable title, so if I may, I will call you that. Gentlemen, may we go where we can talk? Handsome as this room is, it hardly looks like a reception area."

"This way," Jim said, and led the group out and down the hall to the Officers' Lounge. He bowed the Commander in; and the first thing she responded to was not the elegant appointments, or the artwork, or the refreshments laid out, but the large port that looked out on the stars. That starlight was wavering, the uncomfortable starlight of unfiltered otherspace. Nevertheless she looked long and hard at it before she turned away. "The view must be marvelous," she said, "when the ship is not in warp."

"It is," Jim said. "Commander, will you sit?"

"Gladly." Without a moment's hesitation she slipped past the two couches set by the low refreshment table, and sat down in the single chair that faced them both, the chair commanding both the best view of the

couches' occupants and the best access to the table—
the chair Jim had intended to sit in. He smiled, said
nothing, and made himself comfortable on one couch;
but McCoy, fishing around in his medikit for a translator implant and the spray injector to fit it into, caught
Jim's eye and raised one eyebrow before turning his
attention back to business.

"Commander," Jim said, "what can we do for you?"

"For the moment, listen," said the Commander.
"More strenuous service may come later, however, if
you agree with what I have to say. First, though, I have
given you no name. I am Ael."

Spock, who had seated himself beside Jim, looked
momentarily startled, and immediately composed himself. "Your First Officer understands, perhaps better
than most, that we are chary about giving others even
our first names, even when they are already known,"
Ael said. "And there are other names more private yet.
But I can think of no other way to demonstrate my
sincerity to you from the start, since many of the things
I must now say to you will sound incredible. I urge you,
study to credit them. The whole Romulan Empire, and
the Federation, and the Klingon Empire as well, rests
on how seriously you take me."

"Tell us your problem, madam," Spock said.

"It will not be simply told." Seeing that McCoy was
ready, Ael held out her arm to him; he took it, picked a
spot on the inside of the forearm, and used the spray
injector to install the translator's neutral implant up
against the brachial nerve. "How is that? All right?—
Well enough. Captain, have you ever heard of a place
called Levaeri V?"

Jim considered for a moment. "Levaeri is a star in
Romulan space, if I remember right. I would assume
the 'V' refers to a planet."

"It does. Actually, the planet itself is uninhabited; a space station, built for research purposes, circles it. The Empire has been doing research there for some fifteen years into the nature and exploitation of genetic material, particularly the building-block molecule that governs and transmits life, along with its various messenger segments."

"DNA and RNA," said McCoy.

"Correct. The research has been secret, for reasons you will come to understand. But it is very nearly complete now. If the fruit of that research is allowed to escape into our civilization, it will destroy it—and eventually yours. The research has specifically involved the genetic material of Vulcans."

Spock sat up very straight. Jim glanced sideways at him—knowing that putting-it-all-together look from long experience—but for the moment said nothing but, "Toward what purpose?"

"The scientists at Levaeri V have been correcting Vulcan DNA and messenger RNA for the genetic drift that has occurred over the years between Romulan and Vulcan genetic material—so that the drift-corrected material can be used to give Romulans the paramental abilities of trained Vulcans."

"My God," Bones said softly.

Jim sat there wondering if he had missed something. Certainly it sounded dire. . . . "Bones, explain."

McCoy looked as though he would rather have done anything else. "Jim, this research—if I'm understanding Ael correctly—had its earliest antecedents on Earth in some very primitive mind experiments concerning planaria. Flatworms, as they're called. If you teach a flatworm something—takes awhile, I can tell you—and then chop it up and feed it to other flatworms, the worms that ate the first one will learn the same trick the first worm learned, but much more quickly than normal. This is a terrible oversimplification, but RNA and DNA can be passed from one creature to another by numerous means, even simple ingestion. It caused a lot of poor jokes for a while about how 'you are what you eat.' But some of our own chemical-learning techniques that we commonly use in Starfleet for speed learning are based in the same technology, considerably updated and refined."

"We understand one another," Ael said. She looked somewhat relieved, but also unnerved, as if actually discussing the subject in public frightened her. "The process I speak of is even more refined than the chemical-learning techniques, which we also possess—"

"Stolen from us, I believe," Jim said mildly.

Ael gave him a sharp look, then smiled, that wry expression again. "Yes, we are always stealing things from one another, are we not? I would like to come back to that later, Captain. But for the moment let me say that the scientists have refined the techniques to dangerous levels. Some bright creature—the Elements should only have taken him back to Themselves—got the idea that, since we are brother stock to the Vulcans, surely they could teach us what they know of the arts and disciplines of the mind, to our great benefit—"

"Madam," Spock said, leaning forward and looking at Ael with great intensity, "those techniques of the mind were not developed until long after the Vulcan colony ships bearing your remote ancestors had left. In the warlike state of the pre-Reformation civilization, before the Peace of Surak, the techniques could never have been developed at all. And the Romulan civilization as we know it preserves to this day almost exactly the same combative atmosphere as existed on Vulcan before the Reformation—unless you can give us some better news."

"If I could, Mr. Spock," Ael said, laughing with a trace of bitterness, "I would not have had to blow up my old ship to keep word of my actions from getting back into the Empire. I would not have been exiled to the Neutral Zone at all. Perhaps there would be no Zone. But those are all wishes, and I am wandering from my story. The researchers at Levaeri determined that such abilities, the mind-techniques such as mindmeld and mindfusion and touch telepathy, and such lesser physical techniques as the healing trance and controlled 'hysterical strength,' could in fact be successfully passed on to the nontalented, and quite simply—by a procedure involving, among other things, selective neutral-tissue grafts to the corpus callosum and spinal cord, and a series of injections of the DNA and RNA fragments into the cerebrospinal fluid."

"It could be done," McCoy said, looking rather upset. "Certainly it could. But you would need—"

"Donor tissue, yes," Ael said. "Brain tissue, both 'white' and 'gray,' and cerebrospinal fluid cultures, from mentally talented Vulcans. A great deal of it, at first, until cultures had been perfected that were sufficiently innocuous not to be rejected outright by the recipient's autoimmune system. Naturally the researchers at Levaeri could not simply take ship across the Zone to Vulcan and ask for some good-quality live Vulcan brain tissue; any more than the Vulcans would have given it to them for any reason whatsoever. So the researchers began—borrowing—Vulcans."

Spock looked at Jim. "Captain," he said, "this is the reason why I asked the Federation Interstellar Shipping Commission for the data on all recent ship losses. My preliminary studies were showing an odd jump in the curve—a nearly statistical probability that spacefaring Vulcans were going missing more frequently than were travelers of other species. I had hoped very much that I was wrong—"

"But you were not," Ael said. "Romulans were taking them, Mr. Spock. They were taken to Levaeri V—as many Vulcans as the researchers thought could be kidnapped without anyone really noticing—and there they were used as experimental subjects and tissue donors."

Jim looked across at McCoy, who was practically trembling with rage. "This is monstrous, Commander," he said, controlling himself very tightly.

"Certainly it is, Doctor," she said. "What honor is there in taking one's enemies by stealth, giving them no chance to fight back, and then binding and torturing and slaughtering them like animals? But there's worse to come. Surely you must realize the purpose of the research. The Empire's High Command greatly desires the Vulcan mind-techniques for a weapon against its enemies—against you, and eventually against the Klingons, who are swiftly becoming a garment too tight for us. And the High Command has been an unscrupulous lot for some time now. The Command, and the Praetorate and Senate, will demand to be the first to use the newly developed techniques. The implementation would not take long, I understand; a clinic-type surgery, followed by several injections and a very brief period of training. Then— Can you imagine, just by way of example, the kind of place Vulcan would be if its people at large, and its rulers in particular, had never developed the logics of peace and ethical behavior that Surak brought—and had the mind techniques anyway?"

Spock looked more grave than Jim had seen him in a

long time. Evidently the thought had occurred to him at one time or another. "A culture of ruthless opportunists," he said, "violating one another's minds for gain, or for power, or even for the mere pleasure of the act. Turmoil among the great as they struggle for preeminence and domination, trying to keep the techniques for themselves. Rebellion among those who do not have the techniques, and desire to, at any cost. War . . ."

"Worse than war," Ael said. "A world in which no thought that did not agree with the present political 'gospel' would be safe—where a chance whim, a moment's disaffection, could mean death at the hands of those who were listening to your thoughts. A world in which honor and trust would swiftly become devalued coinage, and personal integrity a death warrant, if it crossed the desires of those who controlled the technique, those in power. The process has already started. Right now on Romulus and Remus there is already considerable political infighting going on over who will first get the technique when it becomes available. Who will first read all the others' minds? Who will first learn his enemies' secrets? And of course there are people who must be prevented at all costs from learning one's own secret business. A lively trade in assassination is springing up." Ael said the word as if it tasted bad. "We have already lost four Senators to the ambition or fear of people in high places."

Jim nodded slowly, now fully understanding those deaths by "natural causes."

Ael sat silent for a moment, as if gathering her thoughts. "Gentlemen," Ael said, "I will be open with you. I am a warrior, and I find peace very dull. But honor I cherish; and I see, with the completion and release of this technique, the rise of a new Romulan

Empire that will have lost the last vestiges of the glory and honor of the old one. I have sworn oaths to that Empire, to serve it loyally. To stand by and do nothing about the destruction of the ancient and noble tradition on which that Empire is based, is to put the knife into it oneself. I will not. The research station at Levaeri V must be destroyed before the information and materials stored there can be disseminated throughout the Empire."

Jim and Spock and McCoy looked at one another. It was now very plain what Starfleet's problem had been —for there was no hinting at this situation in the open. If the Klingons heard so much as a word about it, they would be at war with the Romulans instantly, trying to get their hands on the same technology. It might not work as well for them, but that would hardly matter; once they had subordinated Romulan space, which was the buffer between them and the Federation, the next step would be to cross the former Neutral Zone and attack the only remaining enemy. *And*—the thought sent a cold chill down Jim's back—*how many officials in the Federation, on any one of a thousand planets, would be willing to pay any price for such an advantage over their opponents? Even benevolent motives couldn't be trusted. They might start out that way, but they wouldn't stay there. Any power of this magnitude corrupts absolutely. . . .*

"Commander," Jim said slowly, "this is information we've come a long way to hear. And we thank you very much for warning us of this danger. But there's something I don't understand. Why are you telling us this? I can't be said to know you well; we've only just met. But I've fought you often enough to know that you never do anything without a good reason."

Ael looked at him tranquilly for a moment, and

again, very briefly, Jim had a flash of combined admiration and envy of her composure. She then tipped her head back to look around the room. "Captain," she said, "do you have any idea how many times I've dreamt of blowing this ship up?"

It seemed a moment for honesty. "Probably about as many times as I've dreamed about blowing up yours." That sounded a little bald, and Jim added, "Of course, it would have been a great pity. . . ."

"Yes," she said absently, "it would have been a shame to blow up *Enterprise,* too. The workmanship appears excellent." She flashed a smile at him: Jim became aware that he was being teased. "Captain, I come to you because I see my world in danger—and incidentally yours—and there's no more help to be found among my friends. At such a time, with millions and billions of lives riding on what is done, pride dies, and one has recourse to one's enemies. Of all my enemies I esteem you highest; you are a fierce combatant, but you've never been less than courteous with me—valorous in the best sense of the word, a warrior who deals in hard knocks or careful courtesy, nothing in between. Excluding, for the moment, various small subterfuges and thefts in the past." Now she did not smile; this was not teasing. "I too have been ordered in the past to do things I found hateful, so I understand the necessity of what you once did to my sister's-daughter—"

"The other Romulan Commander—she's your *niece*?" McCoy said.

"Was," said Ael. "I agree that sooner or later we shall have to deal with that old business, Captain. But right now there is new business far more pressing. Levaeri V must be destroyed!"

"I agree," Jim said. "But if preventing war is one of

your aims, Commander, then we have a problem. While I am willing to overlook the presence of your ship on this side of the Zone, your High Command would never overlook that of *Enterprise* in Romulan space. I suspect you want *Enterprise* to come in and assist you in the destruction of this base, is that right?"

"Yes."

"But our crossing the Zone would be a breach of the Federation-Romulan Treaty, and an act of war."

"Not necessarily."

"Ael," McCoy said, "we're unmistakably a Federation craft. There's no disguising the *Enterprise* as a Romulan Warbird, no matter what you suggest we do to our ID! How do you propose to get us into Romulan space without getting us discovered and shot at?"

She leaned back in her chair and favored them, one after another, with a look that Jim could only call mischievous. "I was thinking of capturing the *Enterprise*," she said to Jim. "Would you mind? . . ."

Eight

Jim looked quietly at Ael. "If that was a joke," he said, "it was a poor one. And if this is a trap of some kind, good workmanship or not, I am going to reduce *Bloodwing* to its component atoms—or die trying."

Ael smiled at Jim, as if seeing a response she had expected, and enjoyed. "It was no joke," she said. "And it is no trap. I may be desperate, but am I mad, to threaten you under a destroyer's guns? Do you think I don't know *Inaieu* is hanging five kilometers off your starboard side, and *Constellation* is closing in fast as per your orders? Give me credit for intelligence if nothing else, Captain."

"That," he said, "if nothing else, Commander. What exactly are you proposing?"

"That you join with me in a bit of subterfuge that will be, as my son has told you, as much to your advantage as to mine. Working together, we will set it up so that it will appear, to any Romulan observer, that the *Enter-*

prise has been bested in an engagement—disabled, boarded, manned by Romulans from my crew. We will so advertise the situation to Romulan High Command, and prepare to tow your 'conquered' ship in to the Romulus-Remus system. Even if Command should send us an escort—which possibility is difficult to predict, ships for Neutral Zone patrol being grudged right now, due to our problem with the Klingons— there would still be no real difficulty in maintaining the ruse. There is no way to sort the types of life-readings, Romulan from hominid or alien, using our ships' sensors; only numbers can be counted. Your crew would remain aboard your ship, running it possibly from the auxiliary Bridge, where control would reside . . . and the Bridge would be full of Romulans, who would handle all communications with other Romulan ships and otherwise maintain the illusion."

"Now, *wait* a moment!" McCoy said.

"Bones, hold your thought. Ael, assuming I should agree to this outrageousness—what would be our justification for passing by Levaeri V on our way in to Romulus-Remus? Such a high-security establishment as you're describing would surely have traffic routed away from it normally—"

"Normally," she said, "of course it does. But what would be normal about capturing the *Enterprise?* Questions of revenge aside—and there are various people at Command who would be only too delighted to tear you apart limb from limb—there are also the legates, who have multiple warrants out for the arrest of you and Mr. Spock on those old espionage charges. Don't look so left out, Doctor; there are writs out on you too, as I understand it, for aiding and abetting an act of espionage, complicity in the impersonation of a Romulan officer, various other things. . . . But in any case Command would want the *Enterprise* brought in by the swiftest and most straightforward route, to reduce your chance of having time to improvise an escape. From this part of space, our course in to Romulus-Remus lies right past Levaeri V. I planned it so. We drove the destroyer Romulan ship *Cuirass* to this location before engaging it, for that very purpose. Now we have an excuse to be here—and radiation trails that conform to the story we will be telling."

Jim leaned forward a bit, grinning. It was a treat to hear this wicked mind working out loud. The only problem was that there was no way to tell whether what Ael was proposing was on the level. Unless . . .

"Commander," he said, "I make you no promises, but you're beginning to interest me. Tell me 'our story.'"

"Why, only this," she said, smiling back at him; "that *Cuirass*, which I command—at least it will seem to be *Cuirass*, for I have a copy of that ship's ID solid aboard *Bloodwing*, ready to be installed—that *Cuirass* detected *Enterprise* violating our space, and followed her out into the Zone, where she attempted to bring us to battle, but suffered mechanical difficulties—which I suspect your Chief Engineer, whom we also know well, can fake without too much difficulty. That, unable to run, and with damage to your warp engines, we had only to draw you into exhausting your firepower, and then wear your shields down with fire of our own, to reduce you to a position where you (with your well-known compassion for your crew) were left helpless enough to be unable to repel a boarding action. With your Bridge taken and your crew under the threat of having your own intruder-control systems used on them—a swift killer, that gas—you surrendered the ship to buy their lives. My crew manned control positions on your ship, placed her in tow, and headed for home."

It was plausible. It was even doable. "There have been other ships in the area, though," Jim said. "Anyone tracing your iontrail and ours would also note the passage of first *Intrepid,* then *Constellation* and *Inaieu*—"

"True. But it's difficult to accurately place such residues in time, is it not? Their decay is not regular, especially in the space hereabouts, where you have noticed the weather has been bad lately." Ael tipped her head to one side, regarding Jim. "And by the time anyone follows our trails out this far and returns within subspace radio range of Levaeri V, it will be too late. We will already have done what we came for. *Enterprise* and *Bloodwing* will break away from the escort, if any—"

"You mean take them all on and blow them up?" McCoy said incredulously. "How many ships come in an escort, anyway?"

"For *Enterprise,* they would hardly send fewer than two. Four, at the most, would be my guess."

Bones looked incredulously from Spock to Jim and back again. "We're just going to 'break away' from four fully-armed Romulan cruisers, probably those Klingon-model cruisers—"

"You gentlemen will not fail me," Ael said, perfectly calm. "This *is* the *Enterprise,* after all. . . . Once we have scrapped the escort, destroying Levaeri V should not be too much of a problem."

"I imagine not," Jim said. "But, Commander, what about the loss of life?"

"The Romulans doing the research have not been too concerned about that," Ael said coolly, "especially where the Vulcans have been concerned. I did not think that would be so much of an issue for you. Perhaps I miscalculated.''

"Perhaps." Jim thought of about seventy things he wanted to shout at her, none of which would have done him or her any good; this woman might look almost Earth-human, but he had to keep reminding himself that their respective branches of humanity had very different mores indeed. "Mr. Spock," he said after a little while, "opinions?"

Spock looked distinctly uncomfortable. "Commander," he said, turning to her for a moment, "I would ask you not to take anything I say as a slight against your honor."

She bowed her head to him, the gracious gesture of nobility to one almost a peer. Jim started to get very annoyed.

"Captain," Spock said, "the plan is an audacious one. Its odds for success in its early stages are very high. However, I advise you most strongly against it. There are too many variables, unknowns, things that can go wrong at the plan's far end. Even should one of our allies suggest such an operation, having a spare Romulan ship with falsified ID on hand, Starfleet would have no mercy on the plan if it miscarried. And with the suggestion coming from a representative of a power with whom the Federation has long been on the fringes of war—"

"Amen to that, Mr. Spock," McCoy growled. "Whole thing's a pack of nonsense."

"No, Doctor," Spock said, eyeing him, "that it is not. The Commander's plan is excellently reasoned—but the risks in its later stages become unacceptably high. For a Vulcan, at least. Captain?"

Jim looked at Ael. "You say that you are willing to forego pride for the time being," he said. "Then I hope you'll pardon me, but this has to be said. How do we know you're not lying? Or worse—how do we know you haven't been brainwashed into thinking this is the truth you're telling us, so that you can safely lay your honor on the line?"

Ael breathed out once, leaving Jim to wonder whether a sigh meant the same thing to Romulans as it did to his branch of humanity. "Captain," she said, "of course you had to say that. But there is a way to find out, one that strikes to the heart of this whole matter. Ask Mr. Spock if he will consent to subject me to a mindmeld."

Jim looked at Spock. Spock was still as stone. "It's true," McCoy said. "There are ways of blocking or tampering with a mind that won't show up under verifier scan—but will in mindmeld. It would be conclusive, Jim."

"I had thought of it," Jim said. "But I didn't want to suggest it." And he said nothing more.

A few seconds went silently by. Finally Spock looked at Ael and said, very quietly, "I will do this, Commander." He glanced over at Jim. "Captain, somewhere more private would be appropriate."

"Your quarters?"

"Those would do very well. Commander, will you accompany me? The Captain and the Doctor will join us shortly."

"Certainly."

Out they went together, the Vulcan and the Romulan, and Jim had to stare after them. There was something so alike about them—not just the racial likeness, either. "Well, Bones," he said, "get it off your chest."

McCoy leaned forward on the couch, elbows on knees, and stared at Jim. "How much I have to get off," he said, "depends on what you're going to do."

"Nothing, until we have Spock's assessment of what the inside of her mind looks like."

"And what if she *is* telling the truth, Jim? Are you tellin' me you're going to go off on some damn fool chase into interdicted territory, probably get us surrounded by Romulans again like the last time—but this time on purpose? We're just going to *sit* there and be towed into Romulan space under escort! Why don't we just tie ourselves up and jump out the airlocks in our underwear? Save us all a lot of—"

"*Bones,*" Jim said, not angrily, but loudly; sometimes when McCoy got started on one of these it was hard to stop him. Bones subsided.

"I am *not* seriously considering it," Jim said. "Even if she *is* telling the truth. What I'm trying to figure out is what to do about what she's told us. This information is too sensitive to do anything but whisper in a Fleet Admiral's ear; I wouldn't dare send it via subspace radio, buoy, or any other means that might be intercepted, decoded, anything. Too much rests on it—as far as that goes, she's not understating. None of the ships can leave the task force, and I'm sure as Hell not going to send an unarmed shuttlecraft or one of *Inaieu*'s little couriers off with it. Plus I have other problems on my mind." He reached out to the table and hit one of the 'com switches on it. "Bridge. Mr. Scott."

"*Scott here.*"

"Scotty, how're our Romulan friends?"

"*Quiet as mice, Captain. Back on their original course, holding steady at warp five and one light-second.*"

"Any communications?"

"*None, sir.*"

"Very well. Give me Uhura."

"She's offshift, sir," said another voice. *"Lieutenant Mahasë."*

"Oh. Fine. Mr. Mahasë, call the Romulan ship. My compliments to Subcommander Tafv, and we are still conferring with the Commander. No progress to report as yet, should he inquire."

"Right, sir. By the way, Captain, we have another message from Intrepid."

"Live message, or canned?"

"Canned, sir. They left it recorded in a squirt on the satellite zone-monitoring station we just passed—NZRM 4488. The ion storm was holding steady at force six; they expected it to begin tapering down any time. Sensors still show a lot of lively hydrogen up that way, though. We'll be running into it ourselves shortly."

Jim rubbed his eyes. *Damn weather . . .* "Well, keep trying to reach them in realtime—they ought to be appraised of what's going on back here. Anything else I should know?"

"Mr. Chekov wants to take just one shot at Bloodwing, *Captain. Just for practice."*

"Tell him to go take a cold shower when his shift's over," Jim said. "Kirk out. Come on, Bones, let's go see if the truth really *will* out."

Nine

Ael followed Spock silently through the corridors of *Enterprise,* trying to understand the people walking those corridors by studying their surroundings. She could make little of what she saw, except that she found it vaguely unpleasant. The overdone handsomeness of the Transporter Room and the ridiculous luxury of the Officers' Lounge had put her off; she had found herself thinking of her bare, cramped quarters in *Bloodwing* with ridiculous nostalgia, as if she were hundreds of light-years away from it, marooned in *Cuirass* again. But the situation was really no different. *Here as there,* she thought, *I am among aliens—and if what I plan succeeds, I will have to live so for the rest of my life. I had better get used to it.* And she followed Spock into his quarters expecting something similar—something Terrene-contaminated, overdone, something that would make her even more uncomfortable than she already was.

But she got a surprise. For one thing, the room was warm enough to be comfortable. For another, except that they were bigger, the quarters might have been a twin to her own for the general feel of them. The place was utterly neat; sparsely furnished, but not barren; and if it accurately reflected its owner, she was going to have to revise her estimation of Vulcans upward.

There were some things there, such as the firepot-beast in the corner, that she knew enough about Vulcans not to inquire of; like a good guest she passed them by. But other things drew Ael's attention. One was a stereo cube, sitting all alone on the ruthlessly clean desk. In it a dark stern Vulcan man stood beside a beautiful older woman, who wore a very un-Vulcan smile. Ael put out a hand to it, not touching, thinking of her father. "This would be Ambassador Sarek, then," she said, "and Lady Amanda."

"You are well informed, Commander," Spock said. He had been standing behind her, not moving—holding very still, as Ael fancied someone might who had a dangerous beast at close range and did not want to frighten it.

She laughed softly at his words, and at her own thoughts. "Too well informed for my own comfort, perhaps." She turned from the portrait toward the wall that adjoined the panel dividing the sleeping area from the rest of the room, and looked up at the very few old weapons adorning it . . . and breathed in once, sharply.

"Mr. Spock," she said, "am I mistaken? Or is that, as I think, a S'harien up there?"

The look in his eyes as she turned to face him was not quite surprise—more appreciation, if that closed face could be said to express anything at all. "It is, Commander. If you would like to examine it . . ."

He trailed off. Ael reached up with great care and took the sword down from the wall, laying it over the forearm of her uniform so as not to risk fingerprinting the exquisite sardonyx-wood inlay of the scabbard. The sheath's design was lean, clean, necessary, brutal logic and an eye for beauty going hand in hand. The hilt was plain black *kahs-hir,* left rough as when it had been quarried, for a better grip: logical again. "May I draw it?" she said.

Spock nodded. Whispering, the steel came out of the sheath. Ael looked at it and shook her head in longing at the way even a starship's artificial light fell on the highlights buried in the blade. No one had ever matched the work of the ancient swordsmiths who had worked at the edge of Vulcan's Forge, five thousand years before; and S'harien had been the greatest of them all. The pilgrims to ch'Ríhan had managed to take five of his swords with them. Of those, three had been broken in dynastic war, shattered in the hands of dying kings and queens; one was stolen and lost, thought to be drifting in a long cometary orbit around Eisn; one lay in the Empty Chair in the Senate Chambers, where no hand might touch it. Certainly Ael had never thought to hold a S'harien. The sword in her hand spoke, by its superb balance, of things Ael couldn't say; of history, and home, and treasures lost forever; of power, and the loss of it, and the word there was no one to tell. . . .

She looked up at the Vulcan in unspeakable envy and admiration, her voice gone quite out of her. *A fine showing you're making!* Ael thought bitterly. *Struck dumb by a piece of metal—*

"It is an heirloom," he said, as if sensing her momentary loss. "It would be illogical to leave it locked in a vault, where it could not be appreciated."

"Appreciation," Ael said, in a tone that was meant to be light mockery; but her voice shook a bit. "That's an emotion, is it not?"

He looked at her, and Ael saw that without meld, without the use of touch or anything else, Spock still saw her nervousness with perfect clarity. "Commander," he said to her, innocently matching her tone, "'appreciation' is a noun. It denotes the just valuation or recognition of worth."

She stared at him dubiously.

"I believe you are telling the truth," he said. "And if you are, I cannot say how much I honor you for daring to do what you have done, for peace's sake. But for both the Captain and myself, belief will not be enough. We must be utterly certain of you and of what you say."

"I understand you very well," Ael said. "Understand me also; I have given up pride—though not yet fear. However, I demand that you do to me whatever will best convince the Captain."

Spock lifted his head, hearing footsteps in the hall. Ael, considering that it might not be wise for the Captain to come in and find her facing his First Officer while holding a sword, gave Spock a conspiratorial glance and turned her back on him, savoring the feel of the S'harien in her hand for just a moment more. . . .

The door-buzzer sounded. "Come," Spock said quietly. In came the Captain and the Doctor, and as the door shut behind them, they stood uncertainly for a moment, looking at Ael. She turned to face them, and her fear fell away from her at the bemusement on the Doctor's face, the surprise on the Captain's.

"Gentlemen," she said to them, picking up the S'harien's scabbard from the desk and sheathing it again, "I had no idea that the *Enterprise* would be carrying museum pieces. Can it be that all those stories about starships being instruments of culture are actually true?"

And to her utter astonishment, she saw that her cautious flippancy was not fooling the Captain, either. He was looking at her with the small wry smile of someone who also knew and loved the feel of a blade in the hand.

"We like to think so, Commander," he said. "You should come down to Recreation, if there's time . . . we have some interesting things down there. But right now we have other business." And he glanced at Spock much as Ael might have glanced at Tafv when there was some uncomfortable business to be gotten over with quickly.

She bowed slightly to him, sat down in the chair at Spock's desk. The Vulcan came to stand behind her. Ael leaned back and closed her eyes.

"There will be some discomfort at first, Commander," said the voice from above and behind her. "If you can avoid resisting it, it will pass very quickly."

"I understand."

Fingers touched her face, positioning themselves precisely over the cranial nerve pathways. Ael shivered all over, once and uncontrollably; then was still.

Her first thought was that she couldn't breathe. No, not that precisely; that there was something wrong with the way she was breathing, it was too fast. . . . She slowed it down, took a longer deeper breath—and then caught it back in shock, realizing that she couldn't *take* that deep a breath, her lungs didn't have that much capacity—

Do not resist, her own voice said in her head without her thinking any such thing. Surely this was what the approach of madness was like.

No! They are breaking faith with me, they are going to drive me mad—no! No! I have too much to do—

Commander—Ael—I warned you of the discomfort. Do not resist or you will damage yourself—

—oh, bizarre, the words were coming in Vulcan but she could still understand them—or rather she heard them at the same time in Rihannsu, and in Federation Basic, and in Vulcan, and she understood them all. Her own voice speaking them inside her, as if in her own thought—but the thought another's—

Better. Our minds are drawing closer. . . . Open to me, Ael. Let me in.

—impossible not to; the self/other voice was gentle enough, but there was a strength behind it that could easily crush any denial. *Would* not, however—she realized that without knowing how—

—closer now, closer—

—Elements above and beyond, what had she been afraid of? What an astonishment, to breathe with other lungs, to see through another mind's eye, to journey through another darkness and find light at journey's end. . . . That was no more than she did on *Bloodwing,* than she had done all her life; how could she possibly fear it? She reached out for the other, not knowing how: hoping will would be enough, as it had always been for everything else—

—we are one.

She was. Odd that there were suddenly two of her, but it seemed always to have been that way. With the odd calmness of a dream, where outrageous things happen and seem perfectly normal, she found herself very curious about the events of the past few months, the whole business regarding Levaeri V, from beginning to end. Luckily it took little time, in this timelessness, to go over it all; and she took herself from beginning to end in running commentary and split-instant images—the crimson banners of the Senate chambers, the faces of old friends in the Praetorate who solemnly said "no," or said "perhaps" meaning "no." There were the faces of her crew, glad to see her back, outraged nearly to rebellion at the thought of her transfer from *Bloodwing*. There were the hateful faces of the crew of *Cuirass*, and there was t'Liun's voice shouting over ship's channels for her to come to the Bridge. There was Tafv, dark and keen, reaching out to take her hand as she boarded *Bloodwing* again, raising her hand to his forehead in a ridiculously antique and moving gesture of welcome. And her cheering crew, all of them like children to her, like brothers and sisters. There was *Bloodwing's* Transporter Room. And there was another Transporter Room entirely, with men in it. One fair and lithe, with an unreadable face and a very unalien courtesy; one dark and fierce-eyed, with hands that looked skilled; and one who could have been one of her own brothers, if not for Starfleet blue, and the memory of old enmities. . . .

Her sudden curiosity invited her to look more closely at those enmities. She resisted at first—they were old history, and their consideration bred nothing but anger. But the curiosity wouldn't be balked, and finally Ael gave in to it. That image of her sister's-daughter standing before the Senate after her defeat at the Captain's and Spock's hands, after the loss of the cloaking device to the Federation. Ael's impassioned, desperate defense of her before the Senators—useless, fallen on hearts too obsessed with vengeance and fear for their own places to hear any plea. Ael stared again down the length of the white chamber, looking toward the Empty Chair, while around her the voices proclaimed her sister-daughter's eternal exile from ch'Ríhan and ch'Havran, the stripping of her honors from her, and worst, the ceremonial shaming and removal of her house-name. Ael had protested again at that, not caring how it would endanger her own position. The protest had gone unheeded. She stood at marble attention while the name was thrice written, thrice burned, and watched bitterly as her sister-daughter went from the chambers in the deepest disgrace—no longer even a person, for a Rihannsu without a house was no one and nothing.

And where is she now? she cried to that curious, silent part of her that watched all this. *Wandering somewhere in space, or living alone on some wretched exile-world, alone among aliens? How should I not hate those who did such a thing to her?* Nor was there any forgetting Tafv's bitter anger at the exile of his cousin, his dear old playmate. Yet he had come to know cool reason, as Ael had, just as this sudden new part of her had learned it when he was young and occasionally angry. Hate would have to wait. Perhaps some kind shift in the Elements, at another time, would allow her a chance to face her enemies and prove on their bodies in clean battle that they were cowards, who had consented to deal in trickery to achieve their means. Now, though, she needed those enemies badly. Personal business could not be allowed to matter where the survival of empires was involved.

The new part of her agreed silently and said nothing more for a moment. Ael seized that moment, for she had her own curiosity. Here was one of those enemies, inwardly linked to her. Becoming "curious" in turn, she reached out to it; and the other part of her, in a kind of somber acknowledgment of justice, suffered her to do so. Ael reached deep—

She had for years been picturing some kind of

monster, a half-bred thing without true conscience or sense of self, the kind of person who could work a treachery on her sister-daughter with such cool precision. But now, as in her estimate of what his rooms would be like, she found herself wrong again, so very wrong that her shame burned her. Certainly there was the vast internal catalogue of data and store of expertise that she would have expected from a man whom even among the Rihannsu was a legend as one of Starfleet's great officers. But what she had not suspected was someone as torn as she was, and as whole as she was, and in such similar ways. Someone who had sworn himself to a hard life, for what seemed to him a greater good more important than his own, and who had suffered for the oath's sake, and would again, willingly; someone who was also powerfully rooted in another life, a heart's life—based around a planet where he could hardly ever walk, and relationships he could never fully acknowledge, because of what he had chosen to be. No oaths were attached to those choices— just simple will, rock-steady and unbreakable. *That* person she had not suspected. Alien he might be, but there was that very Rihannsu characteristic, the unshakable, unbreakable loyalty to an idea, a goal, a man who embodied it. The best part of the ruling Passion, a banked fire, but burning this man out from within, and never to be relinquished, no matter how much it hurt—

That man she could open to, as she might open to Tafv or Aidoann or tr'Keirianh. And she did, feeling suddenly for the terrible suppressed passions in him, and for one of them more than any of the others—for homesickness. She showed him Airissuin, and the barren red mountains of her home, so like his own; she showed him the farmstead, and the place where the hlai got out, and her father, so very like his; the small dry flowers on the hillside, and the way the sunlight fell across her couch the day after her son was born, and she held him in her arms for the first time without the distraction of pain, wishing his father had lived to see—oh, Liha, lost to the Klingons in that ridiculous "misunderstanding" off Nh'rainnsele! Could there never be an end to such misunderstandings—worlds to walk safely, an end to wars, other ways to avoid boredom and find adventure? Must the innocent die, and must she keep on killing them? *An end to it, an end!*

Her second self was in distress; but so was Ael, and for the moment she had no pity on either of them. This was after all the most important matter, the only one that ranked with truth and hearts and names. Life must go on, and with the implementation of the project at Levaeri, there would be an end to it. Truth would become deadly, hearts would become public places, and names—Better that small wars should flare up and take their inevitable toll, better that she and Tafv and all the crew of *Bloodwing,* yes, and that of *Enterprise* too, should die before such a thing happened. For these were honorable people, as she had always suspected and now found that she had not known half the truth of it. Just the image of the Captain that her otherself held was enough to convince her; his image of the Doctor, very different but held in no less loyalty, was more data toward the same conclusion. Such people, whatever her hatreds, hinted at the existence of many more on the other side of the Zone. They must not be allowed to become obsolete, or dead, as honorable people everywhere would should this technique be carried to its logical conclusion; they must not, *they must not—*

—and her mind abruptly came undone. Not a painful sensation, but a sad one, as if she had been born twins and was bidding the twin good-bye.

Ael opened her eyes. The Vulcan she could still feel behind her—some thread of the link apparently remained; she could feel the stone-steady foundations of his mind shaken somewhat. But of more interest to her was the look the Captain was giving her, both compassionate and bleak. The Doctor was turned toward the wall and rubbing his eyes, as if something ailed them. She realized abruptly that her face was wet.

Spock came around from behind her, his hands behind his back, physically standing at ease; but Ael knew better. "Commander," he said quietly. "I apologize profoundly for the intrusion."

"I thank you," she said, "but the apology is unnecessary. I am quite well."

Glancing up at him, she saw that Spock, also, knew better. The Captain was looking from one to the other of them. "I also apologize, Commander," he said. "If it will do any good . . ."

"It will do none to the exiled or the dead," Ael said, as levelly as she could, wondering how much she and the Vulcan might have spoken aloud in this meld, and fearing the worst. "But for myself, I thank you."

"If you would excuse us a moment," the Captain said, "I must discuss this business with Mr. Spock and Dr. McCoy."

She bowed her head to him; they went out into the corridor together, all three moving as separate parts of one mind. *We are more alike than I imagined,* she said to herself, rubbing briefly at her face and thinking of those times in battle and out of it when she and Tafv and Aidoann functioned as one whole creature in three different places. *If I am not careful, I will forget to hate these people for what they did to my sister-daughter . . . and what will become of me then?*

"*Captain,*" she distinctly heard Spock saying, "*every word she has told us is the truth. She is under no compulsion save that of her conscience—which is of considerable power; her resolve and fear of lost time was what broke the link—I did not.*"

"*Any sign of tampering with her mind at all?*" the Captain said.

"*None. There were areas I could not touch, as there might be in any mind. And one piece of data with unusually powerful privacy blocks around it—an area somewhat contaminated with emotions that I consider similar to human types of shame and regret. But my sense was that this was a private matter, not concerning us.*"

"*I don't like it,*" the Doctor said. "*Did you get a 'sense' of any associational linkages to that block that might reach into the areas that do concern us?*"

"*Some, Doctor. But this blocked material had linkages to almost every other part of the Commander's mind as well. I do not think it is of importance to us.*"

"*Well,*" said the Captain, and let out a long breath. "*Spock, I hate to say this, but Fleet is not going to buy what the Commander's proposing. It's too farfetched, too dangerous, and even though the Commander is an honorable woman, I can't possibly trust all those other Romulans. She tells us herself that the Romulans as a whole are becoming more opportunistic, less attached to their old code of honor. What do we do if some one of them, while aboard the* Enterprise, *gets the idea to try a takeover? Granted that we outnumber them incredibly— if so much as one of my crew should die in such an incident, Starfleet would have my hide. And rightly. I agree with her that we have a moral responsibility to the three great powers—but if we tried to carry off the operation she suggests, and then botched it somehow so that word of what's going on at Levaeri leaked out without our managing to destroy the place—No. I'm sorry. Strategically it's a lovely idea, but tactically, with our present force and numbers, it's a wash. I am going to send for more ships—quietly—and then act."*

The Captain let out another unhappy breath. *"Come on, gentlemen. Let's tell her the bad news as gently—"*

The small viewer on Spock's desk whistled. *"Bridge to Captain Kirk."*

Ael reached out to flick the small switch beside it. "If you will hold one moment, I will get him." *Mr. Spock,* she said through the rapidly fading mindlink, *would you please tell the Captain he has a call?*

A flash of acquiescence reached her. The door hissed open, and in the three came again. "Sorry to keep you waiting, Commander," the Captain said. "Let me handle this first. Kirk here," he said to the viewer.

"Captain," said the communications officer, a gray-skinned hominid who had apparently replaced the lovely dark woman Ael recalled from Tafv's earlier call to *Enterprise, "we have another squirt from* Intrepid. *They were passing by NZR 4486 when they were apparently attacked."*

"By what?" the Captain said, glancing sharply at Ael.

"That's the problem, sir. They didn't know. The ion storm suddenly escalated to nearly force-ten—enough to leave them sensor-blind. It was just after that that they were fired upon. But the odd thing is that they didn't fall out of communication with the relay station until almost a minute and a half after the storm escalated. Then they just cut off communication in the middle of transmission

—not a storm-fade, or a catastrophic loss of signal, as if they'd been—as if something had happened to the ship. Just a stop."

"Keep trying to raise them, Mr. Mahasë. And call red alert. All hands to battle stations. Alert *Inaieu* and *Constellation;* they're to go to red alert as well."

"Aye aye, sir. Any further orders?"

"None at present. Kirk out."

Outside Ael could hear the ship's odd red-alert siren whooping, and people hurrying past the room. "Commander," the Captain said, "what do you know of this?"

"That the attacking ship is almost certainly Rihannsu," she said, "and the ion storm almost certainly our doing. I wish you had told me of this earlier; I have had no news of it from my ship. Unfortunately your sensors seem to be rather better than ours—"

"What do you mean the ion storm's 'of your doing'?" the Doctor said.

"I am sorry, gentlemen," she said, "but it is hard to tell you everything presently happening in Rihannsu space while standing on one foot. Mr. Spock, if you look into your memories of our meld, you will find this information accurate. One research that has been complete for some time now is a method for producing ion storms by selective high-energy 'seeding' of stellar coronae. The High Command has been using it for some time as a clandestine weapon to keep the Klingons from raiding our frontier worlds. Their economic situation has been very bad recently, as you may know, and their treaty with us has been honored more in its breach than in its keeping. However, the technique has also been used on this side of the Zone—to cover the tracks of those who have been stealing Vulcans. How better to spirit away small ships, without anyone noticing, than to have them vanish in ion storms? Everybody knows how dangerous those are—"

"Then the change in the stellar weather hereabouts," Spock said, "has not been natural, but engineered."

"To some extent. There was some concern that changing it in one place would also cause changes elsewhere; so the climatic alterations of which you speak may be secondary rather than primary. However, things now look even worse than they did, gentlemen. The research at Levaeri must be even further along than I thought, for the researchers to take such a large group of Vulcans—and right out from under the noses of a Federation task force. They must be about to start production of the shifted genetic material in bulk, to need so wide a spectrum of live tissue." Ael looked grave. "Captain, if you do not do something, shortly half the Imperial Senate will be reading one another's alleged minds, courtesy of the brain tissue of the crew of the *Intrepid*. . . ."

Spock stood still, appearing unmoved—but again Ael knew better; and the other two stared at her in open horror. "Commander," McCoy said at last, "this is ridiculous! If the Romulan ship tries to capture the Vulcans, they'll die sooner than let that happen—"

"They will not be *allowed* to die, Doctor," Ael said, becoming impatient. "Don't you understand yet that this technique not only reproduces in its users the mental abilities of trained Vulcans, but raises those abilities to a much higher level than normal? What use would it be making touch-telepaths out of the Senate? Who among them would allow anyone to touch him? The technique was designed to enable mindreading and control at a distance for short periods—even control over the resistant minds of Vulcans already knowledgeable in the disciplines! Three or four people aboard a Romulan ship could easily hold the Bridge crew of *Intrepid* under complete control for the short time it would take to make them stop firing, lower their shields and be boarded. Or there are other methods equally effective. Then the Rihannsu would simply take ship, Vulcans and all across the Zone, under cover of the ion storm, and do their pleasure with them."

"But Vulcans with command training—" the Captain said.

"Command training will make no difference to this artificially augmented ability, Captain," Ael said. "We are dealing here with an ability that if developed much further will be able to take on even races as telepathically advanced as the Organians and Melkot."

The Captain's face went very fierce. "We've got to go after them—"

"You cannot. If you do, you and your whole crew will suffer the same fate as *Intrepid*—one not so kind, actually. Your minds will fall under control far more swiftly than those of *Intrepid*'s Vulcans did—and after the Rihannsu move in and arrest you and Spock and the Doctor, they will kill your crew and take the *Enterprise* home to study. The same thing will happen if *Inaieu* or *Constellation* follow you in. No, Captain, if you want the *Intrepid* and its crew back, my plan is the only way. And we will have to be swift about it. They will not wait around, at Levaeri, now that they have the genetic material they need. Processing of the Vulcans will begin at once."

Ael sat still, then, and watched the Captain think. A long time she had wanted to see this—her old opponent in the process of decision, ideas and options flickering behind his eyes. And it was very quickly, as she had suspected it would be, that he looked up again.

"Commander," he said, "I think, for the moment, you've got an ally. Spock, have Lieutenant Mahasë call Rihaul and Walsh. I want a meeting of all ships' department heads in *Inaieu* in an hour. Bones, bring Lieutenant Kerasus with you."

"Yes, Captain."

"Right, Jim."

And out they went. Ael found herself alone and looking at an angry man—one who was going to have to do something he didn't want to, and was very aware of it.

"Commander," he said to her, "am I going to regret this?"

" 'Going to'? Captain, you regret it already."

He frowned at her—and at the same time began to smile.

"Let's go," he said.

Ten

It turned into the noisiest staff meeting Jim could remember in many years of them. The number of people in attendance was part of the reason—all eighteen of *Enterprise*'s department heads, along with Janíce Kerasus from Linguistics, Jim's Romulan culture expert, and Colin Matlock, the Security Chief; and the Captains and department heads of both *Constellation* and *Inaieu*. There they were, crammed into *Inaieu*'s Main Briefing . . . hominids and tentacled people and people with extra legs, all three kinds of Denebians and very assorted members of other species, in as much or as little Fleet uniform as they usually wore.

In the middle of all the blue and orange and command gold and green was a patch of color both somberer and more splendid; Ael and her son Tafv, both in the scarlet and gold-shot black of Romulan officers. They did not bear themselves like two aliens alone among suspicious people. Ael sat as unshaken among them as she had in the Officers' Lounge; and Jim, looking across at the calm young Tafv leaning back in his chair, decided that he had inherited more from his mother than his nose.

He had beamed across from *Bloodwing* at Ael's request, and had looked around *Enterprise*'s Transporter Room with the hard, seeing eyes of someone checking an area for weaknesses, assessing its strengths. Jim had looked curiously at him, wondering how old he really might be; for Romulans, like Vulcans, showed little indication of aging until they were in their sixties. The man looked to be in his mid-twenties, but might have been in his forties for all Jim knew. Then he found himself being examined closely by those eyes, so pale a brown they were almost gold; an intrusive, disconcerting stare. "Subcommander," he had said, and courteously enough the young man had bowed to him; but Jim went away disquieted, he didn't know why.

The department heads of the three ships had been making noise about the Romulans' presence at their council; politely, but they had been making it all the same. Jim was letting them run down. It seemed the wisest course; that way there would be slightly less noise when he told them what he and Ael were planning.

He glanced down past McCoy and Sulu and Matlock toward Lieutenant Kerasus, raising an inquiring eyebrow at her.

She glanced back, shaking her head ever so slightly at some response of one of the Eyrene Denebians to something Spock was telling them about the Levaeri V researches. Janíce Kerasus was Chief of Linguistics, the person primarily responsible for programming of the translation computer and translation of alien documents received by the ship. She was a tall, big-boned, strikingly handsome woman with dark curling hair and calm brown eyes that slanted up at the corners, making her look like a lazy cat most of the time—excepting when she was very interested, as she was now; then she got the look of a cat waiting patiently by a mousehole, eyes a bit wide and a faintly pleased look on her face.

She was waiting for something now, that was plain. The room had settled down somewhat from the restrained uproar that had occurred when Jim had first introduced Ael and Tafv. Mike Walsh had stared at Jim as if he'd gone nuts, and Rihaul had slitted her eye at him in a later-for-you gesture he knew too well from the old days, after some particularly painful tutoring session. But now the other officers were beginning to get the idea that these Romulans might actually have come to do them a service. It was taking a while to sink in, unfortunately, and Jim grudged the lost time.

It was time to kick things in the side. Spock had done the "dirty" work, filling the meeting in on the news Ael had brought them and his confirmation of it. Now Jim stopped Spock from taking another question from one of Rihaul's people. "Gentlebeings," he said, "we've got to get moving here. You've heard what the Commander proposes—"

"It would break almost every reg in the book," Mike Walsh said. "Allowing hostiles into classified areas. Entering into private alliances with foreign powers. Espionage again. Destruction of private property . . ."

"I have those powers, Mike," Jim said quietly. "That's what 'unusual breadth of discretion' is for, after all."

Mike grimaced at him, knowing as well as Jim the pitfalls that awaited him should this operation somehow get botched. "I know. But we're quite literally in an untenable position. We can't stay here; the Romulans monitoring the Zone will get suspicious. We can't leave—certainly not without determining the fate of the *Intrepid*. We can't send for help, communication isn't secure; and we can't send ships to carry a secure message—we need all our strength here. We have to act, and we have to do it now, and much as I hate to admit it, Ael's idea is the best we've got."

Ael threw Jim a glance that reminded him a great deal of one of Spock's appreciative-but-don't-tell-anyone expressions. "Gentlefolk," Tafv said from beside her in his light tenor, "I assure you that the Commander is as little sanguine about offering you this plan as you are at the thought of accepting it. If it succeeds, the Commander and I have nothing to gain but disgrace, irrevocable exile for both of us and for the rest of her crew, and the permanent possibility of being hunted down and killed by Romulan agents for revenge's sake." He looked grave. "We are all willing to risk that for her sake. It's a matter of *mnhei'sahe*." There were curious looks around the table at the word the translator had failed to render, but Tafv didn't stop. "However, we face far, far worse if the attempt fails. If caught in Romulan territory, we and *Bloodwing*'s crew will assuredly die. You and your ships could conceivably fight your way out again—and whatever difficulties you may have with Starfleet Command afterward, you will still be alive to have them."

"Noted, Subcommander," Jim said. "One moment. Lieutenant Kerasus—'mneh'-*what?*"

"'*Mnhei'sahe*,'" she said promptly. "Captain, I'm sorry, but you would ask me to render one of the most difficult words in the language. It's not quite honor—and not quite loyalty—and not quite anger, or hatred, or about fifty other things. It can be a form of hatred that requires you to give your last drop of water to a thirsty enemy—or an act of love that requires you to kill a friend. The meaning changes constantly with context, and even in one given context, it's slippery at best."

"In this one?"

Kerasus glanced across at Tafv. "If I understand the Subcommander correctly, they are returning the favor that Commander t'Rllaillieu has done them by commanding them, by being in turn willing to be commanded. That sounds a little odd, I know, but their forms of what we call 'loyalty' do not always involve compliance. These people will follow her to death . . . and beyond, if they can . . . because they acknowledge that what she's doing is right, no matter what High Command says."

There was a little silence around the table at that. "Commander," Captain Rihaul said quietly, "I hope you will excuse us both our ignorance and our caution. But none of us have ever seen Romulans do anything but make war, and that savagely. That you would also wage peace . . . if forcefully . . . comes as something of a surprise."

Ael smiled at the Deirr captain, a rueful look. "Oh, I assure you, Captain, we know more arts than those of war. But our position between you and the Klingons has left us little leisure to practice them. So we tend to leave their development to others. Our allies . . . or our subjects."

Lieutenant Kerasus lifted her head at that, though she said nothing. Jim caught the look, though. "Comment, Lieutenant?"

"Yes, sir." She looked down the table toward Ael and began to speak, and her quiet voice suddenly had steel in it. "'Other peoples may yet/more skillfully teach bronze to breathe,

" 'leading outward and loosing
the life lying hidden in marble;
some may plead causes better,
or using the tools of science
better predict heaven's moods
and chart the stars' changing courses.
But Roman, remember you well
that your own arts are these others:
to govern the nations in power;
to dictate their rule in peace;
to raise up the peoples you've conquered,
and throw down the proud who resist. . . .' "

Jim saw Ael looking at Kerasus with an expression that looked like surprise, or hope, or both. "That is very well said. But the language sounds old. Those people are no longer with you, I think."

"Their descendants only," Jim said. "Though many of Earth's major languages were powerfully affected by theirs. For the most part, their way is one we've left behind us. But they were a great people."

"If they became less than great," Ael said, glancing around the table at the many sorts of listeners, "it is because they forgot those words and handed their rule over to others—perhaps to onetime enemies, whom in their contempt and laziness they tried to absorb, and forgot to fear. Or else to those who paid lip service to the ancient laws without understanding the vision on which they were founded. Am I wrong?"

The stillness of their faces evidently told her she was not. "That is the danger in which my Empire now stands, gentlefolk. And I will not see five thousand years' civilization fall, as it seems other empires have, due to some paltry cause, to mere sloth, or folly—or the death of honor! I have said to *Enterprise*'s Captain that there was no help to be found in my friends, so that I needs must turn to my enemies. Your Federation says it wants peace among the great powers. Now it shall be seen how much it wants that, by the actions of you its representatives. For if you fail to act now on the information I bring you, with the power to hand, peace will fail you forever."

The room was quiet for a few seconds, and into that quietness came the whistle of the intercom. "Main Briefing," said Captain Rihaul.

"Captain," said the foghorn voice of one of Rihaul's Bridge crew, *"we're now in the area from which* Intrepid *made its last report. The meson residue of her engines comes this far, then stops . . . as if the matter-antimatter converters had been shut down. There's a faint meson trail leading away from here, though—shutdown residue, nothing more."*

"Where does it lead?" Mike Walsh said.

"Bearing ninety mark plus-five, sir. Into the Neutral Zone."

People all around the room looked at one another. "Anything else, Syill?" said Rihaul.

"No, madam."

"All right. Main Briefing out."

"There it is, gentlebeings," Jim said. "One of our starships is missing—and we know where it's gone. If we needed an excuse for crossing the Zone, we've got one now. Not even Fleet will be able to argue with what our sensors show us. And the question of committing an act of war is now also moot. What would you call shanghaiing the *Intrepid?*"

"No argument there, Jim." Rihaul looked across the table at him with great concern. "Unfortunately. Now it falls to us to keep this war from escalating into a full-scale conflict."

"And the only way we're going to manage it is Ael's plan," Jim said. "I'm sorry to have to command you to do things you can't fully support—but I see no alternative."

"Jim," Mike Walsh said, "you misunderstand us. We support you to the hilt. But we don't like this!"

"Bad odds?" Jim said gently.

Mike looked rueful. "They'd be better if you'd take *Inaieu* and *Constellation* along."

"Sorry, Mike, but that's out of the question. At the slightest warning the people on Levaeri will dump their computers and escape with the genetic material—and take *Intrepid* along with them, so deep into Romulan space that none of us would ever get out again."

"We could be taken along in tow, 'captured' as you would be," Rihaul said. But she said it so wistfully that Jim wanted to reach over and pat her tentacles.

Ael, seated not far from Rihaul, laughed very kindly. "Captain," she said, "you do *Bloodwing* such an honor as she has never been done before. But it would never work. One starship I can barely justify catching, on my own reputation as a commander. But with *Cuirass*, and the idiot crew that Romulan High Command knows is aboard her—*three* starships, and one of those a *Defender*-class destroyer? They would know upon detecting us that something was amiss, and flee Levaeri as *Enterprise*'s Captain has said. . . . And besides all that, if I tried to tow so much tonnage, I would burn out *Bloodwing*'s engines. I fear it will not work. But I am sorry to have to answer such *mnhei'sahe* with cold counsel. . . ."

The people around the table were quiet, looking at Jim. "Well, we'd best get started," he said. "Mr. Spock has detailed the Commander's plan for you. We will be following it quite closely. I want *Inaieu* and *Constella-*

tion to continue routine patrols—being careful to avoid this area for several hours on the next sweep; we mustn't have any more muon trails through here than Ael's story will account for—and the phaser fire of the 'battle' we're going to stage will obliterate the trails left by your presence here and now. Ael will be beaming about forty Romulans aboard to man key posts in case the escorting ships decide they need proof of what's going on. Subcommander Tafv will be remaining on *Bloodwing,* while Ael supervises her people's settling in over here. What's our ETA at Levaeri V?"

"At towing speed, about warp two, two days and five hours in your time system," Tafv said. "We will hit their sensor boundary at about one day twenty hours. An escort, should Command decide to send us one, would doubtless scramble and meet us about one day into the journey."

"Couldn't we just sneak in?" Sulu said, from beyond Spock.

"Besides the lack of honor in such an approach," Tafv said with a slight smile, "no. Our side of the Zone is as thickly sown with sensor satellites as yours is; and should we try to reenter the Zone without reporting our presence, Command would know immediately that something was amiss. The ships sent to intercept us would fire first and ask no questions, whether we had *Enterprise* in tow or not—in fact, they would be glad to blow you up and take the credit for it. And as you already know, they count the Commander a nuisance better dead than alive. No, we must declare ourselves, and then prepare to deceive the escort."

"So we'd best get started," Jim said. "Commander, Subcommander, will you beam over to *Enterprise* with Dr. McCoy and Mr. Spock and work out quartering arrangements for your crewpeople with them? We don't have a lot of space in crew's quarters proper, but those who need to be aboard for the ruse should be comfortable enough. And, Uhura, I want you to see if there isn't some way to temporarily block subspace communication in our neighborhood—or at least interfere with it."

"Aye, sir."

"Captain Rihaul, I leave you in command of the task force—what's left of it. Be very clear about this: should something go wrong with this operation, under no circumstances are you to mount a rescue attempt of any kind. You must disavow us if approached. Understood?"

"Jim—"

"No 'buts,' Mike. Acknowledge and comply."

"Acknowledged," said Captain Walsh.

"Yes, Jim," said Rihaul.

"Very well."

"And good luck, Captain," Walsh said.

"If there is such a thing," Jim said, "I accept with thanks. Dismissed, all."

Jim stood; the room emptied—swiftly of Denebians, more slowly of the other species. Finally only the three of them were left—the two hominids and the brown, baggy Deirr, looking uncomfortably at one another.

"It's hardly a pat hand, Jim," Mike said. "I would much rather you cheated."

"I am considering tucking you two up my sleeve," Jim said. "Nhauris, let's go down to your quarters and talk."

Much later, Jim leaned over the helm console and said, "How about it, Mr. Sulu? Do you think you can make it work?"

"No question, Captain." Sulu was seated at the

console, making minute adjustments to a set of programmed flight instructions. Beside Jim, looking over Sulu's other shoulder with great interest, was Subcommander Tafv. He and Sulu had been consulting for nearly an hour now, "choreographing" the "battle" they would fight in Romulan space.

"It's just like the wargames simulations back at the Academy," Sulu said, "except with real ships. We'll have to use phasers at higher-than-minimal power in order to wipe out our muon trail properly and leave the right heat and photon residues to fool any investigator. Screens will be up at normal power on both ships for the first few passes—but see, here in the fourth pass *Enterprise* will 'take a hit' on number four screen, which will go down and allow the damage to the port nacelle that Mr. Scott's arranging—"

"Will be arranging," Jim said, his ears still burning slightly from Scotty's private conversation with him, in one of the turbolifts, about what Jim was planning to do to his precious engines. "I don't think he can bear to start just yet. Go on, gentlemen."

"We will use a separate burst of phaser fire to make the actual cut in the nacelle," Tafv said. "That way there will be less chance of hurting the reinforcement your Chief Engineer will be installing on the inner hull, so that the matter-antimatter converter in the nacelle can still function. That is probably the most delicate part of the operation. After that, Mr. Sulu has programmed the *Enterprise*'s navigations and gunnery computers to make another pass at us and do us some damage—a 'missed shot' at our own port nacelle that will instead hull us in one cargo hold, causing the usual explosive decompression and scattering various supplies all over the area. However, it will not be enough to stop us; *Enterprise* will be 'limping' badly at that point, and we will chase her until she's forced to turn and fight because of 'overheating' in the remaining, overstressed nacelle. We will answer with more phaser fire, while *Enterprise*'s, due to the fueling of phasers from the already overtaxed nacelle, drops off. Then screens will go down, and the Commander will send her message ahead to Fleet Command. At this distance from Romulus we will have some six hours' grace before it reaches them—during which time we will jointly fake whatever else needs faking; the use of the intruder control system, various burn marks and damages from 'fighting in the corridors,' and so forth."

"At the same time," Sulu said, "we'll be transferring control to the Auxiliary Bridge, and coaching the Romulan 'invaders' in how to handle communications and so forth, for when the escort comes along and demands to know what's *really* going on." He stopped then, looking a little disconcerted. "Captain—one problem. What if they want to board, rather than just examining us by ship-to-ship communication?"

Jim shook his head. "The Commander thinks she can prevent that," he said, "but if they do board—well, we'll get some acting practice, that's all. There shouldn't be too many Romulans to fool, anyway—it's not as if a whole crew would beam over and inspect every bit of the ship. We shouldn't have to deal with any more than twenty or thirty Romulans tops—and if we can't fool thirty Romulans—" Jim stopped abruptly, grinned at Tafv. "Sorry, Subcommander. Some habits are hard to break."

"Yes, I agree," Tafv said, smiling slightly. "But the effort is interesting. Captain, will there be anything else? I am going to be needed on *Bloodwing* shortly."

"If you gentlemen are finished, then by all means go ahead," Jim said. Tafv bowed slightly to Jim, waved two fingers at Sulu in a small saluting gesture, and hurried off the Bridge.

When the lift doors had closed behind him, Sulu sat back in his chair and looked up at Jim with an expression both worried and bemused. "Sir," he said, "is it all right to say that I trust you completely—and I wish I could say the same for them?"

"Absolutely," Jim said, "because that's exactly the way I feel about it. However, the only way to prove someone trustworthy is to trust them. I just wish it wasn't my ship and my crew I had to trust them with. . . ."

Sulu looked up at Jim and nodded. "Captain," he said, "we're with you. It's not only the Romulans who have mneh—whatever-it-is."

"Yes, Mr. Sulu," Jim said. "I know. And thank you." He sighed. "I suppose I'd better get down there and see how poor Scotty's doing with 'blowing up' his engine. . . ."

"I bet he's doing most of the 'blowing up' himself," Chekov said quietly from beside Sulu.

"Mr. Chekov," Jim said, "amen to that. Mind the Bridge, gentlemen. We won't be in it for long. . . ."

And so it was that, several hours later, a lone Federation starship ventured out of its own space into the proscribed space of the Romulan Neutral Zone, and was found trespassing there by a ship whose ID read ChR *Cuirass*. The Federation ship tried to escape, but it was too far into the Zone to make it back into its own space before being caught by *Cuirass* and brought to battle. The engagement was brief and fierce, characterized by a virtuoso set of evasive maneuvers by the *Enterprise*'s helmsman, and the dogged, never-say-die pursuit of *Cuirass;* but in the end virtuosity was not enough to save the Federation ship, one of whose engines overloaded during a particularly high-power turn-and-fire maneuver. *Cuirass* was quick to exploit the problem, and though she took some hurt herself in the exchange of fire that followed, she blew a hole eighty meters long in the *Enterprise*'s starboard nacelle. "Oh, m' poor bairn!" someone was heard to moan on the *Enterprise*'s Bridge; but the Romulans who heard the exclamation only laughed softly, and those who didn't began raining phaser fire on the *Enterprise*'s weakening screens. Number four went down, and others followed; a great many Romulans beamed aboard the beleaguered ship, right into the Bridge, securing it before the *Enterprise*'s own security or intruder-defense systems could act. They took that intruder-defense system and used it to their own advantage—gassing most of the crew into unconsciousness and locking them up, then confining the Captain and Bridge crew and threatening him with the death of his whole crew unless he unconditionally surrendered his ship.

Faced with the inevitable, he did so. For only the second time in Federation history, a living captain gave up his command and was locked away to await trial with various of his officers. And a Rihannsu Commander stood proudly on a Federation starship's Bridge, called Rihannsu High Command, and informed them that she had captured the USS *Enterprise*.

High Command had not yet heard from three other Rihannsu ships, in another part of homespace, concerning the sudden disappearance from their area of *Cuirass*, pursued by another Warbird. The three commanders of the ships with the Klingon names were still in conference aboard *Ehhak*, trying to figure out what story to tell Command that would save their necks.

So there was celebration at Command when the message came in; and a three-ship escort was detached from other duty to help *Cuirass* bring the *Enterprise* in. Judges were selected from the Senate for the war-crimes trials, and various people in the Science and Shipbuilding departments of Command became abnormally cheerful at the thought of the happy months of analysis ahead of them. Some Senators and Praetors grumbled bitterly among themselves. There was nothing to be done about t'Rllaillieu; throw the cursed woman into a dungheap and she came up covered with dilithium crystals. There had to be another way to get rid of her.

They would have been pleased to know that there were already various people working on the problem.

Eleven

She could not get used to it—she knew she would never get used to it—this business of standing on the Bridge of a Federation vessel, not as a prisoner, but as an ally.

It was bizarre to look around her and see the Captain sitting there as calm in his center chair as she might be in hers, looking around at a Bridge where Rihannsu worked alongside Terrans and other odd creatures. Her own crewpeople were rather bemused about it themselves, but they applied themselves to their work, and saved their wondering for their few off hours. They had a lot to learn in a very short time.

They were her best. *Bloodwing* had been through its share of trouble over the last three years, and several times had had to be not only refitted but supplied with new people to replace those lost in this or that battle. Of her two hundred crew, only about fifty had been with her for more than ten years—an assortment of canny old creatures who lived almost wholly by their wits, and crazy young ones who had survived this long mostly by trusting her blindly and doing everything she told them. Some of them, by keeping their eyes open and learning from what she did, had become prime command material—though they usually loudly claimed that they would never be as good as she was, did the subject ever come up. Among this latter group were many of her officers; and she loved them dearly, feeling that she had more than one child. They looked up to her like a mother. It was to this younger group that Ael was "susse-thrai"; the elder group just called her "our Commander," and smiled at the youngsters.

"Commander," said the Captain, breaking her out of her thoughts, "anything from *Bloodwing?*"

"Nothing new," she said. "But your Mz. Kerasus was busy translating the last communication from Command a little while ago. She should have it for you shortly. Oh, Captain, it was choice."

He looked oddly at her smile. "How so? I thought it was fairly dry, from what you told me."

"Well." She sat down opposite him at one of the auxiliary science stations. "That is why I suggested the Lieutenant translate it into Basic for you; there were nuances that I am incompetent to render. I am a thorn in the Senate's side, you see; a major annoyance to them. Command likes me no better, since it's the Senate that appropriates their funds, and the retirees holding down desk jobs in Command all study to dance to their masters' harps. They sent me out on Neutral Zone patrol in the first place in hopes I would be killed—an 'honorable' duty assigned for a dishonorable purpose. Lieutenant Kerasus called it 'being sent to Gaul.' Where *is* Gaul, by the way? Some kind of prison planet?"

The Captain shook his head, smiling. "No, it's on

Earth, and the wine there is very good . . . but don't drink the water."

She knew a joke when she heard one, even if she didn't understand it. "I shall not, then. But at any rate, the tone of the communication was, shall we say, rather sour. They had to do me honor—but it annoyed them to do so. Nor did Command dare send me too much 'help' in bringing you home. I might take offense—and should my star rise again in the Senate, as may now seem likely to them, they would be slitting their own wrists in angering me. You will see when you read the communiqué. Lieutenant Kerasus strikes me as a very skilled officer, and I'm sure you will find the text amusing."

Jim nodded. "Three ships, you said?"

"Yes. *Rea's Helm* and *Wildfire,* which I think you know, have been pulled off Neutral Zone patrol in other areas to attend us: and *Javelin,* which usually does courier runs between Eisn and the Klingon borders, was out this way on an errand to Hihwende and is also being dispatched. This is good luck for us, Captain. Two of these, the Commanders of *Helm* and *Javelin,* are old unfriends of mine—too politic to argue with me, though, when I am obviously in a position of power. The third, *Wildfire's* commander, I don't know—but that may work to our advantage as well."

"I've wondered ever since I heard the name," the Captain said, "who 'Rea' was. . . ."

Ael looked at the Captain from under her brows, a mischievous expression. "You would have liked him, Captain. He was a magician whose enemies captured him and forced him to use his arts for them. They told him they wanted him to make a helmet that would make the person who wore it proof against wounds. So he did—and when one of those who captured him tried it on, the demon Rea had bound inside the helmet bit the man's head off. A corpse will not care how you wound it. . . ." She laughed at his wry look. "Enough, Captain. Soon you will be asking me what a 'blood-wing' is—"

"That would have been the next question, yes. . . ."

"Later," said Ael, standing, as Lieutenant Kerasus came in. "And you will tell me what great 'enterprise' your ship is named for. . . ."

She went over to stand by the gorgeous dark-skinned woman, Uhura, and her own crewwoman Aidoann, while the Captain, with occasional snickerings, read the document the Lieutenant had brought him. Aidoann t'Khnialmnae was Ael's third-in-command, a tall young woman with bronze-fair hair and a round, broad face that could be astonishingly complacent or astonishingly ferocious, depending on the mood that rode her. "How are you doing, small one?"

It was their old joke, and here as anywhere else Aidoann flicked her eyes sidewise, stifling a reply until they should both be off duty. "Well enough, khre-'Riov," she said. "Lieutenant Uhura has been very patient with me. I don't doubt I will have the more important features of this board mastered by the time the skill is needed."

"I haven't much needed to be patient, Commander," said Uhura. "The Antecenturion is very quick—"

Aidoann cocked her head at the Lieutenant. "All right, Aidoann, then," Uhura said. "It's a pity she's not—no, I beg your pardon, I mean—"

"Not one of your crew?" Ael said. "No offense taken, Lieutenant. For the moment, at least, she is." She glanced at Aidoann. "How has Khiy been doing with the helm?"

They all three glanced down at the small, slim, dark

147

man sitting beside Mr. Sulu, with Mr. Chekov looking over his shoulder and giving advice. "Rather well, I think," Aidoann said. "At least the ship has not crashed into anything yet."

"Commander?" said the Captain, looking up from his center seat. "What's this about this other ship?— *Battlequeen*, is it?"

"That's the one that will not be here," Ael said, turning away from Aidoann and stepping down into the center again. "Be glad of it. *Battlequeen* is commanded by Lyirru tr'Illialhae, and Lyirru is a reckless, bloodthirsty idiot who would certainly want to beam over here at first sight of you. He has done enough stupid things in the past to be deprived of his command if he were anyone else—but unfortunately he has friends among both Praetors and Senators, and he's the delight of the expansionist lobby in the Tricameron. However, the kind Elements have put him safely out of our way for the moment—there's a rebellion going on out on one of the colony planets, as you see, and he's off putting an end to it. I just hope he leaves the planet there when he's done; it would be just like him to blow it up in a fit of pique."

She saw on the Captain's face what he thought of such tactics, and was heartened. "Fine. As long as he stays out of our way . . ." He handed the report back to Lieutenant Kerasus, who took it around to Mr. Spock. "I see what you meant about the tone of that thing. Bureaucracy doesn't change, does it?"

"Apparently not. —Captain, I want to make the rounds and see how my people are settling in; would you care to come with me?"

"I'll join you later, Commander," he said. "I have some work to finish up here. Just tell the lift where you want to go; once it dumps you out on a given floor, ask it for directions—it'll answer, all the lifts have been put on the translator network."

"Thank you, Captain."

She stepped into the lift. Its doors closed on her, and Ael stood for a moment irresolute, wondering where to go. Then she remembered that Tafv had gone off with Hvaid t'Khaethaetreh, one of her subalterns, to see about accomodations near the Recreation department. "Recreation deck," she said to the lift, and obediently it whooshed off.

The amiable sound of many voices down the hall told Ael which way to go as surely as the computer could have. She went down toward it, her usual purposeful stride slowed to a stroll, as it had again and again over the past few hours. She could not get used to how large this ship was. *Bloodwing* was a hole by comparison, cramped, dark and barren. *I am getting spoiled,* she thought. *If I am not careful, I will begin to covet this ship. And even thinking that thought is dangerous. . . .*

The doors to Recreation were open. She stepped in and was astonished to see how very many people were in there. People of all kinds. That was another thing she was having trouble getting used to. When the Rihannsu had left Vulcan, astronomy had been old, but space-flight was still in its infancy; and generation ships had been all they had. They had met no other species in their travels, and ch'Ríhan had had plenty of animal life, but no other intelligence. For thousands of years the Rihannsu had not dreamed of any other life in the universe; even Vulcan had become almost a legend. But then came the days of starflight, the rediscovery of other species, and the First War that resulted in the setting up of the Zone. What had been mere ignorance and isolation turned rather suddenly into a politically-based xenophobia, the idea that anything not Rihannsu would most likely either shoot at you or steal from you. The Klingons had not helped this impression. Now, though, Ael looked around this bewildering collection of aliens—all these Terrans and Tellarites and Andorians and Sulamids and three kinds of Denebians, and whatnot else—and was bewildered. Four hundred kinds of 'humanity,' the ship's library computers called them. She found that bizarre. There was only one kind of humanity, everybody knew that. But to judge from the way these people worked together, one would think *they* didn't know it. . . .

It would have been the rankest discourtesy, of course, to display that attitude among hosts who thought otherwise. So Ael walked on through the room looking with cool and (she hoped) polite interest at all the weird things with tentacles and the odd-colored men and women, eating and drinking and playing together, and privately wondered how they stood one another.

"Can I help you, ma'am?" said a very polite, very clear voice from her left and down by her feet—a voice that sounded rather like rock grinding on rock, a most peculiar noise. Ael turned and looked down, and Elements have mercy on her, there was one of Them personified—a rock talking to her. At least it looked like a rock, if rocks had shaggy fringes, and if any mineral ever mined came in such odd colors—orange and ocher and black, bizarrely crusted together. The creature glittered as if it were gemmed, and the *Enterprise*'s parabolic insignia gleamed on the small, flat black box fitted into a hollow between excrescences on its back. A voder, possibly.

Ael got hold of herself as best she could and said, "Surely you may, Ensign." The rock wore no uniform, but there were no stripes on the voder, and Ael knew from her study of Fleet protocol that 'ensigns,' equivalent to Rihannsu subcenturia, had no stripes at all. "I am looking for the officer in charge of the billeting of the visiting Rihannsu. Would you know who that might be?"

"Mr. Tanzer and Dr. McCoy are working on it, Commander," the rock said to her, its fringe rippling on one side of it. "May I take you to them?"

There was a cheerful eagerness in the voice that Ael almost smiled at; this was a very young officer, if she was any judge. She thought fondly of Tafv when he was that young, and of Aidoann a few years ago, before battle and friendship had shaken some of the rawness out of her. "Yes, Ensign, thank you."

The rock rumbled off through the big room, and Ael went after him at a leisurely pace, looking around her as she went. A swimming bath, for pity's sake! and banqueting tables surrounded by people eating what would have been a feast by Rihannsu standards, but what Ael suspected was probably just ordinary fare. *They have so much,* she thought. *No wonder they understand us so little, who are so poor. Perhaps they don't even understand the anger that the hungry feel when the full go by, unthinking. . . .* But the anger, the thought of her poor cramped crew who deserved so much better, was shaken out of her somewhat by the sight of her crewpeople themselves. They were standing and sitting, most of them, off in one corner of the great room, looking quite brave and aloof and self-sufficient, and (to Ael's trained eye) rather lost and scared. Dr. McCoy was making his way busily among them, talking to them as kindly as her own ship's surgeon might, as he installed intradermal translators in their forearms. Indeed, Surgeon t'Hrienteh was at McCoy's elbow, carefully watching what he did; and there was an unaccustomed smile on her grim dark face as McCoy patted the forearm of poor nervous tr'Jaihen, spoke some reassuring (though not yet understood) word to him, and slipped the implant in.

"Doctor," Ael said, and to her amusement both McCoy and t'Hrienteh turned to see who called them.

"Oh, there you are, Commander," McCoy said, giving her the casual look someone back on the farm might have given a strayed fvai that had finally come back to the stable. "I see Ensign Naraht found you."

"Indeed he did," said Ael, tipping a quick smile down at the youngster. "Are the arrangements about complete, Doctor? My people and I have a lot of work to do."

"Almost done, Commander. Just a few more translators to go in." McCoy looked around at the corner of the room. "The Recreation Chief has gone off to see about partitioning this area off for your people's sleeping quarters. We didn't have enough room to put them in crew quarters, unfortunately; we're just about full up with our own people right now."

"Doctor, this will suit us very well," Ael said. "We are used to barracks living, all of us, and there's much more room here than even back on *Bloodwing*. Is there a visitors' mess?"

"Not as such, but Mr. Tanzer's reprogrammed the food processors in the lounge adjacent to this area. I've already told most of your people, but now I should tell you; when you use the processor, stay away from anything with a red tag on it—those are the foods that won't agree with your metabolism. Last thing you people need to worry about right now would be coming down with the Titanian two-step."

"Pardon?"

"*LIhrei'sian*," said t'Hrienteh.

"Oh. Thank you, Doctor, you're quite right. . . ."

"Len?" someone said from behind her. Ael turned to find herself looking at a short, well-muscled, silver-haired man with such calm wise eyes that her first thought was *Senior Centurion*. But of course that couldn't be the case; the Captain had not even introduced him at the department heads' meeting, though the man had been there. He looked at her in return, weighed her, and accepted her utterly, all in one swift glance; then said, "I beg your pardon, Commander."

"Please don't," she said, though his courtesy pleased her as much as his assessment had unnerved her.

"This is Lieutenant Harb Tanzer, Commander," said McCoy. "He'll be handling your people's needs, since he's in charge of this whole area. If they need anything at all while they're here—anything nonmedical, that is—they should see him."

"I'll be on call at all times, Commander," said Mr. Tanzer. "We should have enough time before the other Rihannsu ships arrive for your crew to get at least one shift's worth of sleep. When they're ready, call me and I'll block this whole area off for them. I'm sorry we don't have solid walls; we normally use opaque force-fields with a high-positive soundblock."

"Those sound fine," Ael said, wondering what in the worlds the man was talking about. "If there's a problem, we'll let you know."

"Meantime, once they've handled what they have to do aboard ship, they're most welcome to our facilities," Mr. Tanzer said. "In fact, Commander, if I may say so, a lot of the people in here are rather hoping your crew will join them. They're incredibly curious. None of us have ever had the chance to talk to a Rihannsu before."

Ael noticed, to her considerable surprise, that the translator was not merely rendering it from the Basic word "Romulan"; the man was actually saying "Rihannsu"—and with a tolerable accent. "If they wish to," she said, looking more carefully at Mr. Tanzer than she had at first, "they certainly may, and thank you kindly. Will you excuse me? I need to talk to them."

"Certainly."

The Doctor and the Recreation Officer and the rock all went off together, leaving Ael with her little group. With their usual cool discipline they all sank down together, sitting cross-legged on the strange, soft floor as they would have after workout in *Bloodwing's* little gym.

"What of it, my own?" she said. "Are you well, or will you shortly be that way? And can you hold to your oaths in this place, under the eyes of strangers and under these circumstances? For surely none of us have ever been this sorely tested, or will be. Anyone who thinks that he or she might be tempted to do our old enemies evil in an unguarded moment, say it now. I will not hold it against you. You will go back to *Bloodwing* in honor for a bitter truth told, and courage in telling it."

They all looked at her soberly, her faithful group— the many familiar faces that had followed her into battle so many times before. Fair little N'alae with her placid eyes and deadly hands, silent Khoal, great lanky Dhiemn with his farm-child's hands and his sword-sharp mind; Rhioa and Ireqh and Dhiov and Ejiul and T'maekh, and many another—they all watched her, quite silent, and no one moved. "Be certain," Ael said softly. "This is to our everlasting shame and my own dishonor should we fail. Poor tattered rag that my honor will be, once Command finds out what we're up to—yet I would not tear it any worse."

Dhiov, who was always timid except when it came to

154

slighting herself, or killing, said abruptly, "Those things with the tentacles—"

"Are people," Ael said. "Never doubt it. They look horrible to me too, but I make no doubt that their gorge rises somewhat at us." There was soft laughter over that. "They have their own version of the Passion, too; they will defend their ship and their shipmates as brilliantly and as bravely as you will. The same for the blue people and the orange ones and the brown ones and the ones who look like hlai."

"And the rock?" said Dhiemn, with his usual dry humor.

"Especially the rock, I think. Elements, my children, what a start that one gave me. May I be preserved from seeing any more of that kind of thing; if Air or Fire should walk up and speak to me, I doubt I could bear it."

More laughter. They were relaxing, and Ael was glad to see it. "So, we're merry. Have you learned your duties well enough to be sure of them?"

Various heads bowed "yes." "It's not hard, khre-'Riov," said Ejiul. "Most of the positions we're being taught involve only communications. Any consoles we need to read have been reprogrammed for Rihannsu, and the instructions usually coach you along."

"Be certain, now. There will be no room for mistakes once *Javelin* and *Rea's Helm* and *Battlequeen* get here."

There was a sound of indrawn breath. Ael looked over at little dark Nniol, who was suddenly staring at the carpet. "O Air and Earth, khre'Riov," he said. "My sister was serving on *Javelin* last I heard."

Ael looked at him. "Nniol, that's hard. Will your oath hold?"

He looked up, stricken. "Khre'Riov—I don't know."

"Who must we ask to find out?" she said, very softly.

He stared at the carpet again. "We were close," he said. And after a long pause, he said, "I think I had best go back."

She looked at him, then nodded swiftly. "There's *mnhei'sahe* indeed—painful, but pure. Stay with us for the moment, Nniol: I'll speak to the Captain. Anyone else?"

No one spoke.

"Very well. Shall we work out? We haven't had time to stretch as yet today, and we'll need to be limber tomorrow." Ael grinned at them. "Let's show them how it's done, shall we?"

There were answering grins all around, even from Nniol. They rose again, all together, and after reverence done toward ch'Ríhan, in the Elements' direction ("That way," Dhiemn said, pointing at the floor; he always knew), Ael led them through the preliminary stretches and focusing. By the time they had gotten through the first few throws and choke-breaks and had broken into small freestyle groups to work out, some of the *Enterprise* people had drifted over, very casually, to watch them. Ael stepped away from her people as a cheerful free-for-all was starting among them—N'alae and Khoal dominating it as usual, everyone leaping at them and being thrown halfway to the horizon for their pains.

Ael wiped her brow and looked, under cover of the motion, at the *Enterprise* people. They were maintaining very carefully their pose of casualness; but Ael saw plainly enough that some of them wanted to dive into that fight too and try their luck. At least some of the hominids did; there was no telling what that tall purple-tentacled thing with all the writhing eyes might be thinking about—or, for that matter, young Ensign

Rock, who was standing next to it. None of the hominids, at least, looked hostile. They looked hopeful, like children waiting to be asked to play . . . though their faces pretended mild interest and their conversation was calm.

She felt eyes on her, looked up. *Enterprise*'s Captain was coming toward her, along with Lieutenant Tanzer. The Captain was in fact looking slightly past her, at the free-for-all, and if she was any good at reading Terrans, Ael thought she caught a kind of itchy expression on his face that indicated he, too, would like to get in on it. But there was regret there, too. *Poor man*, Ael thought, *he doesn't have the leisure either. . . .*

"Commander," said the Captain, and paused beside her, watching the madness going on in the corner, as little N'alae picked up Dhiemn bodily and tossed him at Lhair and Ameh. They caught him, barely.

"Captain," she said. "Just a workout; 'llaekh-ae'rl,' we call it."

" 'Laughing murder'? Very apt . . . My people tell me that yours have been picking up the parts they'll play very fast indeed."

"I have no time for slow learners, Captain," Ael said. "And to tell you truth, few of them survive long on Neutral Zone patrol, or on our frontier with the Klingons. —I'm glad you came now; for I have a problem. My crewman Nniol t'AAnikh has kin on one of the incoming ships, *Javelin*. I cannot allow him to be at or near a combat station when we engage that ship. I am sending him back to *Bloodwing*."

He looked at her narrowly. "Certainly, Commander. Is it a matter of trust?"

Ael restrained herself from frowning at him, though it annoyed her that he should instantly think the worst of one of her people. "Yes, it is," she said. "He trusts me enough to tell me that he does not know whether he can trust himself in such a situation. It is my responsibility to guard his honor, just as by speaking he guards mine."

Perhaps the Captain got a sense of how nettled she felt, for his face changed quickly. "Of course, Commander. Do as you think best. When he's ready to go back, just send him down to the Transporter Room; I'll see to it that they expect him."

"Thank you. Oh, now, see that. . . ." She had glanced away from the Captain at a sudden lull in the scrapping behind her. There were several of the *Enterprise* crewpeople among her own—a couple of hominids, one blue-skinned and one fair like the Captain—and one of the strange violet-tentacled things with all the eyes. The fairer of the two hominids, a small slim man, was making gestures that approximated N'alae's last throw, evidently asking her something about it; and Ael smiled as N'alae reached out to the man with that demure little expression of hers. The crewman set himself as well as he could to prevent her, Ael gave him credit for that; but all his preparation did the poor fellow no good. He went flying, came down hard and slapped the floor—then bounced up again, none the worse for wear but looking downright delighted.

"Can you all do that?" the Captain said from beside Ael, watching the business with the same rueful delight as his crewman.

"No," Ael said, not without some rue on her own side. Many a time poor N'alae had tried to teach her some of the finest points of llaekh-ae'rl, the delicate shifts of balance that required a mind that could root itself in earth, or the metal of deckplates. But Ael had too much fire and air in her, and could not root. She had become resigned to defending herself with a phaser, or her mind. "N'alae is our specialist in the art."

"Uh-oh," said the Captain, a sound that Ael's translator refused to render. Nevertheless, she understood it, for the tall purple sheaf of tentacles glided over to N'alae and was saying something to her, gesturing with liquid grace and many arms.

"That's a Sulamid," the Captain said. "Mr. Athendë from Maintenance. Hand-to-hand combat is one of his hobbies. . . ."

That joke Ael understood, and she laughed hard for a few seconds, enjoying the sensation immensely. How long had it been since she laughed for pure merriment, not out of bitterness? She saw various heads turn among her crew; evidently it was a sound they were glad to hear, too, and some of the stiffness and formality seemed to fall away from them on hearing it. N'alae laughed also—that dangerous sound Ael knew very well—and held out her arms to the Sulamid, which obligingly wrapped numerous of its tentacles around them like thickvine running up a tree's branches. There was a moment of swaying and straining, long seconds when nothing seemed to happen; and then with startling suddenness N'alae was standing all by herself again, and Mr. Athendë was sailing through the air, eyes and tentacles waving and whipping around. He hit the deck without a sound—evidently the tentacles made good shock absorbers—and bounced up again.

All Ael's people were cheering N'alae, who looked flushed and surprised. But, surprisingly, the *Enterprise* people standing around—and there were quite a lot of them now—were cheering her too; and Athendë swayed and bent double in a deep bow to her, saying something Ael couldn't quite catch, but something that made N'alae laugh.

Ael glanced sideways and saw the Captain's look, thoughtful and impressed. "We could learn a lot from her," he said. "None of us have ever been able to pull that on Athendë—not even Mr. Spock. After we finish our business at Levaeri, would you consider lending that lady to us for a little while? . . ."

"I am not sure we would want to give up the advantage," Ael said soberly. "I shall ask her, however."

The two of them turned away from the rapidly growing group in the corner, strolling away across Recreation. "Your people have been very kind to ours since we came here, Captain," she said.

The Captain raised his shoulders and let them fall again in a careless gesture. "Simple interspecies amity," he said. "The spirit of brotherhood."

The translator made little sense of the last word; but Ael understood why—it having been one of many oddities she had noticed long ago when working on her own translator program. "There is a question you might answer for me," she said. "Why does the word imply male siblings and not female as well?"

"It's an old word," said the Captain, looking slightly embarrassed. "'Kinship' would be closer to the meaning."

"But a word's true meaning, its intended meaning, is always implicit in its structure," Ael said. "Evidently there were those who thought, when your language was forged, that only men were capable of that brand of kinship—and that by implication it was impossible between two women, or between female and male.

How did they justify that in the face of evidence otherwise? Or did they simply wish half your species to think that it could *not* set back to back and fight for life and the things that mattered?"

He said nothing, and there was something about his silence that troubled Ael, so that she pressed her advantage to see what lay under the silence. "What about it, Captain? How is it that only brothers may fight, be valiant, persevere, defy deaths great and small—while judging half your race outside of that burden, that privilege, from the beginning?"

"I have no answer for you," the Captain said, all tact, refusing to be drawn.

"Indeed. One wonders why the other half of your species put up with yours for so long."

"Perhaps they got their revenge," the Captain said, "by letting my half of the species think it was right about them—and letting it go to Hell as a result."

Ael's eyebrow went up in surprised and pleased acknowledgment of the Captain's shot across her bows. He looked oddly at her, as if even through his anger seeing something familiar in her, though Ael had no idea what and at the moment didn't care. "Besides," the Captain said, "there's one characteristic of being a brother that you didn't mention. Liking. Brothers have that for one another, generally. I'm not sure I could have that much of that kind of liking for a woman."

Ael briefly considered the steady, sure relationship she had sensed between the Captain and Uhura—the flashes of humor, the utter trust—and realized with wry amusement that she was being insulted. Why, she wasn't yet sure; so for the moment she put the matter aside and merely considered the Captain's premise. "Liking. Well. Brothers may certainly develop it. It may make living with one another easier. But it's hardly necessary to brotherhood proper. Say my brother and I quarrel; then he falls in danger of his life. Do I let him lie there, because I no longer 'like' him? Or do I save him—simply because he is my brother, because I have said that he is forever someone important to me—and I'm bound by what I have said?"

"I'm not sure that's what I meant."

"Neither am I. But in any case it is *mnhei'sahe*. The bondage beyond reason, beyond hope or pain or escape. The bond that not even betrayal can break—only snarl around the heart until the betrayer's heart scars. The bond of word, of choice. Unbreakable."

"Death—"

"Death avails nothing against it. Your parents, your own brother who is dead—oh, yes, we know. What use is intelligence but for the knowing of one's enemies? Have you come to love your relatives any less for their being dead? Or perhaps more?"

The Captain said nothing.

"So you see the nature of this bondage between beings who fight the same fight," Ael said. "A going in the same direction, for a little while, or for a life, that's all that's needed. The decision to go in company. Liking—" Ael shrugged one shoulder. "What need have allies of such a thing?"

"None," the Captain said, "I'm sure."

They walked along in silence a moment longer. Then Ael paused by a curious thing—a table with a holographic projection above it of a cube divided into many smaller cubes, eight of them to an edge. "What is this?"

"Four-dimensional chess," said the Captain. "Are you familiar with the game?"

"No."

The Captain smiled at her, and a very odd smile it was, one that made Ael curious. "If we have time—"

"I would be delighted to learn. Now, if you like; I dare say I can spare a few minutes to learn the rules."

That smile got wider, and the Captain pulled out one of the chairs that stood by the table, offering it to her. But neither of them had time to sit down; that infernal whooping began again. Heads went up all over the room, and a lot of the people who had been talking to Ael's folk excused themselves hurriedly and ran out.

"Red alert," the Vulcan's calm voice said, made gigantic over the ship's annunciator system. *"Battle stations, battle stations. This is no drill."*

The Captain slapped one hand down on a switch on the game table. "Kirk here."

"Captain, we have a Romulan vessel at extreme sensor range. K'tinga-class vessel, ID'ing as Romulan ship Javelin."

"They're early," Ael said, alarmed.

"Have they hailed us?" said the Captain.

"Not as yet, but they will soon be within range to do so."

"We're going to need some more of your people up on the Bridge, Commander. Mr. Spock, are Antecenturions Aidoann and Hvaid up there?"

"Affirmative, Captain."

"Have them handle any communications that come in. No visual until everyone on the Bridge is covered by an armed Romulan. Transfer control to the Auxiliary Bridge immediately and send Mr. Sulu and Mr. Chekov down there to handle things."

"Done, sir."

"Good. Give me allcall. Commander—"

"This is t'Rllaillieu," Ael said, astonished at how her

163

voice echoed in this flying cavern. "Rihannsu, report at speed to your assigned posts. Helmets all, and make sure any distinguishing insignia of *Bloodwing* about you are removed. If in doubt about any necessary action, consult with your 'prisoners.'" She allowed herself a slight laugh on the word; the Captain looked grim, but his eyes danced all the same. "Remember, you are *Cuirass* crew; do nothing to attract attention to yourselves when we are monitored! Honor to you—and *mnhei'sahe*. Out."

The Captain was looking at her quizzically. "I wished them luck," Ael said.

He shook his head. "I thought that word meant 'love.'"

Ael quirked half a grin at him. "What use is a word that means only one thing? Besides, in this context, they are nearly the same. . . ."

He looked bemused, but only for the instant; then he was all officer again, hard and ready. "You may have something there. In the meantime, I think you'll be needed on the Bridge. Mr. Spock," he said to the intercom, "our presence has been requested at a little theatrical. Would you care to join me in the brig?"

"My pleasure, Captain. Bridge out."

The humor in the Vulcan's voice was so little concealed and so dry that Ael had to laugh again; but the laugh lasted for only a breath, fading at the Captain's look. "Madam—" he said.

"I will care for your Bridge," said Ael. And she turned and was off, hurrying, and feeling his eyes in her back like the points of spears.

Very strange, it felt, to sit there in that soft chair at the heart of airy openness, staring at the big screen and waiting. Ael's heart pounded and her hands were sweating, as they always did before an engagement. She cursed them, as she always did, and rubbed them on her breeches. Around her, her own people failed to notice this business, as usual, and made themselves useful at strange consoles and odd instruments. The only thing missing was Tafv, but he was on *Bloodwing*, lying low for the moment; after all, *Cuirass* was not a place where he belonged. Aidoann was on *Bloodwing*, pretending to be commanding it in Ael's absence; the Commander, Aidoann would be telling *Javelin*, was aboard *Enterprise* making it secure and supervising the tapping and recording of its computer library. Hvaid and N'alae sat at the helm console; Khoal manned the science station, and Lhian the communications board. How cool they all looked, how very competent . . . a shadow of the look they had been wearing down in the Recreation deck, while the *Enterprise* people had been watching them. *And how I sit here and twitch like a broody hlai,* Ael thought. *Fire burn it, we can build a device that can cloak a whole starship, but we can't find a way to keep people's hands from sweating—*

"Communication from *Javelin*, khre'Riov," said Lhian, exactly as if they were back on *Bloodwing*.

"Accept it," Ael said.

The screen wavered and settled down, and Ael took a long breath and relaxed. Oh, that bland, round, foolish, familiar face. It was LLunih tr'Raedheol, and the Elements had been kind to her after all, for if anyone in space needed killing, it was this one. A coward and a fool, and one who thought everyone else was just like him, too lazy to do more than exhibit just enough energy to keep Command off his back. "Commander tr'Raedheol," Ael said, companionably

165

enough, "welcome to the Outmarches. You see we have found something rather interesting floating around out here. . . ."

"*Yes,*" LLunih said, and the greed, jealousy and hate distilling behind LLunih's eyes should have killed the man on the spot. Unfortunately, he was immune to his own venom, like the *nei'rrh* he was. "*So Command said. I should appreciate the opportunity to beam over and examine this tremendous prize for myself.*"

And try to figure out a way to cheat me out of it, you mean, Ael thought. "Oh, LLunih—may I call you LLunih?"

"*Do,*" said the repulsive creature, and smiled.

Ael kept herself from shuddering in loathing. "I couldn't allow that as yet. We are still in the process of learning to handle the command systems aboard this ship. Its officers are understandably annoyed with us, and they have not been as cooperative as would have been wise. These screens, for example; we were working with raising and lowering them, this morning, and we thought they were down—but in an evil moment someone from *Cuirass* tried to beam over and hit a 'phantom' screen of which our intelligence had failed to warn us. An outgrowth of the cloaking device, actually; quite clever." She smiled whimsically. "But unfortunate, since one of my minor officers is now floating around this part of space, reduced to his component atoms." *Oh, I will pay for* that *one sooner or later. . . .* "Until we're sure, I would rather you didn't take the chance. . . ."

"*Oh, Ael, I quite understand. . . .*" She lost his next few words, thinking of the old saying that a soiled name may only be washed clean in blood. *He has enough of it in all that flab to wash all four of them clean, I'll warrant. We shall see.*

". . . *find it hard to not want a look at the famous Captain Kiuurk*. . . ."

"Oh, as to that," Ael said, looking wicked, and not having to try too hard this time, "I dare say I could let you see a bit of what would please you. In fact, I have been hearing complaints from the Captain concerning his present lodging; I was about to go down there and settle them with him when you called. If you will hold a moment, you may watch the proceedings."

"*Surely.*"

Ael rose and nodded at Lhian: the screen went blank. "Warn them," she said.

"Khre'Riov," Lhian said, with one of his dark-browed looks, "we're being scanned. Shields are up, but there's some signal leakage, and anything on ship's channels might be overheard—"

"True," she said. "Well thought. Wait till I'm about halfway down the deck eight hall, going toward Detention; then pick me up on visual and pipe it over to *Javelin*, following me. Hvaid, come along."

Young Hvaid leaped up from his post, and the two of them hurried into the lift. "Detention, deck eight," Ael said. "Hvaid, when the lift stops, run ahead and warn the Captain and his officers. Tell them who has called and that we must play this very broadly; LLunih is stupid and unsubtle, and nods and winks will not do. If we do convince him, though, he'll convince the other ships when they arrive, and save us the trouble of doing all this again. —Then you'll have to run about to the various departments and tell everyone not to say anything damning on the ship's intercom until we are sure we're not being scanned, or can find a way to plug the leaks. Find some others of us to help you. Pull Lyie and K'haeth and Dhisuia off their posts; they're quick on their feet." The lift stopped. "Go now!"

Hvaid ran off down the hall. Ael leaned against the open door of the lift for a long, easy count of twenty, doing her best to slow her breathing down. It did not slow much, but finally she had to get out and walk, and found that the trembling in her knees wasn't nearly as bad as it had been. "Are you with me, *Javelin?*" she said cheerily to the air, using her upward look to disguise a glance around the corner she was approaching. Scan could not see it, but Ael could see Hvaid hurrying out of the door to Detention, around another corner and out of sight.

"We see you, Ael," said LLunih.

"Good. Here we are—"

She swung around through the door into Detention and saw the sight that many a Rihannsu had long desired to see: the Captain of the *Enterprise* and his formidable officers, one and all, crammed into a cell in the brig and every one of them looking ready to commit murder that would have no laughing about it. There was the good Doctor, his strange blue eyes flashing, and handsome Uhura looking as if she wanted a knife; and Mr. Scott with arms folded and eyes narrowed. He turned away from the sight of Ael as she came in; *a pretty touch,* she thought, *and probably based on reality*—for Mr. Scott had not yet forgiven her for the wounding of his precious engines. Even the Vulcan looked murderous—though in a restrained and decorous fashion. And the Captain, the courteous, genteel Captain, was from the look of him far gone in a cold rage that would have done the best of Ael's old commanders proud. Ael nodded the outer guards away from the forcefield controls on the door—poor Triy and Helev, looking as grimly triumphant as they knew how, and, Ael suspected, ready to break up laughing as soon as they knew they were no longer watched.

"Captain," Ael began, courteously enough; but the Captain didn't let her get any further.

"It is about time you found your way down here, lady," he said, with a stateliness of language that sorted bizarrely with his anger. *"What are you doing with my ship!* And my crew! You are in violation of—"

"You are in a poor position to be talking about violations, Captain," said Ael, motioning Triy to kill the forcefield. "You were the one we caught in the Zone—"

"Surely you would not mind if my crew watched this, Ael," said LLunih's voice from the intercom.

"Who the devil is *that!*" the Doctor shouted.

"Of course not," Ael said, as she stepped into the room and her eye fell on Nniol, who was doing inside guard duty.

O, by my Element, Ael thought, for Nniol's sister was on *Javelin,* and there was no possible reason for him to be on *Cuirass*—and there he was, his face shielded by a fortuitous angle for the moment, but the instant he moved a breath's worth, or she did, the pickup would catch him all too clearly. Her back was to it, at least; her eye flashed alarm at Nniol—there was nothing else she could do—

Then the fight broke out. At least it would have looked like a fight to any observer who did not stand where Ael did, who did not see the Captain swiftly cock back one fist and turn a little in the doing, just enough to exchange glances with the Doctor. The Doctor instantly put his head down and economically, savagely, butted Nniol in the gut with it. Nniol doubled over, his face safely out of the way of the pickup; but on the way down he clubbed McCoy two-handed and sidewise in the legs, and the Doctor came crashing down on top of him, concealing him further. Mr. Scott and the

Vulcan got in the way, but Triy and Helev, shouldering in past Ael and the Captain, shoved or slapped them back out of trouble—rather easily, in the Vulcan's case, though the phasers pointed at his midsection and at the Captain, and their meaningful looks, might have had something to do with it. And as for the Captain's punch, that had started all this, it never fell. Ael blocked it, hard, blocked the second one harder, heard something snap, and didn't dare hesitate, but carried through, slamming the man backhanded across the face. He went flying, crashed up against the wall, sagged down it, didn't move.

Ael glared at Uhura and Scott and Spock, who stood at bay in the corner of the cell, with phasers held on them. "I had thought to offer you honorable parole," she said, "but I see now it would have been a fool's act. Have them bound," she said to Triy. "All their other people, too; I dare say this boorishness and treachery is typical. And tend to this one." She nudged Nniol with her boot. Nniol, who lay sprawled face down under the Doctor, stirred and groaned, but very prudently did not move otherwise.

Ael stepped over the carnage and out of the cell, dusting herself off. "Llunih," she said, while Helev assisted the doubled-over Nniol out of the cell and Triy sealed the cell up again, "I would stay for conversation, but you see that I have business to be about—interrogations and so forth; and these people are not going to make it easy for me, that's plain. I do hope you'll excuse me."

"Any assistance I can offer, Ael—"

"LLunih, I will surely ask. In the meantime, I would count it a kindness if your navigator and mine would consult together, so that yours can match my course."

"Certainly."

"Then a good day to you; I will pay you a courtesy call tonight or tomorrow, if you would be so gracious as to receive me. Perhaps we might have dinner." *Though I say nothing of keeping it down for long.*

"Ael, I would be delighted."

"Until later, then." She turned back to the glaring group in the cell and eyed them until Lhian said from the Bridge, *"They have closed channels, khre'Riov. Shall I send a security detachment?"*

"No, we're secure," Ael said. "As you were, Lhian."

"Commander."

—and she stepped forward and killed the forcefield, and bent down hurriedly to the Captain, as the others did. "That crawling slime," she said bitterly as she helped the Captain to his feet. "He so loves the sight of others' shame that he cannot resist spreading it around for the delectation of his whole crew. Captain, I have done you a great discourtesy! I shall do you a better turn some other time."

The Captain, for the moment, found nothing to say but a groan. She helped him stand from one side, while Spock assisted him on the other, being very careful of the injured arm. "There's this good at least come of it all," she said. "LLunih will gossip so to the commanders of *Rea's Helm* and *Wildfire* of how he saw *Enterprise*'s great Captain struck down that they will give us no trouble. In fact, I would lay money on the creature's having recorded it to show them. —Doctor, I heard something break, I didn't mean to hit him that hard—"

The Doctor was running a small whirring scanner up and down the Captain's left arm. "Greenstick fracture of the ulna, Commander; that's this forearm-bone here. Nothing serious. Jim, are you slipping in your workouts? Since when do you cross-block backward like that?"

"You could do it better?" said the Captain, looking humorous through his pain.

"Well, I—"

"Never mind. Commander, that *was* the youngster you were going to send back?"

"Yes. I had no idea he was going to be here, though, else I would have warned him out. . . ."

"Murphy's Law," the Captain said. "At least we managed to cover for him. Nice work, everyone. —Bones, how long is it going to take to regenerate this thing?"

"About an hour. Less if you don't squirm when it itches."

"Captain," Ael said, "who was Murphy, and what was his Law?"

"One I should have learned the last time," said the Captain. "Never eat at a place called 'Mom's'; never play cards with a man called 'Doc'; and don't start fights with Romulan Commanders."

That was when the punch came that the Captain did *not* telegraph; and it slammed Ael back against the nearest wall so hard that the effect was the same as being hit twice, once in front and once from behind. She rebounded from the wall, tried to stand, staggered. Things spun.

"But if you *do* start one," the Captain said with an absolutely feral grin, "always finish it."

The room would not stop rotating; and Ael's mind was in such a whirl of rage, relief and merriment that she scarcely knew what to do. "Captain, your hand," she said, holding hers out and considering—just briefly —showing him that trick of N'alae's that he had so admired. But there would be no honor in doing it to an injured man. . . . He took her hand, and then grinned.

"Yours sweat too, huh?" he said.

"Captain," she said, "what a pity you're not Rihannsu. . . ."

"I bet you say that to all your prisoners. Let's get back up to the Bridge."

174 · DIANE DUANE

Twelve

Jim sat in his center seat and wondered at the strange-
ness of the world.

Here he was, deep into Romulan space, surrounded
by Romulan ships; not even under way, his engines
only producing enough power to run ship's systems and
keep themselves alive. Another eighteen hours would
see the *Enterprise* towed into a Romulan starbase. Yet
he sat in his chair, and turning to one side, he could see
Scotty leaning back in his station's chair, grumpily
eyeing the nonexistent power conversion levels in the
not-really-blown-up port nacelle, while delivering a
rapid-fire lecture on the difficulties of the restart procedure to the slim dark Romulan man looking over his
shoulder. Hvaid, that one was. Turning the other way,
there were Mr. Spock and Lieutenant Kerasus and
young Aidoann, Ael's third-in-command, deep in conversation about Old High Vulcan linguistic roots and

their manifestations in modern Vulcan and Romulan. And Uhura would be—

She wasn't, though. Jim's train of thought was temporarily derailed. "Mr. Spock, where's Lieutenant Uhura?"

"She went down to Recreation, Captain," Spock said. "I did not catch the entire conversation, but there was some communications problem to which she felt Mr. Freeman from Life Sciences had the answer."

"Fine. Where's the Commander?"

"I believe she is also down in Recreation, Captain. Lieutenant Uhura requested the Commander's presence there shortly after she left."

Jim got up, stretched—and stopped the gesture abruptly; his neck muscles still ached from the backhand the Commander had given him. "All right, Mr. Spock, mind the store till I get back."

"Acknowledged," Spock said. He moved down to the center seat, and Kerasus and Aidoann moved with him, the analysis of Vulcan phonemes missing hardly a beat.

"Sickbay," Jim said to the lift, and off it went. He leaned against the wall, rubbing his neck.

There was something bothering him about this whole business. Not a feeling that Ael or her people might betray him—not that *specifically*. But the whole matter of where the *Enterprise* was, of both capture and escape being out of his hands . . . Out of his control. That was it.

The old problem, Jim thought, with some chagrin. He remembered all too vividly that little incident back on Triacus with Gorgan the *soi-disant* "Friendly Angel," in which that fear, his worst one, had been inflamed to paralyzing proportions. *This isn't nearly that bad,* he told himself severely. *And I did choose to do this. It was my decision.* But all the same, it had been Ael who came to him with the idea all ready-made; and even when he had been ready to refuse her, damned if circumstances didn't force him to accept her plan.

Circumstances. Very convenient circumstances, too . . .

Oh, stop that! That's paranoia!

Still, it was difficult not to be paranoid about this woman. A Romulan, to begin with . . . Well, that by itself wasn't reason to mistrust her. But she had admitted to Jim that she had rigged most of the circumstances that had brought the *Enterprise* here—even to the point of paying a considerable amount in bribes to have the information about "something going on in Romulan space" smuggled out to Starfleet Command, planted where they would hear it. She had angled specifically and with great precision for *Enterprise* to be sent here—and she had managed it. And now his Bridge was full of her officers, and his Rec deck was full of her crew . . . and his neck ached.

She had him right where she wanted him . . . wherever that was. It was the not knowing that made him crazy.

Loss of control . . .

The lift slid to a stop. Jim stalked out of its open doors and down the hall toward Sickbay, brooding. It might have been slightly easier to handle if the woman were at least likeable . . . if she weren't so relentlessly manipulative, as sharp and cold as the sword she had been admiring in Spock's quarters. If only she didn't constantly seem to be maneuvering events with the same cool virtuosity that Spock exhibited while maneuvering pieces in the chesscubic. Though not *quite* the same. Spock's terrible expertise was always tempered, at least with Jim, by that elusive, almost mischievous compassion.

Then again, he couldn't set aside that wicked, merry, understanding flash of Ael's eyes at him, just after he had punched her out. . . .

He breathed out in disgust, gave the problem up as something he couldn't do anything about but would be pleased to see ended, and swung into Sickbay. And there it all was again, for here was Ael's chief surgeon, t'Whatever-her-name-was, those Romulan words were pretty to hear but impossible to remember—with Lia Burke beside her, showing the Romulan woman how to use an anabolic protoplaser in regenerative mode. They were working on the Romulan's own arm, apparently removing and regenerating the tissue of an old scar a little bit at a time, so that the Romulan surgeon could get a feel for the instrument's settings. "No, watch that, you'll involve the fascia and get the cells all confused," Lia was saying, her dark curly head bent down close together with the Romulan's bronze-dark, straight-haired one. "Try it a little shallower. One millimeter is deep enough where the skin is this thin. —Good afternoon, Captain; how's the neck?"

"I have a pain in it," Jim said, thinking more of the figurative truth than of the literal one. "Where's Dr. McCoy?"

"In his office, sir. Paperwork, I think. Can I be of assistance?"

"Possibly. Would you excuse yourself, Lieutenant?" Jim walked on through Sickbay to Bones's office in the back; Lia came after him.

"Bones?"

McCoy looked up from a desk cluttered with cassettes and computer pads. "Come on in, Jim. What can I do for you?"

"Close the door after you, Lieutenant. Would you mind," Jim said to the nurse, "telling me what was going on out there? My orders were that our 'guests' were not to be given any nonessential information. We are still going to have to answer to Fleet after we get out of this mess—always providing we *do*."

Bones opened his mouth to say something, but Lia beat him to it. "Captain, with all due respects, complete healing of the wounded, no matter how old the wound is, hardly strikes me as 'nonessential.' And in this area at least, my oaths to Starfleet—and other authorities—are intact."

"'Other authorities'?"

"'I shall teach my Art without fee or stipulation to other disciples also bound to it by oath, should they desire to learn it,'" Lia said, that dry, merry voice of hers going soft and sober for the moment.

"'. . . and this I swear by Apollo the Physician, and Aesculapius, and Health and Allheal His daughters, and by all the other Gods and Goddesses, and the One above Them Whose Name we do not know. . . .'" Bones said, just as quietly. "The Romulan version turns out to be a lot shorter—but the intent's the same. Some things transcend even the discipline of the service, Jim."

Jim's neck throbbed worse, and he opened his mouth —then closed it again. *Gently. Gently. Loss of control . . .* "Sorry, Lieutenant," he said. "You're quite right. Bones, my apologies."

McCoy raised both eyebrows. "For what? Nothin's normal around here just now—no reason for *us* to be. Lia, get the Captain ten mils of Aerosal, all right?"

"Better make it twenty," Jim said.

Lia looked from McCoy to Kirk and back again—

then, significantly, up at the ceiling. She nodded. "Fifteen it is," she said, and went out.

McCoy looked after her with rueful amusement. "They don't make nurses like that anymore," he said.

Jim sat down and laughed at him. "Just as well, huh Bones?"

"Well," McCoy said, "I *was* about to say fifteen. I think that woman's been taking lessons from Spock—though I don't want to know in what. Don't get comfortable, Jim; I was just going down to Recreation."

"Isn't everybody?" Jim said. "Can't keep the crew away from the Romulans. . . ."

"I didn't think you would want to. We're going to be working pretty closely with those people over the next twenty-four hours or so, on some pretty crucial business. The more comfortable the crew gets with them, the better."

"Theoretically, at least . . ."

"Misgivings?" The small transporter pad on McCoy's desk sang and sparkled briefly, and a spray hypo and an ampule of amber liquid appeared on it. McCoy picked it up, checked the label on the ampule three times, almost ceremonially, slipped it into the hypo and came around the desk to Jim. "Stop twitching."

"The arm still itches."

The hypo hissed, and McCoy tossed it onto the desk. "If I were anything but an old country doctor, I would suspect your itch of being elsewhere."

The throbbing in Jim's neck went away. "I'm nervous," he said.

"See, the truth *will* out after all. Guess what? So am I."

"And who do you tell about it?"

"Christine. Or maybe Lia. Then they tell Spock, see, and Spock tells the ceiling. A carefully arranged chain of confidences. The nurses talk only to Vulcans, and the Vulcans talk only to God. . . ."

Jim snorted. It was a lot harder to be paranoid when he wasn't in pain. "That explains where he gets his chess strategies, anyway. . . . Bones, there's a question I wanted to ask you. Where'd you learn to play like that?"

"Watching Spock, mostly. And watching you."

"With a talent like that, you should be in tournament play."

McCoy started to laugh quietly as the two of them left his office, heading down the hall to the lift for Recreation. "Jim, you haven't looked at my record since I was assigned, have you? . . . My F.I.D.E. rating is in the 700's somewhere."

Jim stared at McCoy as they got into the lift. 'The F.I.D.E.' was the Federation Intergalactique des Échecs; its members got their ratings only through Federation-sanctioned tournament play, and the 700's, while hardly a master's level, were a respectable neighborhood. "No kidding. Why don't you play more often?"

"I'm a voyeur. —Oh, stop that. A *chess* voyeur. I use it mostly as a diagnostic tool."

"Come again?"

"Jim, chess isn't just good for the brain. It's a wonderful way to get a feeling for someone's attitude toward life and games and other people. Their response to stress, their ability to plan, what they do when plans are foiled. Their attack on life—sneaky, bold, straight-forward, subtle, careless, what have you. Humor or the lack of it, compassion, enthusiasm, the 'poker face,' all the different things that go toward 'psyching' an opponent out . . . A string of five or six chess games can make a marvelous précis of a personality and the ways it reacts in its different moods.''

"An intelligence test?"

The lift stopped and they got out. "Lord, no," McCoy said. "On this ship intelligence is a foregone conclusion . . . and in any case, it's hardly everything. It's hardly even *anything,* from some psychiatrists' point of view. You want to get a feeling for where someone's personal style lies, their 'flair.' Spock, for example. Why do you think he gets so many requests for standard 3D tournament play when we're close to home space? It's not because he's brilliant. There are enough brilliant chess masters floating around the Federation to carpet a small planet with. But Spock's games have elegance. My guess would be that it comes partly of his expertise in the sciences—the delight in the perfect solution, the most logical and economical one. But if you look at his games, you also see elegance— exquisitely laid traps that close with such precision, it looks like he micrometered them. There's a great love of the precision itself: not just of its logic and economy, but of its beauty. Though Spock'd sooner die than admit it. Our cool, 'unemotional' Vulcan, Captain, is a closet aesthete. But you knew that.''

"I did? Of course I did.''

"I should make you figure this out yourself," Bones said. "Still, none of this is anything you haven't already noticed from long observation of him in other areas. That aestheticism is a virtue; it shows up in his other work too. But it's also a hint at where one of his weak spots might be. He will scorn blunter or more brutal moves or setups that might produce a faster win. Why do you think he has that sword on his wall? But this is where you get lucky sometimes, because you tend to go straight for the throat. Spock gets busy doing move-sculpture—and enjoying himself; he loves watching people's minds work too, yours especially—and he gets lost in the fun. And then you come in with an ax and hack his artwork to pieces with good old human-brand unsubtle craziness. Note, of course, that he keeps coming back. The win is obviously not the purpose of the game for him."

"Obviously. Bones, is this something I can take a correspondence course in?"

McCoy grinned. "Psychology by mail, huh? You might have trouble. Not that many med schools teach diagnostic chess, and they wouldn't be able to help you with 4D anyway. In fact, Lia is one of the few people I know who's managed to find a course in even 3D diagnostic. She routinely plays at least a game or two with her patients whenever she can. She's not much of a tactician, but she says she doesn't mind losing . . . she's more interested in finding out about other people."

Bones chuckled as they stepped into Recreation together. "You should have seen her playing with Jerry Freeman the other week . . . poor Lia found out a little more about him than she wanted to. Jerry wasn't paying attention to the game at the beginning, and Lia put him in a bad position pretty quickly. So he bided his time and fought a holding action until she got up to answer a page, and while she was gone, he quietly programmed the cubic for 'catastrophic dump.' When she got back, she tried to move a piece, and the cubic blew up. Pieces flying everywhere . . . I wish you could have seen her face."

Jim wished he could have too. "And what did she deduce from that?"

"If she's smart, the same thing I did after I played with him a couple of times; that Mr. Freeman is quite bright, and knows it, and occasionally gets incautious. What is *not* occasional about him, though, is his extreme dislike of looking dumb in front of people— and he will sometimes resort to very unorthodox solutions to save his game."

"You call that a save?"

"It was for him. The next game he played with Lia—"

"There was a next game? I would have killed him."

"They used to call them 'the gentler sex,' didn't they once? Let's wait and see if Freeman can still walk after his yearly injections next week. Anyway, next game, he wiped the Rec deck up with her. Then he fetched her a drink and was the picture of gallantry. He's a very good winner."

Jim chuckled. "Bones, do me a favor, will you?"

"What?"

"Play 4D with Ael."

At that Bones looked somber, and pulled Jim a bit off to one side, well away from the freestyle demonstration of Romulan hand-to-hand combat that seemed to have resumed over in the far left corner of the room. McCoy eased himself down into one of a pair of chairs in a conversation niche, and said, "I already did, a few hours ago."

Jim had a sudden sinking feeling that that line of Ael's about learning the game in "a few minutes" had not been mere casual braggadocio. *Damn* the woman! "And?"

"She blew me to plasma."

"She beat *you!*"

"Don't look so shocked. Don't go all sorry for me,

either! I learned lots more from the loss than I would have from the win. But it wasn't a pretty picture."

"What did she do?"

"Oh, no, Jim. I leave that as an exercise for the student. You'll find a recording of the game in my office running files under the password 'Trojan Horse.' She knew I was recording it, by the way."

"And?"

"She didn't care. She knew what I was up to and just didn't care. Chew on *that* one, Jim."

"Later. There's Uhura and your demolitions expert; I was looking for them."

"Not for Ael, of course."

"Of course. Come on, Bones."

"One thing, Jim, before we go over there."

"What?"

"Get some sleep this afternoon. You're looking a bit raw . . . and besides, a brain full of lactic acid by-products and short on REM sleep makes for poor command performance."

"Noted. . . ."

They walked together over to the massive control console for the holography stage. Very little seemed to have changed since several days ago. There was Uhura, working at the controls on top of the console; and there was the lower half of Lieutenant Freeman, sitting cross-legged between the pedestal-legs of the console. The upper half of him was inside the works of the console; as Jim and McCoy came up, one arm came out from inside, felt around for one of the tools littered about, grabbed a circuit spanner, and went back inside again. The only addition to the scene was Ael, looking over Uhura's shoulder with an interested expression.

"Got it, Nyota," said the muffled voice from inside. "Try it now."

"Right." Uhura looked up at Jim, grinned happily, and said, "Say something, Captain."

"Certainly. Aren't you supposed to be on the Bridge?"

"HEUOIPK EEIRWOINVSY SHTENIX GFAK HU MMHNINA AWAH!" the console said, or at least that was what it sounded like.

"What the devil was that?" said McCoy. "Sounds like you've got a problem there, Lieutenant. A malfunction that shouts."

"No, Doctor. It's taken us the last half hour to get it to do that." Uhura beamed at Jim. "Captain, I'm on my break at the moment. But this is the answer to that little poser you handed me the other day. And also the antidote, incidentally, to the trouble we had with signal leakage while Ael's people were running communications."

"I'm all ears," Jim said. "One moment, though. Mr. Freeman, are you just shy, or did Lieutenant Burke finally lose her temper and do a hemicorporectomy on you?"

The half-a-person whooped with that very distinctive laugh of his—an even funnier sound than usual, smothered as it was inside the console—and carefully came out from under, brushing himself off as he stood. Regardless of his age (in the mid-thirties), his six-foot height, and his silver-shot hair (now somewhat disarranged from being inside the console), Jerry Freeman always struck Jim as one of the youngest of his crew. The man was eternally excited about something—for example, right now, those old sterries—but though the subject of the enthusiasm might change without notice, his total commitment to the subject of the moment never did. "What are you two up to?" Jim said.

"Words of one syllable, please," said McCoy.

"Oh, come on, Bones. You have to learn some big words sooner or later. E-lec-tron. Can you say that? *Sure* you can. . . ."

Freeman took a moment to smooth his hair back in place. "We're confusing the intercom system, Doctor," he said. "Among other things. But what the Captain needed was a more effective jamming system for subspace communications than Fleet has bothered to design for wide-area use. Mostly they've tried to handle the 'beam-tapping' problem in deepspace communications by avoiding it . . . defeating it at sending and receiving ends with 'unbreakable' codes, hypercoherent wavicle packets, all that silliness. But what technology can produce, technology can sooner or later decode or unravel."

Uhura was leaning on one elbow beside Ael with a humorous look on her face, watching her protégé lecture. "You can't solve a problem that way," she said. "Fleet has been ignoring the medium through which the messages travel, considering deepspace too big and unmanageable to handle. And it's true that 'broadcast' jamming of the sort done in a planet's ionosphere is impossible out here; while the relatively small-scale jamming already available to us is useless for our present purposes. So what Jerry and I have been doing is finding a way to make space itself more amenable to being jammed . . . a method that's an outgrowth of the way Jerry's been making digital documents more amenable to being rechanneled."

"Mr. Scott helped," Jerry said. "We used material from the parts bank to build a very small warpfield generator of the kind used in warp-capable shuttlecraft. We attached that to one of the little message buoys that the ship jettisons in jeopardy situations. Then we adjusted the warpfield generator so that it would twist space just slightly over a large cubic area, causing the contours of surrounding subspace to favor randomly directed tachyon flow along certain 'tunnels' at a certain packet frequency—"

"Good-bye," McCoy said. "I'm off to do something simple. A hemicorporectomy, possibly."

"It makes subspace much easier to jam," Mr. Freeman said, sounding rather desperate. "That's all."

"Why didn't you say that?" McCoy muttered.

"I did."

"It also takes a lot of power," Jim said thoughtfully. "Even a hefty warpfield generator would only have a limited life expectancy."

"Yes, sir. Four hours is our predicted upper limit. But for those four hours, nobody trying to use subspace communication is going to hear anything but what sounds like a lot of 'black noise'—stellar wind and so forth. And whatever they try to send will be perverted into the same noise."

"Range?"

"Presently about a thousand cubic light-years, Captain. If you want more, you can have it, but the life of the generator becomes inversely shorter in proportion to the extension of the jamming buoy's range."

Jim nodded—he had rather expected that. "All right. How many of them can you put together for me in the next four hours?"

Uhura and Freeman looked at each other. "We'll need more people—"

"Get Scotty and the Engineering staff on it."

"We don't dare overdrain the parts bank, sir," Freeman said. "Will three more be enough?"

"They'll have to be. Ael, how about it? How fast are your people likely to understand this if they come up against it?"

The Commander looked dubious. "Hard to tell, Captain. They are not all idiots like LLunih, or as complacent as t'Kaenmie and tr'Arriufvi, who're pacing us in *Helm* and *Wildfire*. I would delay as long as possible before deploying such a device; that would give any interested observer less time to become suspicious and start deducing what was going on."

Yes, Jim thought, *you would say that, wouldn't you? No matter what you were up to.* But he put the thought aside for the moment. "Agreed," he said. "At our present rate we should be hitting the 'breakaway' point, where we drop our pursuit, in about five hours, correct?"

"That's so, Captain."

"Fine. We'll drop one of those buoys there as we begin the engagement, to keep your three friends from yelling for help. One we'll drop in the area of Levaeri when we reach it. To the third one I want the fourth warp generator attached so that it has starflight capability as well as the subspace alteration function. We'll send it off past Levaeri, along the likeliest vector of approach for an unexpected ship. Think about that, Commander, and let me know."

Ael blinked at Jim. "But if the ship is unexpected—" Then she smiled. "Ah, Hilaefve's Paradox, eh Captain? Very well. I will think about it for you."

"Good. Uhura, Mr. Freeman, take what people you need and get on it. One thing before you go: *why* have you taught the holography console to shout gibberish?"

Uhura chuckled. "Captain, it takes months of practice and skill to handle a ship's communications board so that there's no signal leakage through the shields. The problem is, after working with a board for awhile, a comm officer does that without thinking of it—and I didn't think to warn poor Aidoann. Not that she would have known what to do about it—I haven't had time to teach her all the board's little tricks. So Jerry took the same random number generator he used in the jamming buoy's tachyon-switching protocols and adapted it to the multi-use programmable logic solid that every intercom in the ship has inside it. The solids will now encode and decode voices and data at their sending and receiving ends; signal along the circuitry, which is where the leakage comes from, will now only manifest as that gibberish you heard—so that even while Ael's people are handling our intercoms, we can say anything we have to without worrying about being overheard, or needing people to run around with notes. . . ."

"Nice work," Jim said, and both Uhura and Freeman looked exceptionally pleased. "Now I need another four hours of it. Uhura, have Lieutenant Mahasë cover for you on the Bridge till you're done. Both of you scoot!"

They did. Jim watched them go, and Ael moved around to join him and McCoy. "If we're to be in battle in four hours," she said, "I'd best go see to *Bloodwing* and make sure my people are ready."

"Sounds good to me, Commander. Bones, I'm about ready for my nap. Have me paged at point six, unless something requires my attention sooner."

"Right."

Ael went off in one direction, and the Doctor in another. Jim just stood there for a moment, watching them both out of sight—then headed down to his cabin, via Engineering, thinking very hard about chess.

He was still thinking about it two hours later, after his nap turned into a tossing-and-turning session, and even one of McCoy's mild soothers left him completely awake. On Jim's desk screen, the ship's computer had obligingly translated the chesscubic's holographic display of McCoy's game with Ael into a 2D graphic, and displayed it for him. It made a fascinating study—the first moves sure on McCoy's part, tentative on Ael's; then roles reversing—McCoy moving with more of an outward show of caution, apparently seeing what Ael would do if offered the run of the cubic. There was a point at which the computer recorded a long interval between moves; she had hesitated. Jim could almost see those cool eyes of hers across the cubic, suddenly lifted to assess not only the tactical situation but the man who sat across from her—who was, at the moment, himself a tactic. And then came a series of moves that were, to put it mildly, insulting. She became "polite" to McCoy. She moved out into the cubic, but genteelly, almost as if not wanting to beat him, almost as if they were playing on the same side. McCoy put up with it for about ten minutes, then timed about half his pieces out, preparing to dump them on her like a ton of neutronium in six very visible moves. He could seem insulting too, when it suited his purposes.

And she derailed Bones as totally as Bones had derailed Spock. Three of her pieces timed out, not even critical ones. Three moves later, McCoy's pieces all came back—into cubes that were suddenly no longer vacant. Annihilation, all over the board. McCoy had one stronghold left for his king and both of his queens.

Ael sacrificed both her queens to his—and checkmated his king with three pawns and a knight fork.

Her first game.

She didn't even care, Jim. Chew on that.

He did. It tasted awful.

—and the red alert sirens started whooping, and there was no time to waste worrying anymore. *Trust her,* he told himself bitterly as he leapt up from the chair, pulling the velour on over the undertunic. *Or don't. But make up your mind.*

He ran out, seething. The corridors were alive with his people, and with Romulans, too, scrambling for posts. He dashed into the lift at the end of officers' country and found tall pretty Aidoann already in there, breathing hard. "Where's the Commander?" he said, as the doors closed on them.

"Beamed back over to *Bloodwing,* Captain," Aidoann said. She looked at him with those big brown eyes of hers, and Jim had a sudden thought that she looked rather like Uhura, the same slant to the eyes. . . . "Sir—" she said.

It was the first time any of them had called him anything but "Captain." *Something cultural?* he wondered. But whatever, suddenly she wasn't a Romulan anymore; she was a young crewperson, looking nervous before a major engagement. "Antecenturion?"

"Do you have things you believe in?"

Impossible not to answer such directness. "Yes," Jim said.

"I hope They're with us now," Aidoann said. "Those three will blow us all to Areinnye if they can."

"Aidoann," he said, grateful that he could pronounce that word at least, "your Commander and I have other plans."

She grinned at Jim, a quick flash through the otherwise Romulan intensity. The Bridge doors opened for them.

I just hope they're the same ones, Jim thought, and swung down toward the center seat.

Spock got out of it with his usual quick grace and hurried back to his station. "Captain, we are running slightly ahead of schedule," he said over his shoulder as he went. "Registering a group of large masses at most extreme sensor range. Their location and arrangement agree closely with *Bloodwing*'s estimates for ephemerae of Levaeri V and its primary. The station is not yet detectable. On the revised schedule, we are now five minutes from scheduled 'breakaway.'"

"Good. Mr. Mahasë"—Jim turned to the gray-haired, gray-skinned Eseriat who was holding down Uhura's post, with Aidoann standing by if she should be needed. "Get me Engineering."

"Aye, sir."

"Engineering, Scott here . . ."

"We're running fast, Scotty—in range a bit early. How are Uhura and Freeman doing?"

"They're just helping my people put the finishing touches on the last buoy," Scotty said.

"Fine. Load one of them up; we're about to lay an egg."

"Already in photon torpedo tube one, Captain."

"All right. Hold on to it, Scotty; I'll let you know when. Thirty seconds tops. Out. Aidoann, please call *Bloodwing* and give them the prearranged signal."

"Yes, sir," she said. And then, after a moment, *"Bloodwing,* this is *Enterprise;* t'Khnialmnae."

"Tr'Rllaillieu," said Subcommander Tafv's voice, cool and calm as usual.

"Subcommander, we have an emergency," Aidoann said, not having to fake a small tremor in her voice. "A small party of Federation personnel have broken out of group detention—"

Mahasë killed the frequency between the two ships. Jim hit the intercom button on his chair. "Okay, Scotty, *now!*"

The ship held steady as always, but there was a small muffled noise, much quieter than the usual dull thump of a photon torpedo on the way out. "Buoy away, Captain," Chekov said, "heading one eighty mark minus twenty."

"Activate it."

Chekov hit a control on his board. "Operational, Captain. Subspace communications are jammed."

"Allcall," Jim said to Mahasë; and when he spoke again his voice rang through the ship. "Battle stations, battle stations! Secure for warp maneuvering!" He made a kill-it gesture at the Eseriat. "Screens up, gentlemen, deflectors on full. Mr. Sulu, kick the engines up to warp three. Break out of *Bloodwing*'s tractors and maneuver at your discretion. Closest Romulan vessel—"

"Rea's Helm, sir."

"Lock on phasers. Fire at will. Mr. Chekov, photon torpedoes—"

"Tubes three through six charged and ready—"

"Mr. Sulu, why aren't we moving!"

"Bloodwing has increased power to her tractors, sir—"

Why that—! She was supposed to— "Break them," Jim said tightly.

"Engine overheat, Captain—"

"Risk it. Break free!"

Sulu's hands swept over his board. "No good, sir—"

"Increase warp."

"Sir, no result, *Bloodwing*'s too close—"

"Rea's Helm has put its shields up, Captain," Spock said, staring down his viewer. "Hailing us."

"Ignore. Mr. Chekov, fire on *Bloodwing.*"

Aidoann's head jerked up; her face was ashen. "Shielded, Captain—" Chekov said.

"I note that. Scan for weakest point and fire phasers

right there. Look for areas of screen overlap, those spots are sometimes poorly protected—"

"Shields going up on *Wildfire* and *Javelin*, Captain," Spock said. The ship shuddered as something hit the screens. "Fire, Captain," Spock added. "From *Bloodwing*. Phaser fire, clean hit on number six screen, screen efficiency decreased to sixty percent—"

Damn! Damn! DAMN! "Return fire at will, Mr. Chekov. Mr. Sulu, if you don't break those tractors in about a second, I'm going to tell Lieutenant Renner who stole her clothes from poolside last month!"

Next to Chekov, who was firing the phasers in blast after blast, Sulu went pale. Jim didn't see what he did, but the ship lurched mightily, and suddenly space on the screen in front of them was clear again. "Damage?" he said.

"Minimal," Spock said. "A very quick burst at warp eight, most precisely angled. Well done, Mr. Sulu."

Yes," Jim said, sweating and grim, but grinning nonetheless.

"Four clean hits on *Bloodwing*, Captain. Her forward screen is down to thirty percent efficiency, and her port screen has failed altogether. Further fire—"

"Forget her," Jim said. "Sulu, Chekov, *get me those three ships*!"

"Positions on screen," Spock said. There they were in schematic: *Bloodwing* lying a little to one side, coming after *Enterprise* but losing speed; *Rea's Helm* closing in from port and above, *Wildfire* coming in faster yet from the starboard, *Javelin* arching around toward the rear. "Mr. Chekov, watch out for him—"

"Firing rear tubes, standard spread," Chekov said, eyes flicking back and forth from his board to the screen. "Recharging."

"Clean misses," Spock said. "*Javelin* is in evasive

maneuvers. Dropping back—now closing again—
Rea's Helm is in close approach—"

"Fire!" Jim cried at exactly the moment Chekov
did so. White fire lanced away from the *Enterprise*,
hitting the Romulan ship exactly in a screen overlap
zone over a nacelle. There was one of those seemingly
month-long pauses, and then *Rea's Helm* blew up,
blazing, matter and antimatter making a small sun of
her. Sulu brought *Enterprise* curving about and threw
her right into the expanding cloud of debris, letting the
deflectors take it.

"Steady on, Mr. Sulu," Jim said, leaning forward
in the center seat. "We're leaving a trail—"

"Yes, sir, I know," Sulu said. "Warp six—" He
was working on his console again, while behind them
sensors showed *Wildfire* screaming in from the starboard, *Javelin* trailing somewhat, and *Bloodwing* at
the rear of the pack, building speed but still far behind.

"*Wildfire* is closing," Spock said calmly. "Firing to
her port—" Spock paused a moment, looking down
his scanner. "Explosion, Captain. She has destroyed
jamming buoy. *Wildfire*'s range now five hundred
thousand kilometers—four hundred thousand—"

Sulu's eyebrows went up as his hands flickered over
the console. Jim watched him with uneasy delight. He
was doing something Jim had seen done in starships in
warp, but always at slower speeds: deforming the
warpfield itself, broadening and flattening it forward,
tightening it to the rear. And the ship was responding
in the only way she could—slowly, gracefully nosing
downward as she flashed through the *Helm*'s remains,
then nosing down faster, harder, pitching forward until
she was literally flying "vertically," nacelles and the
broad side of the disk forward.

It was not a position a ship could fly in for more than

a few seconds, in warp. Yet if this worked . . . "Mr. Sulu—" Jim said.

"I know, Captain," Sulu said, and kept *Enterprise* rolling forward—a slow somersault through otherspace at seven hundred twenty times the speed of light, while behind her, seeing nothing but the unchanged shape of her defensive screens, *Wildfire* came charging in—right into the teeth of her forward phasers. If Sulu could get her around in time! She was flying "diagonal" now, easing out of it, flattening out—flying upside down and backward, and right into their faces, now, here came *Wildfire*, firing phasers— "Hits on number one shield, number three shield," Spock said, beginning to sound a touch grim now, "number one buckling, Captain; reinforcing—"

"No! Belay that!" Jim could feel Spock glancing at him, ignored it for the moment. "Another hit on number three," Spock said, "down to twenty percent—"

"Ready, Mr. Chekov?"

"Ready, Captain—"

Wildfire swelled on the screen, coming right down their throats, and now that the Romulan ship could see what was happening, it was too late— *"Now!"*

Mr. Chekov pounced on his board. *Enterprise*'s deadly forward phasers lashed out where *Wildfire* had expected only the lesser rear ones, or photon torpedoes. And suddenly, *Wildfire* was gone in a bloom of light—

—*Javelin*, following behind, vanished.

"Cloaking device," Spock said.

"Defeat it, Mr. Spock—"

"The cloaking countermeasure is not functional, Captain, it's a function of subspace communication."

Oh no! Jim stared at the empty screen, in which there was nothing but *Bloodwing* now, soaring in toward them faster than she had been. *He'll go off in some other direction—*

He stared at *Bloodwing,* and it hit him. "Mr. Chekov, fire! Everything we've got, right at her!"

"Captain!" That was Aidoann, a child's cry for a betrayed mother.

Chekov fired, photon torpedoes and phasers both at once. "Sulu, hard about!" And at the same moment *Bloodwing's* phasers lashed out at the *Enterprise—*

—and their combined armament hit what lay directly between them, what Jim had somehow known would be using *Bloodwing* as cover, only from in front. "Spock, the shields!" he cried, but Spock had already reinforced them. Nothing else saved *Enterprise* from the point-blank explosion of another starship right in front of her. She screamed through the wreckage and the swiftly dying fire, while *Bloodwing,* plunging toward them at warp five, angled up and over them, deforming her own warpfield in a crazed, congratulatory victory roll.

"They do that too. . . ." Jim said, slumping back in his seat.

"Local traffic, Captain," Spock said sharply, looking down his scanner. "A small ship, bearing— Too late. It's cloaked."

"Our friend the 'crawling slime,'" Jim said. "LLunih."

"I would say so. Evidently he suspected *Bloodwing* of complicity with us—and sacrificed his ship to test the theory."

"A wonderful person," Jim said. "Hail *Bloodwing.*"

The screen lit up. There was that cramped little

control room, and in it, Ael, sweating rivers and looking haggard. *"Captain,"* she said, *"is your ship all right?"*

"We're fine. Ael, you know more about 'the better part of valor' than anyone I've ever met."

"Probably. Why do you think I went to dinner with LLunih the other night? I wanted to see what he had hidden in his engineering room—and I got him to show me. It was an Imperial courier: that little creature in which he just saved his skin. Some day I shall have it for a pot-scouring rag."

"His courier ship?"

"That too. What could I do, until you deployed your jammer and I knew it was working, save increase my efforts to hold on to you as if your escape was genuinely a surprise? He will report to the Senate in doubt now—knowing that you apparently willingly fired on me to kill—and thus keep us both clear of the suspicion of complicity. They will argue—and the ship that might have gotten here from Romulus in four hours will perhaps not come for ten, or twenty."

"I have a question for you."

"Ask."

"What the devil took you so long to figure out that the damn buoy was working?!"

"Captain, our sensors are not as good as yours, especially in the high ranges, you know that. . . . I could know nothing until my subspace communication with one of the other ships failed."

Jim sighed and said a bad word in his head, for that was true. "All right, Commander. We'd better get started for Levaeri V. . . ."

"I agree. I'll be over in Hsaaja *in a few moments."*

Jim looked at her, not liking what he was thinking. "What do you need *Hsaaja* for?"

"I don't need it," Ael said, *"but you will. One of your warpdrive generators is destroyed. Your second one will be needed to power its companion along the 'least expected' course out of the Levaeri system. Another will be dropped in the system itself. The last one we'll install in Hsaaja and send on Llunih's trail—thereby slowing down his report to the High Command a bit more. Even minutes may be precious later."*

Jim nodded. "Ael," he said regretfully, "that's a sweet little ship. . . ."

"If I'm dead," she said drily, *"I won't be able to fly him anyway."*

And suddenly the light dawned, and Jim sat straight up in his chair and said, "Ael—that was *five* warpdrive generators—"

"So it was," she said. *"Wasn't that how many you ordered made?"* She smiled at him wickedly, and closed the channel down.

Damn the woman!!

Thirteen

"Captain, would you kindly hand me that little silver spanner there?—no, the other one."

"Commander," said the Captain, "is it going to be 'Captain' all the way back *from* Levaeri, too?"

Ael looked up from the hatch in the floor of *Hsaaja*'s cockpit, pushed a strand of sweaty hair out of the eye into which it had fallen, and said, "Oh. You think we are going to *make* it back, then?"

"Commander—"

"You may call me 'Ael.' The Doctor does. Even Mr. Spock does." She bowed her head again, reaching down into the guts of the autopilot and starting the last of the connections to the jamming apparatus.

"Well . . . I wasn't quite sure I'd been given permission. You 'gave' us your name. But it's not the same. And permission to the Doctor, and Spock, is not necessarily permission to me."

That was perceptive of him, an insight she wouldn't

have expected him to reach. "You're quite right," she said. "I was withholding it."

He started to ask why, then stopped. That, too, was something she wouldn't have expected; restraint. Just as well; she wasn't certain of the reasons herself. "As for you," she said slowly, touching a connection open, reading the charge on it, and closing it again, "I can't quite pronounce the name after 'Captain.' And it's unwise to mishandle names."

"You said that before. . . ." He looked thoughtful. "Can you say 'Jim'?"

She gasped and started to laugh, so hard that she almost dropped the spanner. And when she was sure she still had it, and looked up again, the Captain looked so bewildered that it just made her laugh harder. "Oh, Elements," she finally managed to say, sitting back against the seat cushion of the pilot's chair, "is that truly your self-name?"

"James, actually. 'Jim' is a contraction. . . ."

"Oh, oh my." Ael started laughing again, still harder, so that all she could do was sag back against the seat and wave the spanner weakly at him. *Reaction*, she thought clinically, in some remote part of her. *Wouldn't t'Hrienteh look askance at this? or even the Doctor. . . .* And indeed the poor Captain was looking rather askance himself. "No, no," Ael finally managed to gasp, when he showed signs of getting up and leaving. "Oh, Captain. 'Jim.' Jim, I will call you that gladly, but I beg you . . ."

He made a questioning look at her.

"Don't ask me what it means! . . ."

"Well, all right. Ael, then."

"Jim," Ael said, and studied to keep her face straight. "Well enough. Let me finish this, we don't have all day." She busied herself with the spanner again, sealing the last connections. "The other name, the long form: what does it mean?"

"Nothing embarrassing, thank heaven." He cocked an eyebrow at her, and Ael wondered fleetingly whether he had stolen the expression from Spock, or Spock from him? "I looked it up once—it means 'supplanter,' or something like that."

"The translator didn't render that word."

"Someone who takes other people's rights or positions away from them."

That made *her* put an eyebrow up. "You had best be careful with a name like that," Ael said. "It could lead you into trouble. . . . But then what other position than this one could you possibly want?"

He shook his head. There was no other, and he knew it as well as she did. "And what mighty 'enterprise' was this ship named after?" she said.

"Not one particular one. Just the spirit of enterprise in general. And there were many other ships with the same name, an old tradition. . . ."

He trailed off when he saw that she was staring at him again. "Oh, no wonder," she said softly, more to herself than to him. "All of ch'Ríhan has wondered why this ship has been through so much trouble, so much glory. . . ."

"Do enlighten me."

It was sarcasm, but gentle; he genuinely didn't seem to know what she was talking about. "Ca— Jim, it's dangerous to name anything, a person, a vessel, after an entire unmitigated virtue. The whole power of it gets into the named one, makes it go places, do things too great for man. . . . Glory follows; but sorrow too. . . ."

"That's usually the way with people, no matter what the ship's named." Still, he looked thoughtful.

"Tell me your thought."

"Funny, actually . . . There were other ships called *Intrepid*, you know. A lot of them got in trouble all the time. One of the most famous of them, the one in mothballs in New York Harbor—"

"This translator is having problems. You have little round flying insects on Earth that are eating a ship named *Intrepid*? And *you* ask *me* about the danger of names?"

"The ship," Jim said with careful dignity, giving Ael a dirty look that needed no translation, "is in honorable retirement. Preserved as a museum for many, many years. But she had a reputation among her crew for being a bad-luck ship. Gallant—but unlucky. They called her the 'Evil I.' Probably that won't translate; 'i' is both the name of the letter *Intrepid*'s name starts with, and a sound-alike for the Anglish word for this." He pointed at his eye.

"Evil eye, yes; I see the pun. We have a sign you make against it."

"Yes. This old ship kept getting torpedoed, running aground—it was a wet-navy ship. All kinds of annoying things like that. Well, then comes our *Intrepid,* the first starship by that name, and it serves hardly more than a few years before being attacked and destroyed by a spacegoing creature, a kind of giant amoeba. And then the new *Intrepid* is built, and this happens to it. . . ." He waved vaguely in the general direction of Levaeri.

Ael nodded. "You see the problem. Name a ship for the spirit of fearlessness, and it forgets to fear. A bad trait. Worse when the ship is full of Vulcans . . ." She checked the last connection, pulled the autopilot's door down over the opening again, and sealed it. Her glance up at Jim showed her a face that looked rather skeptical.

"Not your belief, I see," she said, standing up carefully, both to keep from banging her head on the canopy and because of the ache in her back. "No matter. Let's send this poor creature on his way." She flicked switches on the consoles, looking with sorrowful longing at the familiar arrays, the screen that made her eyes hurt, the place where she had dropped the wrench once and scratched the flawless, shiny black front panel. It was a shame to send this ship out into the cold nowhere, to run alone, finally to run out of fuel and drift alone forever. But there was nothing else for it; the *Enterprise*'s shuttlecraft, which Jim had offered, didn't have *Hsaaja*'s range or speed. And both would be needed.

"You always were good at throwing things away when you had to," Jim said from behind her. "I remember once—it was the Battle of alpha Trianguli, wasn't it?—you emptied out two whole Rihannsu cruisers and left them drifting there crewless in space— doubled up their crews with those of two other ships and ran away, while poor Captain Rihaul went crazy over two empty ships rigged on automatic and firing at her. You didn't even have to hurry to get away. . . ."

There was rueful admiration in the tone, and something more; compassion, consolation. It sounded as if he understood what she felt.

Bizarre idea. "Yes," she said, "I remember that. Come on, Jim, he's on the timer. Let's get out of here."

They did, and on a screen in a briefing room near the hangar deck watched the sleek black ship rise up on its thrusters and glide out into the starry night. The hangar deck's doors closed, then, and Ael, standing there watching them, felt cold enough to shudder. It might have been a piece of her going away.

It is. Why must I love things so? They pass away, one and all. . . .

She straightened up. "We have another meeting, don't we, Jim?"

"Preattack briefing," he said. "The chief of Security, the department heads, some other people. We'll keep it short . . . everybody needs rest, and we've only got about six more hours before we hit Levaeri sensor range."

She nodded, and they left the little briefing room together, heading for the lift. "This business of names . . ." Jim said.

"It's not names specifically. Just words. Even in your world, people have died for words. Sometimes they've died *of* them. One learns to be careful what one says in such a world. And like anything so powerful, like any weapon, words cut both ways. They redeem and betray —sometimes both at once. The attribute we name as a virtue may also turn out to be our bane. So we watch what we call things—in case we should turn out to be right."

Jim looked thoughtful at that too, but this time Ael left the thought behind the look alone. "We treasure names," she said. "They're the most powerful words, and our favorites. After all, what makes you respond more immediately than your name being called? . . . As long as a Rihannsu has someone to speak his name, or even if it's written, or remembered, that person is real. Afterward . . . nothing. The shadows, some say. The place where the Elements are unmixed, more *real* than here, say others." She shrugged. "But either way, names are life. . . ."

Jim appeared to be considering that for a moment as the lift doors closed in front of them. "You never did tell me what a 'bloodwing' is," he said at last.

Ael laughed softly. "The name is hardly as noble as *Enterprise*'s, I'm afraid . . . but then it's not as peril-ous, either. It's a flying creature we have on ch'Ríhan, and my House's sigil-beast. A big, slow, ugly scaven-ger, so big that it can't fly without a long takeoff run, and you can keep one captive just by putting a small fence around it. But once it's in the air, nothing can match it for speed or power of flight."

The lift opened, and they walked out together toward Main Briefing. Coming down the hall toward them, there were Spock and McCoy. "Gentlemen," Jim said to them as they all headed into the briefing room, "you're early."

"Spock and I wanted to take our time going over the roster for the strike force," McCoy said. He sat down at the table, Spock beside him, and began sorting through a pile of cassettes he had been carrying. Ael sat down opposite, so as to see their faces better; Jim sat beside her. *For the same reason?* she wondered briefly.

"This is the best of the group," McCoy was saying as he dropped a cassette into one of the table's readout slots. "Low stress factors, good with weapons or with hand-to-hand. A lot of security people there—"

"Bones," Jim said, "let's not be too picky. What we need here is numbers."

"Numbers will not help us," Spock said, "unless they are the right ones. There is going to be very little margin for error in this operation, Captain; but we are nevertheless taking care not to understaff you. Go on, Doctor."

"Here's the recommended list, then. Abernathy, Ahrens, Athendë, Austin, Bischoff, Brand, Brassard, Burke, Canfield, Carver, Claremont. . . ."

It went on for quite some time, a long list of unfamiliar names, and Ael leaned one elbow on the table and rested her head on her hand, bored. Not bored, exactly. What she had just done was beginning to catch up with her, as she had known it would . . . but this was no time for reaction. Nevertheless, it claimed her. *How many more lives have I spilled to prevent those phantom billion deaths?* she thought unhappily. *How many Rihannsu went back to the Elements today, cursing my name, and Bloodwing's? Sooner or later this will be paid for. Sooner, I fear. . . .*

A horrible thought intruded itself on her slowly, and refused to go away. *Suppose something has gone wrong with the researches at Levaeri—and instead of the Intrepid's disappearance being a sign of their readiness, it was instead a signal of a failure—something the Levaeri people did to cover their tracks in some manner, buy themselves time, hide the fact that there's something wrong? Suppose the mind-techniques never actually come to fruition . . . then what am I? A murderer, a traitor, many times over—and for nothing, not even in a good cause—not that the ends ever extenuate the means, at least as far as the Elements are concerned. What one does is what one does, and one answers for it. . . .*

"—Khalifa, Korren, Krejci, Langsam, Lee, Litt, London; Maass, Donald; Maass, Diane—"

"I didn't hear 'Kirk' in there," Jim said rather sharply, bringing Ael back to the moment.

Spock and McCoy looked at each other, all innocence. Ael saw that there was more teasing going on. "Mr. Spock, how did we miss that?"

Spock looked mildly surprised. "Habit, no doubt. The Captain never goes anywhere. . . ."

". . . but just this once . . ."

". . . considering that the armed escort will be ample. . . ."

"Gentlemen!"

"Gotcha, Jim," McCoy said.

Jim's smile took awhile about appearing, but finally managed it. "All right," he said. "I consider myself warned. But if you two are going to play 'mother hen,' don't either of you be surprised if you find me holding your hand."

"Fine by me," McCoy said. "But watch it with Spock. People start the damndest rumors about this ship's crew, even without provocation. . . ."

"Doctor, how *does* one hold hands with a mother hen?" Spock asked innocently.

"Gentlemen!!"

Ael kept her laughter to herself. ". . . Malkson, Matlock—"

The door opened, and the Elements were apparently joking with them all, for in came Colin Matlock, the Security Chief, whom Ael remembered from the briefing on *Inaieu*. He was a tall, good-looking, dark-visaged young man, half frowning all the time, even when he smiled. At the moment he chiefly looked embarrassed. "Sorry, Captain, I'll come back later—"

"No, take a seat, Mr. Matlock. We were going over the strike group. Go on, Bones."

"Where was I?"

"Matlock," Jim said, and then paused, looking slightly surprised. He glanced at Ael.

She glanced back, keeping her face quite straight, and let him wonder. ". . . McCoy, Miñambrés, Morris, Mosley, Muller, Naraht—"

"Too young," Jim said.

"Jim, he's got to go out sometime," McCoy said. "And he's got an incredibly low anxiety level. As low as a Vulcan's, nearly."

"But not enough experience—"

Ael straightened. "Jim, is this that young Ensign Rock of yours?"

Jim stared at her, then laughed. "Yes."

"Of your courtesy, take him. I ask it."

"Reasons?"

"I have none that I can explain to you." *Knowing what you would probably think about the Elements, from how little you think about names.*

"Hunch, Commander?" Spock said.

"Yes," she said.

"Well, I had one too," McCoy said. "Jim, ride with us on this one."

Jim waved his hand. "All right. Go on."

"Norton, Oranjeboom, Paul . . ."

On and on it went. At last McCoy stopped, and he and Spock looked at Jim for his final reaction.

"That's almost all of Security," Jim said, "and easily half the crew. . . ."

"Captain," Spock said, "you were quite right about needing numbers."

He looked over at Ael. "And Levaeri has about a hundred and fifty staff, you said."

"Yes, Jim. But they have the advantage of the ground. They will know how to hold the place against us—how to set up ambushes, seal whole sections. The more people, and with the more expertise and fire-power, the better. Our chief advantage lies in this, that the station is far inside Rihannsu space and will not be long on armaments."

"How do they protect it, then, if the installation's such a high-security business?"

"High-intensity deflector screens," Mr. Matlock said. "The specs the Commander's given us indicate shields of much higher power than any mobile facility, such as a starship, can support. We'll have our work cut out for us getting those down."

"It will have to be subterfuge again, Captain," Ael said to him. "And there's worse to come; for as I told you, this is *Battlequeen*'s patrol area. There is no telling when Lyirru t'Illialhae might turn up—all Elements preserve us from the happenstance. I much fear that LLunih will try to find *Battlequeen* and bring her here. In any case, we must not linger in this neighborhood, or stop to sample the wine."

The door hissed open again. "The Rihannsu make wine?" someone said. It was Mr. Scott; and much to Ael's surprise, the scowl with which he traditionally favored her was only about half there.

"Yes," she said, slightly puzzled. "It's not quite as ruinous to the throat as our ale is . . . but it's considerably stronger."

"Stronger?"

"We have some on *Bloodwing*," Ael said, still puzzled, but the look of anticipation on the man's face was impossible to miss. "Perhaps I might make you a gift of some to atone for what I did to your port nacelle. A hektoliter or so? . . ."

Scott looked at Spock incredulously. "Why, that would be . . ."

"Twenty-six point four one eight gallons," Spock said, with the slightest trace of amusement showing. "Or six thousand one hundred and two point four cubic inches at—what is your wine's specific gravity, Commander?"

"Gentlemen . . ." Jim said wearily.

"We can handle this later, Mr. Scott," said Ael.

"Oh, aye!"

More people began coming in—Sulu, Chekov, then Harb Tanzer and Uhura, until finally all the department heads were present. "Captain," said Mr. Matlock, "one thing before we start . . ."

"Certainly."

"Commander," the dark young man said to Ael, "what color are the halls in that station going to be?"

"White, mostly, or bare-metal silver."

"Captain," Matlock said to Jim, with a faintly ironic expression, "I don't think it would be wise for us to attempt a board-and-storm operation dressed in bright blue and black, or gold and black, or green and black—or especially orange and black. Everyone in the party would stand out like zebras in the snow; and as for my people, they might as well have targets painted on them."

"Noted, Mr. Matlock. Order light gray battle fatigues for everybody."

"Already done, sir," said Matlock, just a little sheepishly. "Quartermaster's working on it now."

"Colin," Jim said, "I have great hopes for you. Just be careful."

"What are these fatigues, Captain?" said Ael.

"Light-colored coveralls and overboots."

"Would you give orders that they also be provided for all of my people who will be going along?"

Spock looked up from some report-pad he had been studying. "Captain, that is an excellent idea. It could very well confuse the station's complement of Rihannsu into thinking that our allies are not Rihannsu at all, but Vulcans attached to Starfleet . . . perhaps even *Intrepid* crew, escaped from confinement, or previously concealed."

"They won't think that for long, Spock," McCoy said. "Remember, Rihannsu and Vulcan culture have been diverging for thousands of years . . . and most of the subconscious cues buried in their respective kinesics, their 'body languages,' will also now be very different. A Rihannsu would know you weren't one, if he looked long enough, not from any physical divergence—but just from a wrong 'feel.'"

"But none of them will be getting 'long looks,' Doctor, not if this works correctly," said Spock. "They will look, be briefly confused, be surprised—thinking that they are seeing Rihannsu. They will hesitate, possibly hold their fire briefly, in many cases. That will give our people an extra second to act. We cannot afford to be so proud that we throw away the advantage of surprise. Captain, I would recommend that every one of our different striking parties have at least one or two of Ael's people with it."

"That's an excellent idea. So ordered. Ladies and gentlebeings, let's get this started, shall we? Commander, please begin."

She hunted among the switches before her on the table, made her connection to the ship's computer and brought up a three-dimensional graphic above the holography pad in the center of the table. There it hung before them all in spidery lines of light, the Levaeri V station: a big rectangular prism, about twice as long as it was wide, like a brick hanging in space. "This is the research facility," she said. "You can see that it is large and complex—about two miles long and a mile wide. Not all of it is in use at this time, to the best of my knowledge—the structure you see here is a standard Rihannsu design, purposely built larger than it needs to be, to make later additions simpler. There are potentially eighteen levels, each one much divided by corridors, as you can see. At present I believe only the 'outer' six levels to be staffed; much of the inner is empty, or occupied by computer core and therefore airless."

"Commander," Scotty said, "how'd you come by this information?"

"I was there about two years ago, your time," she said. "A VIP inspection tour, before the mind-technique research was moved there. The rest of the data comes from both the Praetorate and my family's spies in High Command. This project, for all its 'secrecy,' has been as leak-ridden as any other."

Scotty nodded.

"Most of the laboratory space where I believe the actual work is being done is on the inmost level, near the computer core and the computer control rooms. This project has been most prodigal of computer hardware, since most of the actual gene-splitting and other microsurgery used to correct the 'drifted' linkages of the DNA is performed by the computers. They are in fact all that makes it possible—for each cell of genetic and neural material must be individually corrected, and thousands of years' worth of human labor would be needed to make even a gram of the stuff. The computers are the heart of the business. Put them out of operation, and part of the danger is done."

She folded her hands, staring at the schematic as it rotated. "But only part. The surgical computers are innocent enough by themselves; but the computer banks containing the actual locations of the linkages that are corrected, and the nature of the corrections, must also be destroyed. I have reason to believe that this data is extant only here, reproduced nowhere else in the Empire—partly due to the wonderful paranoia of the Praetorate, which is terrified that some other party they don't approve of might get hold of it. Destroy this information, all this data, and then you have truly destroyed the menace. It would take them years to reproduce their results—if that's even possible, for there are literally thousands of linkages in each molecule of Vulcan DNA that are corrected in the operation. No one could remember them all."

"Pity we can't just blow the place up," Mr. Chekov said.

"I agree," Jim said. "Unfortunately, I don't think the crew of *Intrepid* would appreciate it. . . . Ael, where do you think they will be?"

"My guess would be here," she said, reaching into the hologram to indicate a large area off to one side of the labs. "It is convenient to the laboratories, large enough to hold several hundred people without too much trouble—and sealed off on three sides by structural bulkheads too strong for even the massed strength of Vulcans to damage." She looked somber. "If they are able to manage anything at this point. I would hypothesize that their captors, not wanting to take chances with such a dangerous resource, have them constantly drugged, or mind-controlled, or both."

"The mind control is likeliest," Spock said, looking grim. "It would do less harm, chemically speaking, to the brain and neural tissue that the researchers are after. Which raises another problem, Commander. Do you have any idea where the already corrected tissue would be kept?"

"None."

"Why, Spock?" Jim said.

"Because it, too, is alive," Spock said, "and we must find it. It would be not only immoral but illogical to rescue the crew of the *Intrepid* and leave other living Vulcan material behind."

Ael watched Jim open his mouth, then close it. "Spock," he said, "I want you to know I'm no happier about the killing that has happened—and may soon happen—than you are. But this is just . . . I don't know . . . just meat. . . ."

"It's alive, Jim," McCoy said, very quietly. "He's right. If there's any chance, we can't leave the stock-piled material there. Not only for ethical reasons; for tactical ones as well. Any remaining material can be used to work backward and recreate the research. If we can't take it with us, it must at least be destroyed. But it must be found."

Jim looked at McCoy and Spock, then nodded. "All right," he said. "That makes things even more compli-cated, but what're a few more complications among friends? Mr. Matlock, let's talk about the actual plan of attack."

"Yes, sir." Matlock stood up with a small control-pad in one hand and began setting markers, small dots of light, into the hologram. "We will be dividing our attack force into four parts, and hitting the base in four different areas. Here, in what the Commander has identified as staff and crew quarters, to secure those station personnel who aren't on duty: here, in two different places near the labs, flanking the area where the most resistance is likely to occur immediately on our arrival; and here, where the Commander suspects the Intrepid's crew to be held prisoner."

Matlock eyed the station schematic with what looked to Ael like genuine relish. "The four groups, once the station's screens have been reduced, will beam down simultaneously and each secure its assigned area, while also sealing off the unoccupied parts of the station to prevent our being attacked from several different 'rears.' Additionally, each of these two groups"—he pointed at the attack forces near the labs—"will secure the transporters to prevent any of the station people from utilizing in-station beaming. Just in case, once we leave, the *Enterprise* will have her screens up to prevent any counterattack from the station should our hold on the transporters be broken at any time."

"That is well thought of," Ael said. "Captain, gentlefolk, a Rihannsu is at her most dangerous when her territory is threatened . . . we are rather atavistic that way. Even scientists will be able to fight with terrible ferocity; and remember that at the moment this is still partly a military facility. Not starship personnel—but soldiers nonetheless, people with a deadly hatred of the Federation. And a worse hatred of you, if they find out who you are: my sister-daughter had many friends." She looked across at Spock. "Do not hesitate to kill. They will not hesitate to kill *you* after that first second's confusion."

Spock lowered his eyes, said nothing. "The ship will be scanning constantly," Mr. Matlock said, "monitoring the situation on the station and advising the attack parties via scrambled communications of developments. Once the indicated areas are secure, the computer attack group—Mr. Spock and the people he'll name for you shortly—will assemble, locate the computers, and begin that part of the operation. Sir?"

Spock looked up. "Along with the Commander, Lieutenant Kerasus, Mr. Athendë, and several others from the Commander's staff and from Security, we will tap into the computers and either remove or destroy all pertinent information concerning the mind-technique researches. In the case that complete removal of the information proves to be impossible, I have with the Commander's assistance developed a 'virus' program that will infect the computers the next time they are brought into operational mode, dumping and wiping their total memories. Once the 'infection' is successfully accomplished, we will attempt to activate the computers and obtain the location of the already manufactured genetic material. In the case that either of these objectives proves unattainable, we will destroy the computer installation and rejoin the main attack group."

"Which, as soon as the transporters are secured, will be locating and freeing the Vulcans," Mr. Matlock said. "Our sensors are sufficiently accurate at close range to tell the difference between Vulcan and Rihannsu life-readings—unlike the Rihannsu instruments. Once the Vulcans are freed, we will call the ship and begin beaming them back aboard the *Enterprise* via cargo transporters."

"Gonna be crowded up there," McCoy said softly. "What about *Intrepid?*"

Ael shook her head at him. "That's an unknown, Doctor. My guess would be that they will have her inside the screens, held by tractors; and it's likely they will have shut her engines down. Mr. Scott, how long does a restart cycle take?"

"That depends on how long the engines have been cold," Scott said. "Postulatin' worst case, and the *Intrepid*'s refitted engines, fifteen minutes."

"The best estimated in-and-out time for this operation is forty minutes, Mr. Scott," Matlock said.

"Well, let's hope we can get at her early, then, if her engines are down. A cold matter-antimatter mix can't be hurried."

"And if for some reason we have to get out of there before she's restarted," Jim said sadly, "we can't leave her there to be taken apart and analyzed. We'll have to blow her up."

There was silence all around the table at that, except for Scott. "Ach, the poor lass," he said.

"That's all, Captain," Mr. Matlock said. "After we beam back with the *Intrepid* crew and the genetic material, there'll be nothing to stop us from heading out of Rihannsu space with *Bloodwing* at warp eight."

McCoy was going through his cassettes again. "That's all, he says."

"Very well," Jim said. "Any questions?"

"Only one," Ael said quietly.

"Commander?"

"Why did you let me talk you into this? . . ."

Jim gave her a cockeyed look. There were chuckles around the table, but Ael noticed that he did not join in them, and neither did Spock or McCoy. "We'll go into that after we've successfully completed the operation, Commander," he said. "As for the rest of you—brief your departments: get your timings from Mr. Matlock: and get into your battle whites. We assemble in Recreation in two hours. Dismissed."

Out they went, obedient and quick and looking eager. Ael turned to glance at Jim, who said, "Cold feet, Ael?"

She stared at him. "My boots are fine."

"I mean, are you—" He stopped. "What a stupid question. I beg your pardon. Come with me and I'll take you down to the Quartermaster's department to be fitted and armed—"

"I have my own weaponry, Captain," she said, "and I'll do best with it, I think. But as for your uniform—I shall be proud to wear it."

"Why, thank you."

". . . Just this once."

"We wouldn't want to keep you in it a moment longer than necessary," Jim said, getting up with an utterly indecipherable expression.

Ael followed him out of the room, shaking her head

in unaccustomed perplexity. She had said something wrong again. Or was it as it seemed, that this man kept his pride on the outside, waiting for someone to tear it? Why did he do that? There was no understanding him. . . .

Curses on the man!

Two hours later she stood on the Bridge of the *Enterprise* again, feeling even stranger about it than she had; for there was Levaeri V ahead of them—within sensor range, though they had not yet hailed her. "I'll wait a bit," she said to the man who stood with his two hundred gathered crewpeople, down in the Recreation Room. "It would not be like me to hurry in this situation, Captain. I would let them have a long, long look and be amazed."

"Anything so long as we catch them by surprise," Jim said.

"Yes. Aidoann reports that control is now completely transferred to the Auxiliary Bridge, and your other people left aboard ship are under 'guard' with various of my folk from *Bloodwing,* so that we will pass an inspection if necessary."

"Is Scotty all right down there?"

"He reports all systems operational, and the next two subspace jamming buoys dropped. Meanwhile, there are no *Enterprise* people up here at all now, and I tell you it looks strange."

"I bet," said the cheerful voice. *"Is Subcommander Tafv with you?"*

"Here, Captain," Tafv said, from the communications console.

"Take care of my ship, Subcommander," the voice said.

"Sir, I shall. Commander, Levaeri is hailing us. We

are nearing the shield boundary—and sensors are showing a starship tethered inside the shields. No ID running—but the sensor readings match its shape to that of *Intrepid*."

"Well," Jim said, "it's showtime." He sounded annoyed, and pleased, and terrified, all at once. "Commander, will you join us?"

"As soon as the screens are down. Don't wait for me, Jim. Get your people down to the cargo transporters. I have your coordinates, and my whites are in the lift."

"*Ael—good luck.*"

"And the Elements with us," she said, "for we'll need Them. Out."

She turned to Tafv, seeing on his face the same mixed excitement and dread she felt. "Open a frequency for the station, son. They've looked long enough."

"Madam," he said, demonstrating that same lovely and unnecessary courtesy he had shown her on coming back aboard *Bloodwing*. Ael sat straight in the center seat, finding her control, stripping the fear out of her heart.

"*Levaeri station to* Bloodwing," said a female voice.

"This is Commander-General Ael t'Rllaillieu," said Ael, very calm, very proud, "presently aboard the captured vessel USS *Enterprise*. To whom am I speaking?"

"*Centurion Ndeian tr'Jeiai, Commander.*"

O, by my Element, no—not Ndeian— "Ndeian," she said, merry-voiced, "what in the Names of Fire and Air are you doing all the way out here? I thought you were on ch'Havran by now, raising fvai!"

"Reenlistment," Ndeian said. "*They're desperate, Ael; they offered to make me rich. The funny thing is that I believed them—*"

"You always were credulous." Ael's heart cried out inside her. "Ndeian, are you commanding?"

"No, Gwiu t'Laheiin is; but we've heard of your coming, we have orders—"

—her stomach twisted itself into a knot in a single second—

"—to give you anything you ask for if you stop. Forgive me, Ael, but I don't think they want you to stay. Our orders were to 'expedite your arrival and departure.'"

"We won't be here long, Ndeian. I need some provisions for *Bloodwing,* and some of my people are in need of better medical help than we have here on the ship; we had a difficult time getting hold of this bright prize. You don't seem to be doing too badly in that department yourself, though."

"No," Ndeian said, *"Battlequeen brought that one in. Ael, just settle into standard orbit and we'll drop screens for you and your technical people and the doctor."*

"Assuming standard orbit, Ndeian. See you in a bit. T'Rllaillieu out."

She waved at Tafv, heartsick. He closed down the channel, then looked at his instruments and said, "Screens are down, Commander. We're in orbit under them."

"Well done." She got up, hurried out of the Bridge, looking around at the place—bizarrely open, bright, lovely for an instrument of destruction. Ndeian's destruction, and a thousand others'— "Keep her well, Tafv," she said; and it was all she could manage. The lift doors opened for her. She picked up her white coverall, that lay neatly folded on the floor, and began struggling into it—sparing a hand from the business to hit the communicator button on the lift wall. "Recreation!"

"We heard," the Captain's voice came back. *"We're on our way. Out."*

The lift stopped, opened its doors. Ael ran down the hall, into one of the cargo transporter rooms, pulled out her phaser and leapt up onto the platform, with a great group of her own people and Jim's. The young man behind the transporter console set the delay, headed for the platform himself, and they all dissolved in shimmer together.

It must have been something different about the Federation transporters, something unsettling in their engineering—or maybe just Ael's own suppressed fear, crying out in her mind—that made her think she heard, as she dematerialized, the sound of phaserwhine outside the Transporter Room, and a scream. . . .

Fourteen

Montgomery Scott paced the Auxiliary Bridge like a caged creature. "This will be the last batch going," he said to the universe in general, and to Uhura and Chekov and Sulu, who were in there with him, along with Khiy and Nniol and Haehwe. "And I don't like it, indeed I don't."

Sulu and Chekov exchanged glances, which Scotty noticed and filed away; they didn't like it either. "It's a fool's errand, that's what it is," Scotty said, looking over Chekov's shoulder at a trim control and reaching down to uselessly check its calibration.

"You should have said something in the briefing, Mr. Scott," Uhura said softly from her station.

"Aye," Scotty said, letting out a long breath, "but what good would it ha' done, lass? You know how the Captain is when his mind's made up. After that, it's the Universe that'd best bend, for it won't be himsel' that's doing it."

He paced around the little room one more time. That was the problem with it, he decided. It was little; too much power crammed into too small a space for the people who had to handle it. Like *Bloodwing*'s poor little scrap of a bridge, if you could even dignify it with the name. A black hole, it was. And this was too. Squeezed in between the armory and the downstairs food processors, a ridiculous spot— "Are they ready?" Scotty said.

"They report ready," Uhura said. "—There they go."

"Good luck to them," Sulu said, staring down at the uncomfortable view on the little screen. Levaeri V station hung there right beneath them, an ugly great sheet of metal stuck all over with pipes and stanchions and antennae and whatnot else. It offended Scotty's sense of design, and confirmed a lot of his private thoughts about Romulan engineering. "Prefab space stations," he muttered. "Where's the sense in that? Probably fall apart if you looked at it."

"They do," said Khiy quietly from the Engineering station. "They're shabby, sir."

"Aye lad, I daresay." Scotty gave one last disgusted look at the thing, then turned to Uhura. "Are they transported safe?"

"Yes, sir, they report arrival—"

"Well enough. I just wish I were down there with the Captain—"

Someone shrieked. Someone did it again, and again, and Scotty recovered from the involuntary attempted leap of his heart from his chest at the sound of his ship screaming. It was the intruder alert siren, a sound like no other. "Screens," he cried at Sulu, "screens, man!" —and leapt for the board himself. Sulu had already hit the control, and the banshee wailing of the ship cut sharply off; but Uhura had turned to the rest of them with a look of terrible alarm on her face, one hand to the transdator in her ear, the other flicking switch after switch on her station's panel. "Mr. Scott, intruders on decks four, eight, nine, twelve—"

"Where from!"

"Already transported, Mr. Scott. Not traceable—"

"*Bloodwing,*" Scotty said bitterly, and swung on Khiy.

"No!" Khiy cried. "Mr. Scott, the Commander would never—"

"Not the Commander, lad," Scotty said, feeling himself turning red. "But I'll bet I know who. Why didna the Captain see it? Khiy, seal us off from the rest of the deck—bring down all the bulkheads south of thirty. Never mind—" and he headed over to the Engineering station and did it himself; poor Khiy was out of his depth, no shame to him. "Lieutenant Uhura, find on what's goin' on out there."

"Confused, Mr. Scott. Fighting on six and eight. Other parts of the ship calling in and asking what the problem is—"

"Tell them. No, wait. Chekov, help Khiy. I want every door in this ship locked. Cut power reversibly if you have to, we'll worry about the details later."

Chekov jumped out of his seat and hurried over to Khiy. "No good, Mr. Scott. Several Jeffries tubes have been disabled, some major system junctions are out—"

"Bloody. Excuse me, Uhura. Pavel, disable the transporters, the whole lot o' them. The Captain will be usin' the Levaeri transporters to come back anyway, and I'll not have that divil Tafv usin' mine for intraship beaming. If he wants the *Enterprise,* he can fight for every inch. Also—" Scotty took a deep breath. "Override the emergency protocols and seal off the Engineering hull. Those creatures'll not get at my engines."

Chekov worked bent over at the board, pointing out controls to Khiy, explaining things under his breath. Several moments later there was another horrific screaming through the ship as she announced her own traumatic amputation—the sealing off of the lower, cylindrical Engineering hull and nacelles from the upper disc. The two were able to function separately, though it had been done so infrequently and in such disastrous situations that Scotty hated to think of the results. Nevertheless, all it would take now would be an explosive-bolt sequence, and the two parts would separate, leaving the lower hull and nacelles, with the warp engines, free of Romulans and still able to escape with the Captain and his party and the rescued Vulcans. If they managed to escape . . .

Till then it was his business to hold that avenue of escape open for them; and Scotty vowed that should the landing party come to grief, Levaeri V would go up in one of the biggest bangs since *the* big one. He still had the self-destruct option, after all, and that option exercised in this particular spot would take the station and *Intrepid* and *Bloodwing* with it. The thought was not comforting, but he put it aside in case he should need it later. Meanwhile there was other business. "How're you doing, lad?" he said to Chekov.

"Executing, sir. The Engineering hull's secure."

"Forty people trapped down there, Mr. Scott," Uhura said. "They're all right, though. A mixed group, our people and the Commander's."

"Aye. . . ." That was the whole problem. These Romulans, that went around behind one another's backs so easily . . . no telling what they were thinking

— But Scotty caught himself. That was hardly fair— look at poor Khiy here, keeping the faith, and doing the best he could for them. "All right. What about the transporters?"

"Out now, Mr. Scott," Chekov said.

"Aye," Scotty said. "We may be trapped here, but so are they, with the shields up . . . and we can have good hope that some of them were transportin' when the shields reestablished. A few o' them'll have hit the shields and gone splash, at any rate. Uhura, call about and find out who's where. What's our strength without the landing party?"

"Two hundred eight, Mr. Scott."

"We could call the Captain—"

"And he would do what, lass? Our people and Ael's doubtless have their hands full enough just now, else we'd have heard more from them than just the news that they'd arrived in the station. No, we've got to handle this ourselves . . . no use in botherin' him. Two hundred and eight . . ." Scotty made a disgusted noise. "And scattered all over the ship. . . . No matter. Call around, Uhura." He paced around the room again, scowling. "Now if I were that black-hearted traitor of a Tafv . . . where would I be heading?"

"Here, sir."

"Aye, Mr. Sulu. And here we sit all alone on this deck, and sealed away from help. He'll have to fight his way here, burn his way through bulkheads and through our people—but he'll do it, and not count the cost."

"But, Mr. Scott, what about intruder control?"

"Ah, Khiy, lad, you didn't look at that board too closely, did you? He's a clever creature, that Tafv: he took it out with those Jeffries tubes, may he roast somewhere warm. Woe's the day we ever let him near the computers. . . ."

Scotty paced. "So . . . He may have taken out the most vital systems he could learn quickly. But we still know the ship better than he does. And possibly . . ." he stopped in mid-stride. "Mr. Sulu," he said, "call up a schematic of the crawlways between here and the main Bridge. While he's at it, Uhura—get into the library computer and transfer it to voiceprint operation. I don't want it working for anyone but *Enterprise* personnel. And if you can rig a program so that individual terminals'll blow their boards if a nonauthorized person uses them, so much the better. . . ."

"You don't ask much, do you, Mr. Scott?" Uhura said drily. But she bent over her board and got busy.

"Mr. Scott," Chekov said, "what about the Romulans on the main Bridge, our friends?"

"Aye, what about them?" He turned to look over his shoulder. "Uhura?"

"Aidoann and Khiy and Nniol all filed voiceprints with me," Uhura said, not looking up, but smiling slightly.

"And Tafv?"

Uhura looked up in mild surprise. "Scotty, I never got one from him. He was always off on *Bloodwing.* . . ."

"Aye, indeed," Scotty said, sounding bitter. "I hate to say it, but it looks as if some of Ael's crew haven't as much of that mneh-whatever as she thought. 'Twill break the lass's heart."

"*Mnhei'sahe,*" Khiy said unhappily. "Mr. Scott . . . some of our crewmembers are newer than others. There are some who were talking about . . . about the opportunity . . ."

". . . of taking *Enterprise* for real, aye lad?" Scotty's eyes grew hard.

"Even the thought was disgraceful. Some of us told

some of the others so. They stopped talking about it . . . but it seems they didn't stop thinking. And when the Commander chose the people who would be working on the *Enterprise*—"

"How *did* she choose them?"

"Only volunteers were considered. Some of those she left behind—not many. But it was odd that none of the ones who had talked about taking *Enterprise* actually came here. . . ."

"Our friend Tafv, it seems, has his own ideas about what to do with this situation," Scotty said. "Well, we'll spoil a few of his guesses if we can. Mr. Sulu, Mr. Chekov, let the board be for now. You two are going for a walk."

"Sir," Sulu said, slowly getting that particular feral grin of his on his face, "the armory *is* next door. . . ."

"Aye, we're thinking in the same direction, Mr. Sulu. But this isn't going to be easy."

"What do you have in mind, sir?" Chekov said.

"Well, if Tafv and his people are going to be making their way *here,* it's to gain full control of the ship, aye?" They nodded at him. "Well, then, lads, can't you just see his face when he gets here and finds this room either sealed or destroyed—and control transferred back up to the main Bridge where it belongs?"

Chekov started to smile too. "It's a very long way to the Bridge, sir," he said.

"Aye, lad. So you two had best slip next door to the armory and pick up anything you think you might need for the trip. Take plenty; should you feel the urge to leave a few boobytraps in the corridors for the unwary to trip over, I think I'd be inclined to condone the extravagance. And bring all the rest of it in here too. No use letting Tafv have it, and Uhura and Khiy and I may need it for one thing or another."

"Mr. Scott," Uhura said softly as Sulu and Chekov hurried out, "Sickbay wants to talk to you. Dr. Chapel."

"Aye, put her on."

"Scotty, what the hell is happening!"

"Treachery and mayhem, Christine," Scotty said merrily. "Not much else. Some of Ael's people have turned coats on her, it seems, and they're thinking it would be nice to have the *Enterprise* for their own uses."

"Oh my God."

"So if I were you I'd lock the Sickbay doors and not open them to anyone you don't know. Area bulkheads have been sealed, but there were Romulans beamin' down all over the ship for a while there, and there's no tellin' which of them are 'theirs' and which of them are 'ours,' or even where 'ours' are—"

"Scotty, don't be silly," Chapel said sharply, and the reply was so unlike her usual tone that it brought Scotty up short. *"Of course we can tell them apart."*

"Well, for pity's sake how?"

"Scotty," Chapel said with rather exaggerated patience, *"you were standing right there the other day, watching me stick intradermal translators into people, and complaining about the terrible annoyance it was, having to manufacture so many cesium-rubidium crystals for them in bulk—"*

"Selective tricorder scan," Scotty said softly. "Any Romulan with an armful of cesium-rubidium is one of ours—"

"—and you can do what you like with the others," Christine said. *"Scotty, what I want to know is, are there any casualties? If there are, M'Benga and I have to get out there and do something. We can't just sit here and play doctor."*

"Check with Uhura," he said, for Sulu and Chekov were just coming into the room with their first load of munitions from the armory, and Scotty's eye had just fallen on a sonic grenade; the sight had triggered a wonderful memory of how to rig one with a time delay and— "Uhura, handle it. Chekov, lad, let me show you something. . . ."

The two of them labored busily together for some minutes, while Sulu and Khiy went next door again and again, emptying the contents of the armory into the Auxiliary Bridge. When they finished, the walls were stacked three feet deep in phasers, phaser rifles, and disruptors, and the floor was piled with six different kinds of grenades, several semiportable fixed-mount phaser guns, and various other implements of destruction.

"All right," Scotty said finally, looking Chekov and Sulu up and down. They were hung like Christmas trees with explosive ornaments; Chekov carried an armful of phaser rifles as if they were a load of firewood. "Take the safest way you can find to the Bridge. It'll have to be crawlways most of the way, with the bulkheads down—but you've got the advantage of the ground. Pick up as much help as you can along the way . . . there have to be a lot of our people holding out in little pockets all over the ship."

Uhura looked up from her station with an unhappy expression. "Six decks up," she said. "That's a long way—"

"Sir—"

They all turned. Khiy was standing there looking extremely upset. "Mr. Scott, let me go with them!" he said. "I'm not much good to you here. But I know how to fight—and it's my honor that's been debased too. We swore, the whole crew swore, to be as brothers to

231

you . . . for a while. Now Subcommander Tafv has shamed us all, betrayed us . . . and if we don't get control of the ship back, he'll surely leave our Commander here to die—or kill her himself. I can't let that happen—none of us can!"

Scotty looked at the young man, thinking how very like Chekov he looked, even with the pointed ears. "Go ahead," he said. "Take some more of the guns, Khiy. Uhura and I will hold this position down till you three call us from the Bridge. Ael's people were there before everything broke loose; the locked bulkheads should have kept them safe in there, and kept Tafv's other people away. We don't dare warn them you're coming —chances are Tafv has tapped into Uhura's scrambled 'com. Just get into the Bridge and signal us when you're ready."

"Mr. Scott—" Chekov looked as unhappy as Khiy. "When Tafv and his people get here and there's no one but you and Uhura to hold this place—and you transfer control—the overrides will cut in and the bulkheads will go up again."

"We'll handle it, lad," Scotty said, though he had not the slightest idea of how. "Get on with you, you're wasting time."

"Yes, sir."

Sulu went to the door. It slid open, and he peered cautiously out; no one was in the hall—the deck was so far deserted. It was eerie in a ship normally as busy as the *Enterprise*. There came a shock, and a muffled sound, and all of them looked up in surprise and unease. Explosives, somewhere not too far away, were detonating inside the ship; and they heard the whine of phasers, very remote, but sounding venomous as a swarm of bees.

"Out with you," Scotty said. "Don't do anything stupid."

Sulu and Chekov and Khiy headed out.

"And if you do," Scotty said to their backs, more softly, "—sell yourselves dearly."

They paused—then were gone. The door closed again. "Come on, Nyota darlin'," Scotty said. "The youngsters will do what they can. Let's you and I go out there real quick and leave our unexpected guests some presents in the hall."

"Sounds good," Uhura said. She got up, picked up a string of sonic grenades, and started setting them for sequential detonation.

Another shudder, much closer, and another explosion, much louder, ran through the fabric of the ship.

"This deck," Scotty said.

They worked faster.

Fifteen

"Phasers on heavy stun," Jim whispered to the group behind him. "Stand by. . . ."

Silent, hardly breathing, his crewpeople waited. And waited, and waited. Jim pulled his head back from the corner he'd been peering around and held his breath. All four parties were beamed down, and it was still that golden period before one group or another started breaking into things, and setting off alarms. This party, of about fifty, was dedicated to securing one side of the computer areas. Right behind Jim stood Spock, and Ael, and Mr. Matlock; then more assorted crewfolk, Security people, and crewfolk of *Bloodwing*, with McCoy and Lia Burke and Naraht and some more Security types bringing up the rear. They were all utterly silent, as Jim had never heard such a large group be before. *Nerves,* he thought. And then, with grim humor: *They should be glad they don't have* mine.

Right behind him, Spock was scanning with a tricorder from which he had prudently removed the warble circuits. "The corridor ahead of us is nearly clear, Captain," he said softly. "Considerable computer activity ahead and for the next two levels down. We are adjacent to the core."

"And the control areas?"

"If I read this correctly, they are off the main corridor that runs at right angles to the one we're facing."

"What about the *Intrepid* crew?"

"Sir, I do not scan them . . . and the tricorder is not malfunctioning. Possibly they are in some shielded area; there are many sections of this base that incorporate forceshielding in their wall structure, purpose unknown, and tricorder scanning at a distance is therefore distorted and uncertain—"

"What the—" someone said in amazement from way behind them.

"Don't fire!" Jim would have hissed had there been time. There was none; seemingly all at once he heard the surprised voice, turned, saw a dark-clad Romulan figure staring at them from the T-intersection at the end of the hall in which Jim's party stood momentarily concealed. Then he realized, with some astonishment, that he needn't have worried. The last white shape at the rear of the group leaped away from the wall in a blur, and did something too sudden for Jim to clearly make out—except that when it was finished a blink later, the Romulan was lying on the floor with his head at an odd angle, and slender little Ensign Brand was staring down at him, looking rather shocked.

Jim nodded grim approval at Brand, and mouthed at her, "Stunned? Dead?"

She bent down beside the Romulan, then glanced up again, making a cutting motion across her throat, and a little "Sorry, Captain" shrug of her hands.

He jerked a thumb at the side corridor; Brand, and the Andorian Ensign Lihwa beside her, nodded and began to drag the man out of sight. Jim turned back to Spock. "We've got to get moving, Mr. Spock. If a group comes along and finds us here, we might not be so lucky."

"Affirmative. The corridor ahead is clear for the moment. Scan shows movement in the others, but it seems routine enough, and we couldn't wait for it all to die down anyway—"

"All right, let's go." Jim waved the hand holding his phaser at the column pressed up against the walls behind him, then headed out into the hall.

His people closed in around him from behind. Ael moved silently at his left, a tiny shape looking unusually pale in whites—or perhaps from some other cause. Spock paced to Jim's right, never taking his eyes off the tricorder. "We turn right at the next intersection," he said. "Then down to the next left, and ten meters along it to the main corridor—"

A horrible klaxon began howling through the hallways, echoing off the bare white walls. "That's torn it," Jim said out loud. There was no use for whispering anymore. "People, let's go. Close formation, watch the rear, stun first and ask questions later!"

And they were off and running. Unfortunately, at the sound of the alarms, so were the Romulans. Turning right at the next intersection, there came a crowd of Romulans in dark coverall-uniforms, ten or fifteen of them—by bad luck or fast scanning running right at Jim's party. Jim took his own advice, leaping aside to fire—then became suddenly aware of Ael pounding past him, with Spock pacing her. The Romulans at the head of the group looked at the two, saw 'Romulans,' hesitated—and from behind Jim ten or fifteen phasers screamed together. The Romulans went down in a heap.

"Armed," Jim said. It was upsetting; the Romulans' response time was too fast. "Destroy their weapons and follow," he said to Matlock, and led the rest of the party on at a run while Matlock's people attended to it and then came after. "Where now, Mr. Spock?"

"Past them, Captain, and the next left—"

They ran. And around that corner came more Romulans, not hesitating at all, firing Romulan-style blasters and disruptors. Reacting before he was sure what he was reacting to, Jim threw himself toward Spock—at the same time felt someone tackle *him* from behind and take him down, so that the three of them crashed to the floor together, out of the way of the massed beams that would have burnt them dead. The three of them rolled to the sides of the hall and came up firing, while behind them Mr. Matlock and his group fired from the hall or from cover, taking the Romulans out one by one. Jim got his feet under him, saw that Spock looked slightly shaken but otherwise all right, and then reached sideways to help up the person who had knocked him down to safety. There was Ael, scrambling to her feet with a smile on her face and a most dangerous look in her eye. "Thanks," he said as they helped each other up.

She cocked an eyebrow at him, then turned to Spock, who was leaning against the wall and looking more than just a little shaken. He was going pale. "Spock?" Ael said, a husky whisper through the howling of the sirens.

"Mr. Spock—" Jim said. "Bones!"

"No, Captain," Spock said, his voice definitely not as strong as usual. "There is something—pressing on my mind. An urge not to move, not to think—making any action pain. The effect got much stronger as we came around that last corner."

"A person?" Ael said as McCoy and Lia Burke hurried up to join them.

"No. Power of mind—without personality—" Spock actually made an expression, right out there in front of everybody: loathing. "Mindless. An abomination—"

"A machine," Ael said bitterly, "working through cloned Vulcan brain tissue."

"Too strong—" Spock said, struggling for control.

"A great mass of brain tissue," McCoy said, getting a look of loathing very much like Spock's. "A tank full of Vulcan gray matter cloned from a single brain cell. No personality—but terrible power, programmed for some single purpose, and performing it mindlessly. Just another computer—"

Jim's stomach turned. "This has to be the weapon they used on the *Intrepid*."

"Or one like it," Spock agreed, straightening, gasping. "Captain, *Intrepid*'s crew must be around here somewhere. The Romulans would hardly have set this weapon up in expectation that I would arrive."

"But the Vulcans should have been on another level," Ael protested.

"Maybe they—" The sound of shouting voices cut that conversation short. Mr. Matlock and about ten of his people leapt past Jim and Bones and Spock and Ael into the main corridor, opening fire before the approaching Romulans could. Jim shouted warning at them, and a few of the Security people managed to turn and meet the second group of Romulans who were coming at them from behind. Only several of these were armed; but this second group came crashing in among them with such speed and force that suddenly phasers were useless, there was too much mixing going on, too many chances to stun or kill a friend.

Jim broke into a whirl of hand-to-hand, relishing it terribly as a release for all the anger and tension and helplessness of the past week. He knew he would pay the price later—his body always ached for days after one of these orgies of anger. Or maybe he would pay for it right now, since every one of these Romulans was about as easy to handle, one-on-one, as Spock.

But training regularly with a Vulcan had its advantages; and though the Romulans might have drifted considerably from the Vulcan norm in terms of genetics, physiologically they still had the same weaknesses. The Vulcanid head and ears were relatively vulnerable, and as for leverage, Romulans flew through the air as well as anyone else. Jim busied himself with that—a double chop to the collarbone here, a broken kneecap there, a bit of *tal-shaya* that Spock had taught him over here. Every now and then he caught a glance of something that would have made him laugh, if he'd had time to breathe; tiny Ael, for instance, slamming a Romulan man nearly twice her height into a wall, putting a foot in his gut, grabbing one of his arms, and neatly relieving the poor man of his sidearm and dislocating his shoulder, all in one quick, rather casual motion. In the middle of a chop-and-kick combination Jim saw Lia Burke come up unnoticed beside a burly Romulan woman who was firing uselessly at the angrily advancing Ensign Naraht. Phasers, at least phasers on the conventional "one" setting, don't work on Hortas; but the unfortunate Romulan woman didn't have time to readjust her phaser, even if she knew that was what needed doing. Lia simply reached up a bit—the woman was tall—and swung her slender little fist sidewise into the Romulan's trachea, like a hammer. Even over the howling alarm klaxon, Jim could hear the crunch of cartilage. *Goodness,* Jim thought mildly, while breaking a Romulan's arm backward at the elbow, *if Mr. Freeman is this good too, his yearly shots are probably going to be a very interesting event. I wonder if Bones'll be selling tickets? . . .*

—and suddenly the fight was over, except that there were still shouts coming from further down the main corridor. Jim dropped the unconscious Romulan he found himself holding and looked swiftly around at his people. They were mostly gasping, some still crouched for combat, unable to stop being ready. "Injuries?" he said.

"Lahae's got a broken arm," Ael said, jerking her head at one of her people. "But she's well otherwise."

"A few burns, Jim." said McCoy. "Harrison got it bad. I've treated him, but we need to get him back topside."

"It's going to take a while, Bones. Mr. Athendë, carry Harrison. Spock?"

"Captain," Spock said, stepping out of a pile of unconscious Romulans, and still looking very unwell, "there is some direction to this mental pressure. That way." He pointed down the corridor, toward all the noise.

"That's it, Ael," Jim said. "The Vulcans *are* on this level, after all. Evidently this is one of those operations in which everything's going to go wrong right away. . . ."

"Saves us wondering," McCoy said. "Spock, can you function?"

"Barely, Doctor. As you delight in reminding me, I am half Terran—and for once that fact is serving me somewhat. My mother's side of the family has a history of being almost relentlessly non-psi sensitive. But as we get closer to the mechanism, the mind-damper, I will surely grow weaker."

"There's no guarantee that the Vulcans will be where the damper is," Ael said.

"Of course not. But if we can put it out of commission, they'll be free to try to escape—and that would make the odds a little more even."

"Well then," Ael said, putting her head around the corner—pulling it back quickly and getting shot at for her trouble—"time to do something. Raha, give me a spare phaser, will you?"

One of Ael's people tossed her a phaser. Ael detached it from the pistol grip, turned it over in her hands. "Where—Oh, here it is." She twisted the supercharge control on the back of it all the way, and tossed it lightly once or twice in her hand as the upscaling scream that signaled imminent overload began. "How long before it goes?" she said to Jim.

"Five seconds! Ael—"

"Three, two," she said, and put her head and her arm around the corner again, and threw the phaser right down the length of the corridor—an astonishing southpaw pitch, fastball swift and going a good four hundred feet down the corridor before it even hit the floor. And as the phaser hit, right among the Romulans massed and firing at the end of the corridor, it blew. The station shuddered slightly, and the concussion struck back down the corridor at the *Enterprise* group, a blast of hot wind and light that knocked Ael back into McCoy's arms and both of them hard against the wall of the side corridor.

"Now!" Jim shouted, and led the way down the corridor, his people pouring down after him. The corridor's end was ugly, blackened by the explosion, and spattered green with Romulan remains and Romulan blood where it wasn't. *Oh, God,* some part of Jim cried in anguish, but the rest of him was far gone in the necessities of the moment, and paid the pain little heed. There was a large door at the end of the corridor. He tried his phaser on the middle of it; no response. A quick experiment on the walls and the doorframe produced the same result. "Refractory," he said. "Too thick. Spock, can you gimmick the lock? If we burn it, it'll probably just seal this permanently shut—"

"Jim," Bones said, "forget it." He was supporting Spock from one side, and Mr. Athendë, already carrying the badly burnt Harrison in his tentacles, was holding Spock up on the other; the Vulcan slumped between them, nearly unconscious, trying to fight the mind-damping effect and failing. Little spasms of pain twisted his face as he kept fighting. Until they got this handled he would not think again, much less speak or move.

"Who's here?" Jim said desperately, for he heard more shouts back in the direction they'd come: a lot more. "Electronics—" But most of his people were Security, and the others were from Medicine, Linguistics, Defense—

"Let me try, Captain," someone said, pushing his way through the group; and there was Mr. Freeman, his usual neatness much the worse for wear. He was singed and smudged and bruised and had a black eye, and his hair was all over the place. But already he was on his knees by the door, snapping open a pouch at one side, fishing for tools. He pushed his hair back in his everyday get-neat gesture while using a decoheser to pop the flush cover off a small panel by the right side of the door. "Oh damn," he said at the sight of the panel's innards, an incomprehensible welter of circuits and chips. "It's all solids."

"Mr. Freeman," Jim said grimly. The sounds of approaching Romulans were getting much louder.

"I know, sir—" Freeman said, poking around in the circuitry and doing God only knew what.

It was taking too long. "Lay down covering fire," Jim said to the people behind him. "Ael—"

"I can't help you here, Jim," she said, giving the panel only a glance and turning away. "Not a format I'm familiar with. Hilae, Gehen, Rai, over there to the side. You—Rotsler, Eisenberg, Feder, the other side. Fisher, Remner, Paul—here with me. The rest of you, mind the Captain and Mr. Spock, and fire as you like. Mr. Athendë, one of your phasers. Hate to use a trick twice—"

"Mr. Freeman!" Jim said.

"Captain, this isn't just something you can—"

"Jim," McCoy said quietly, and rather sorrowfully, "the boy can't manage it, that's all. Back off."

Jim looked up at McCoy in surprise—and so would have missed the look that settled down over Freeman's face at McCoy's words, had McCoy not been looking so fixedly at the young man's back. Jim, who could see Freeman's face from his angle, saw suddenly written on it a rage so terrible that for a second he wondered if Freeman was going to blow up like an overloading phaser himself. Then Jim wondered if he'd seen the look at all, for Jerry's face sealed over into an expression as cool as one of Spock's. Freeman did something brief and precise to the circuitry, changed tools, did something else to a particular logic solid in one quick fierce motion.

The door sprang open.

Behind Jim there were explosions, cries, shouts of anger and triumph. He ignored them and ran into the room. There was equipment of some kind, three walls' worth of it, all studded with controls and switch-lights; there was a fourth wall with a great window in it and another refractory door. And there were Romulans. One of them Jim stunned; the other, too close, he kicked right between the legs, where even Romulans are vulnerable, and Romulan females no less than the males. The third he never had a chance at, for Mr. Athendë, while still carrying the burned Harrison and supporting Spock on the side, had swept into the room right after Jim and thrown one of his major handling tentacles and various minor ones around the remaining Romulan's head and body, squeezing the man's disruptor right out of his hand so that it clattered on the floor.

"Nicely done, Mr. Athendë," Jim said to the Sulamid, panting.

The Sulamid curved several stalked eyes in Jim's direction. "Must protect wounded, Captain," he said; but even his eternal humor sounded a little grim at the moment.

"All right," Jim said to the remaining Romulan. "Which of these controls the damper?"

The Romulan, still straining against the tentacles that held him, turned an enraged look on Jim. "I'll tell you nothing!"

—and the man suddenly gasped and began to turn an astonishing shade of dusky green-bronze. "Suggest you change your mind," Athendë said sweetly, as the great handling tentacles, as thick as tree limbs, began to squeeze. "Might lose temper otherwise. Or start to feel hungry. Love it when prey struggles."

The Romulan made a sudden anguished sound for which Jim could see no reason—until he noticed a runnel of green making its way down the lower leg of the man's uniform, one of the only exposed parts of him. Jim reflected briefly that he still had no idea where a Sulamid kept its mouth, though now the question of whether the mouth had teeth in it seemed to have been resolved.

"Have tasted better," said Mr. Athendë mildly. "But shame to waste. Better say something fast or will bolt my lunch and get on with work."

The Romulan shuddered and moaned and gasped, turning darker—then cried out again. "Over there!" he said, his eyes flickering to the leftmost of the consoles.

"Ael," Jim said. She had hurried into the room with several of her people, and together they went to the console and began touching controls, reading screens. "This is it, Captain. We can crash the effect itself easily enough—" and Ael reached out and tapped at a keypad, then hit several switches in rapid succession. "But I don't see any control for crashing the whole system from here."

"No matter," Jim said. "We'll find the tank with the brain material and stick a sonic grenade in it." He turned around and gave his attention to that large window. Mr. Freeman was already down on his knees by the door adjacent to the window, working on another circuit panel. Looking through the window, Jim could see why; littered all over the floor of the great room were hundreds of bodies in Starfleet green and blue and orange. Some of them were stirring feebly.

"Captain," said a weak voice. It was Spock, whom Athendë was still half-cradling in some spare tentacles. McCoy went to him, helping him to stand. "Jim—that mechanism is full of living material—"

"Mr. Spock, I would like nothing better than to transport it out of here and find it a nice home on Vulcan," Jim said. "But the ship's screens are up, and she's not answering anyway, and we can't do it. If we leave the living material alone, it can be used against us again."

"Not easily, Captain," Ael said. "If we destroy this board"—and she touched more switches—"this whole setup will go, and the connections to the brain tissue will fuse. In any case, it's time that we did one thing or another and got moving. It is getting noisy out there, and not even *our* people can hold that corridor forever."

"All right," Jim said. "The computers at least. Everybody out of the way."

Athendë and the others cleared away from the console side of the room, heading for the door to the large room where the Vulcans had been held. "Get in there and help them," Jim said. "Mr. Spock?"

"A great pleasure, Captain," Spock said, unholstering his phaser and aiming at the key computer board. He blew it to bits.

"'Pleasure' is an emotion, Mr. Spock," Ael said from behind them as the last few crackles and fizzes died out.

Jim turned, wondering what that meant, and found Ael looking at Spock with a rather cockeyed expression. Spock gave it right back to her. "So I hear, Commander," he said, and together they turned and headed for the room full of Vulcans.

Jim hurried after them, for the noise out in the hall *was* getting pretty loud. Many of the Vulcans were on their feet now, and more every moment. From across the room one staggered across to him. It was tall young Sehlk, the *Intrepid*'s First Officer, and Jim reached out and steadied Sehlk as he almost fell over upon reaching him. "Mr. Sehlk, are you all right?"

Sehlk stared at Jim, his face (in the cool Vulcan fashion) bewildered in the extreme. "Captain," Sehlk said with a brief, most unVulcan access of emotion, "it is most illogical for you to be here!"

"Is it really?" Jim said, suspecting that he was going to have to get used to hearing that from every Fleet officer he met for a while. "I'm not doing anything for you and your Captain that he wouldn't probably do for my people, were our places reversed. . . . Meanwhile, I would rather beg the question—"

"As you wish, sir."

"Very good. Where's Captain Suvuk?"

"Not here, Captain," the young Vulcan said. "The Romulans took him from us shortly after we were brought here. Logic would seem to indicate that they are attempting to force classified information from him—most likely the *Intrepid*'s control codes and command ciphers, that being the only information he would have and we would not that would be of use to them."

Useful indeed. With those codes and ciphers the Romulans could drain *Intrepid*'s computers dry of all kinds of useful classified data—Federation starship patrol corridors, troop strengths and distributions— "Mr. Sehlk, they didn't harm him, did they?"

"They tortured him, Captain," Sehlk said with terrible equanimity. "But that did them no good; mere torture will not break Command conditioning, as you know. The Romulans then attempted to bring their mind-techniques to bear on him. We tried to defend him at a distance, by taking the brunt on our own minds—and for a short while we succeeded in standing the Romulans off. Their techniques so far work better for large groups than for single persons. But the techniques they are using are apparently mechanically augmented in some way; once our interference was discovered, they put us all under the damper at such intensity that some of us, the more psionically sensitive, died of it." Sehlk's eyes grew cold. "Can you imagine what it is like, Captain, to lie paralyzed for hour after hour, with a mind forcibly emptied of thought, of volition—though not of the knowledge of what has happened to you, or probably will?"

"Mr. Sehlk," Jim said, "may those of us who have not be preserved from it."

"We will see to that," Sehlk said. "Captain, when Suvuk realized that they were going to use such artificial augmentation to force his mind, he drove himself purposely into *kan-sorn*—a mental state similar to coma, but with this difference, that any attempts on the integrity of a mind in kan-sorn will destroy both mind and body. He made himself useless to them—and so he lies, somewhere in here, comatose. Captain," Sehlk said, "we must find him." And though the statement was certainly based in logic, there was more to it than that: there was the ferocious, unconditional Vulcan loyalty that Jim had come to know very well indeed.

"We will," Jim said. "First we have to get you people out of here. Our position at the moment isn't the best—"

"Acknowledged," Sehlk said, and detached himself coolly from Jim's grip, heading off a little unsteadily to see to his own people. They were recovering rapidly, more than half of them on their feet now, going about the room as swiftly and efficiently as they could. Jim spent about half a second simply being astonished at how many different kinds of Vulcans there were. On some level he had become conditioned to their being dark, and usually tall. But here were gigantic seven-foot Vulcans and little delicate ones, Vulcans slimmer even than Spock and Vulcans much burlier—none of them actually being overweight; Starfleet regulations to one side, Jim suspected nonglandular fat of being, as far as Vulcans were concerned, "illogical." And there were fair Vulcans, blond and ash blond and very light brunette, and, good Lord, several redheads—

Most important, there were four hundred and eight of them. Jim could think of a lot of worse things than having four hundred Vulcans, all coolly furious over the loss of their Captain, at his back in a charge down that corridor.

Ael came up beside him. "Well, Captain," she said, "that's half our job done."

"A third," he said. "Their Captain's not here, Ael—we have to find Suvuk yet. Then the research computers and the genetic-material stockpile."

"And how are we going to find one Vulcan in this place full of Romulans?" she said, looking askance. "Jim, we've already been here more than thirty minutes! The whole population of this station is going to come down on us shortly—"

"Let them," Jim said. "The numbers are a little better right now."

"Yes, but these Vulcans aren't armed! And what about your ship? Why haven't we heard from Mr. Scott?"

"That," Jim said, his guts clenching inside him, "is something I intend to find out as soon as possible. In the meantime, your first question—"

Jim turned around to call for Mr. Selhk, but he was already heading toward Ael and Jim, with T'Leiar and the calm round Sopek in tow. "Captain," he said, "we're ready to move. What are your orders?"

"Well, first of all we're going to have to locate Suvuk."

"Captain," said willowy T'Leiar, "leave that to us. Several of us have had occasion to mindmeld with the Captain before; so we are quite familiar with his basic personality pattern. And now that the mind damper is no longer operational—"

"You can track him," Jim said. "What do you have to do?"

"Sehlk and T'Leiar will hold the pattern," Sopek said. "The rest of us, even those not trained in the disciplines, will also be of use; we will lend them—I think the most precise Basic word would be 'intention.' We will require several minutes' concentration to set up and implement the state."

"Very well, gentlemen, ladies; carry on. I'm only sorry I can't offer you some peace and quiet for what you're doing. . . ."

"Quiet is not necessary," Sehlk said, for a moment looking very like Spock did while he discussed matters Vulcan and private; reserved, intense, and hiding (not well) a great weight of feeling. "And as for the peace, it is inside us, else no outward peace would be of any use."

Jim looked up. All around, slowly surrounding him and Ael and Spock and McCoy and Athendë and the rest of their party, the Vulcans moved in close. There was nothing mysterious about it, no outward sign as in the personal mindmeld. Sehlk closed his eyes; T'Leiar simply folded her arms and looked down at the floor. But Jim suddenly began to become aware of a frightening sense of oneness settling in around him, as seemingly palpable as the Vulcan's bodies, as invasive and inescapable as the air. He told himself that it was frightening only because he had not been brought up to it—to this certainty, seemingly common in Vulcans, that any given group was far more than the sum of its parts, and the parts all infinitely less for the loss of one of them.

Or is it so strange? he thought, as all around him the many parts reached for the one in whom their wholeness best rested, and ever so slightly, mind-blind as Jim usually was, he found himself caught up in the search. *Ael's crew has certainly done the same kind of thing for her. And how many times has mine done it for me? Always, always we're more alike than we dare to admit—*

The air was singing with tension and resolve, though physically no one moved. Outside, the sound of the explosions, the cries and the phaser fire, all sounded very far away. The battle was inward now, one great mind swiftly turning over the thoughts of many smaller ones—some inimical, some desperate, some valiant or preoccupied or blood-mad, all frightened in one way or another. Very few parts of the great searching mind knew anything just now but a terrible, cool, controlled anger they would have rather not admitted to. One part knew that brand of anger, and other emotions as well, and accepted them all together. Two other parts knew mostly rage, and fear for their crews and their ships. All together the power of their emotions, admitted or not, and the power of their intention, wound together, reached outward, pierced—

"There!" cried T'Leiar, and as suddenly as it had coalesced, the great mind fell apart. But the memory and direction of what it had found—a single unconscious Vulcan mind—lingered still. Jim opened his eyes—amazed to find they had been closed—and felt as if he were attached to a rope, with the other end of it fastened to Suvuk. He could have found the man with his eyes closed. Involuntarily he looked up at the ceiling.

"Two levels up," he said. "Next door to the master research computers. Ladies and gentlemen and others, let's go!"

Sixteen

Mostly Ael knew about Vulcans what she had been taught as a child. Their remote ancestors had also been the remote ancestors of the Rihannsu; they were a Federation people now; and like all Federation peoples, they were hopelessly spoiled—rich, soft, and unable to take care of themselves. The inability was a matter of ancient history. There had come a time, long ago, when they could no longer cope with the constant fighting that was the inevitable heritage of a warrior people. Those who could cope had been "invited" to leave the planet. Leave it they had—supposedly without much regret. And those who remained had embraced a frightening, demeaning, bizarre discipline of nonemotionality—bottling inside them emotions that they began pretending not to have, as if that would make them go away. The Rihannsu, hearing about this after all the thousands of years, found it a choice irony.

The meek had, after all, inherited Vulcan; the Rihannsu had gone out and conquered the stars.

There was nothing wrong with logic *per se;* it could be as uplifting as song, as intoxicating as wine, under the proper conditions. But it was hardly bread or meat—there was no living a whole life on it. To throw out love, hate, pain, desire, ambition, hunger and hunger's satisfaction, that was asking too much. That was to turn life into a thin, etiolated shadow, lived like one long, dry, joyless mathematical equation.

Or so Ael had always thought. After first meeting Spock, she had begun to wonder whether her preconceptions had anything to do with reality at all. But then Spock was half Terran, and Terrans, though nearly as soft as Vulcans, still had virtues; courage and joy and wit and many other useful or delightful attributes. Spock, she had thought, would probably not be truly representative of a Vulcan. His inner divisions, his lights and shadows, and the reconciliations he had made among them, had turned him into far too complex and powerful a character.

Now, though—as she raced up a hall surrounded by living, breathing Vulcans, and not by her ideas about them, Ael wondered with some shame whether her brain (as her father had repeatedly insisted) was in fact good only for keeping her skull bones apart. The people around her spoke and moved and fought with a frightful cold precision that spoke more of the computer than of the arena; yet at the same time their ferocity matched that of the angriest Rihannsu she had ever seen. Their courage, as they charged unstoppable down hallways full of Rihannsu firing at them, was indomitable. And as for skill, phaser beams seemed to simply miss them, and if the station personnel threw grenades at them, the Vulcans simply managed somehow to be elsewhere. Some of it might be the mind-disciplines that seemed so much like magic to a Rihannsu. She wondered if their embrace of peace might somehow, paradoxically, have made their fierceness more accessible to them. But in any case Ael began to suspect that her belated perception of the Vulcans' virtues was like that of a child who grows up and finds, abruptly, that her parents aren't so stupid as they used to be when she was younger.

It was an annoying realization, but it was the truth; and as such, she wouldn't have given it up for anything.

She stopped at the head of one more endless corridor, leaned up against the corner, and put her hand back. This had been something of a ritual for the past four corridors, and was proving a great success. Into the hand Ael reached out, someone—perhaps Jim, or Spock, or one of her own people—slapped a phaser or other small disposable object. Ael tossed it out into the corridor. If nothing happened—well, that step would be handled as it came.

Nothing happened.

She put her hand back again. Another object: a Rihannsu disruptor, this time.

She threw it out there. And white light and heat blew up practically in her face as a disruptor blast from down the hall exploded the disruptor she'd thrown.

"There they are," she said to the people behind her. "Jim?"

"Right," he said. And out they went into the corridor, as they had the last three times: diving, rolling, shooting, throwing overloaded phasers and whatever else seemed useful. There was a limit, though, to how many overloaded phasers they could use. Ael was praying for an armory somewhere around here. In the meantime, the Elements did for those who did for

255

themselves, and who stayed alive to keep doing it. She concentrated on staying alive.

It took about ten minutes before this particular knot of station personnel was reduced to unconsciousness or death. It had been some time now since the subject of the ethicality of killing had even crossed Ael's mind. She ached all over; she wanted to be back in her own bed on *Bloodwing* so badly that she could taste it; and it would be hours, maybe weary days, before there would be time for that, she knew. The only satisfaction that would come anytime soon was their arrival at the spot where the Vulcan Captain was being held. Ael could feel the line inside her, stretched tight toward the man, around this corner and to the left.

"Clear, Captain," one of Jim's people out in the hall was saying. Jim grunted softly, pushed himself away from the wall. He had taken a wicked phaser burn along one arm in the intersection before last, and when he knew no one was looking, his face showed the same kind of weary misery that Ael felt. But let someone look at him, and there was suddenly energy in the eyes, erectness about the carriage, power and stern command. *Fire and air,* Ael thought. *The fire will burn bright until there is suddenly nothing left. . . .*

"We're close," Jim said.

Spock was right behind him, looking at Jim with concern, but saying nothing about that; his face was locked in a controlled fierceness much like the other Vulcans'. "Very close," he said. "On the close order of fifty yards."

"Tricorder scan—"

"Ineffective, Captain. All these walls are force-shielded."

"Wonderful. Let's go."

The leading part of the group headed around the corner of the T-intersection, going left. Down at the end of the hall was something that surprised them all: nothing. The hall was empty. That was bizarre, for all the way up here, practically every foot of the way had had to be viciously contended. Now nothing—

"A trap," Ael said. "Jim, have a care."

"I don't think so," Jim said, eyeing the great door at the hall's end. "Spock, scan it."

The Vulcan did, and his face grew grim as he did so. "Captain, we have a problem," he said. "That door and the walls around it are solid hyponeutronium."

Ael looked up in despair. "Collapsed metal? We have nothing that can possibly break that—"

"Ship's phasers, perhaps," Sehlk said from behind them. "Nothing else."

Ael turned and walked away from the door, reduced to simple annoyance. "There are no guards here because they know they don't need any," she said bitterly. "And Suvuk is on the other side of that door somewhere."

All the Vulcans who had managed to fit into the hallway stood staring at the door as if sheer loyalty or logic would be enough to break it, phasers lacking. Spock and Jim and Sehlk were talking desperately at one another, hypothesizing hurriedly. *It will do them no good,* Ael thought. *We have at last come up against a problem all our fellowship and resourcefulness and cleanness of heart can't solve. . . .*

She walked right up to a wall and thumped it angrily with one fist. *It isn't fair!* And as usual, the old cry brought her father's old reply up: *The Elements aren't fair either. . . .*

Elements . . . it was a silly time to get religious. But

what was the old saying? Meet a problem with another problem to make a solution. Meet fire with fire, and earth with earth, and water with water. . . .

Earth!

She ran back down the hall where the many Vulcans and *Enterprise* people and her own crewfolk leaned against the walls, silent or whispering, waiting for orders. One of them would not be leaning. He would be flat down on the floor, glittering, answering everyone with the same solid, cheerful, gravelly voice. . . .

She had to trip over him to find him, finally, which was all right, for that was how Ael usually came by her solutions. "Mr. Naraht," she said, catching herself on the wall with both hands, "come quick, we need you!"

"Yes, ma'am!" the rock said, and Ael hurried down the hall with him coming after in a hurry. People got out of Naraht's way when they saw him coming, knowing by experience (or hearsay, in the Vulcans' case) how fast a Horta can move when it was excited.

She led him back around the corner and up to the Captain and Spock and Sehlk. "Gentlemen," she said, "I have a question for you."

They turned to her, and their eyes fell on Ensign Naraht, and Jim looked up at Ael in astonishment. "No," he said, "I think you've got an answer for us!"

He got down with some care on one knee—one of his own people had misaimed a kick, in one of the countless fights behind them, and had nearly crippled Jim as a result. "Mr. Naraht," he said, "would you see if you can eat through this door in front of us?"

"It is hyponeutronium," Spock said.

Naraht rumbled and shuffled his fringes about on the floor. "Sirs," he said, sounding pained, "I don't know if I can. I've rarely eaten anything denser than lead. But I'll do what I can."

The Horta shuffled over to the doorway, reared up a little way against it. There was a hissing and a sharp smell of acid in the air; the deckplates under Naraht began to smoke.

"Careful, Mr. Naraht," someone said from beside Ael. It was McCoy, watching the whole process with tired amusement. "Don't go through the floor."

Naraht didn't answer—just held his position for several seconds more, then slid down. There was a great ragged patch of the dark hyponeutronium metal missing, about an inch thick and shaped like Naraht's underside.

"Go on, Ensign, you're doing fine," Jim said.

"In a moment, Captain," Naraht said, sounding distressed. "It's awfully rich. . . ."

Both McCoy's eyebrows went up. Ael watched Jim get up and turn most carefully away from the door, hiding a terrible smile. "Proceed, Ensign, if you please," Spock said very gently. "We are quite short of time, and the success of this entire operation may now lie with you. . . ."

Naraht said not a word. He reared up again and laid himself against the door. The hissing and fuming of acid in the air became terrible, so that people had to retreat from the corridor, and McCoy went hurriedly about spraying something into everyone's eyes to protect them from damage. Long minutes, it went on. Ael got herself sprayed and went out into the corridor again . . . just in time to see Naraht, with a strangled little cry, flop forward through a two-meter-wide hole in the door. From inside, disruptor fire hit him, ineffective as usual . . . which was as well, for Naraht didn't move.

"*Now!*" Jim shouted, as if all the lost energy had suddenly returned. "*Don't touch the edges!*"

And immediately after the Captain dove through the

door, the sound of phaser fire broke out on its far side; and Spock and McCoy and many another dove through that door after Jim and Ael, none of them being too careful about the edges, and none of them caring. This room was rather like the large control room near which the Vulcans had been kept; full of consoles, control areas and data pads—and only slightly full of Romulans, several of whom lay stunned on the floor. Ael stood with Jim, turning in the smoky room to pick up the directional line again—and found herself looking at a simple, blastable door and being powerfully drawn toward it. She didn't wait. She blasted it.

She was halfway through the door already by the time the smoke cleared, Jim and Spock and McCoy coming after her. The room was set up as a wretched little barracks—a 'fresher, a food dispenser, and several cots; and on one of the cots lay Suvuk, in fetal position—still unconscious, but alive.

"Bones, take care of him," Jim said. "Spock, the computers. Ael, please go with him, assist him if you can—we've got to get that virus program running. Send Sehlk in here when you have a moment."

They did not have to; Sehlk pushed in past them as Ael and Spock were heading out. "I will need an input station," Spock said quietly. "This looks like one—"

"Here's the initializer," Ael said, and began touching switches. The computer was not unlike the library computer on *Bloodwing,* a later model of a brand she knew well. "Astonishing that these things run at all," she said, as she brought the main operating system up.

"Lowest bidder?" Spock said.

She grinned and kept working. "There you are. Can you access from this command level?"

"Easily. Now then—" His hands flickered over the keyboard with almost insulting ease. Ael turned from him to see one of the stunned Romulans slowly recovering, looking around him at the incredible wreckage, and (with considerable trepidation) at a roomful of angry Vulcans.

One of them was giving him her particular attention. T'Leiar, with two or three of her security people about her, was holding the man by the front of his coverall and conversing with him in no amiable tone. "You will introduce us," she said, "to the head of this research project."

The man glared at her. "I am its head. And it will be my pleasure to see you all executed for the damage you have been doing it—"

"We have not done nearly any damage to the heart of it as yet," T'Leiar said, "but we shall. And as for the pleasures you expect to enjoy, I suggest you reckon them up quickly. We have business with you after which the probability is high that you will no longer understand pleasure—or anything else."

The man laughed at them, such a scornful sound that Ael had to admire his courage, while at the same time wanting very much to step over there, relieve T'Leiar of him, and strangle him with one hand. "You think you can force information from me?" he said. "Do your worst. I was one of the first Rihannsu to obtain the Vulcan mind-techniques directly from your genetic material. It was I who assisted in the capture of your ship by the cruiser *Battlequeen*. Your minds hold no terror for me—"

"Oh, indeed," T'Leiar said, very softly. "But you were using an enhancer, were you not?—several thousand cubic inches of brain matter added to your own, endowing you with much more reach and scope than you have in your own mind. No," said T'Leiar, as from outside the room more and more Vulcans slipped in through the hole in the door, "I can feel you striving for control of my mind; but even my own self alone is too much for you. Now you begin to feel the weight, do you not? So we felt under your damper; and worse is to come."

The air in the room was becoming strained again, full of that awful tightness. There was no affection about this, though, no affinity, no searching, as there had been for Suvuk. This was an inimical pressure, the weight of many minds leaning together, bearing in and down, harder, sharper, their attack narrowing down to a crushing spearhead of thought. "You may tell us the location of the stockpiled genetic material," T'Leiar said in that light, passionless voice of hers. "Or you may try to withhold it."

The Rihannsu researcher lay there, his face straining into awful shapes, and twitched like a palsied thing. "No, I—" he said, in a voice more suited to groaning than to speech; and then more loudly, "No!", and again, "No!", almost a scream. And then the screaming began in earnest. No one touched him, no one moved; T'Leiar sat back on her heels beside him, motionless as a carving, her eyes hooded; and still the man screamed and screamed. Ael watched, approving on some levels, but on others horrified beyond words. The screaming went on—

—and then broke. The Rihannsu research chief gasped, and his head thumped down to the floor with that particular hollow, wet sound that Ael recognized as a dead man's head falling. His eyes stared at the ceiling, wide and terrified, and the Vulcans around him got up, or straightened, and went away, leaving him there.

Ael found herself staring at T'Leiar as she got up.

The young woman caught Ael's glance and said, with utter calm, "He fought us."

"You didn't get the information, then?"

"We obtained it." She started toward the door of the little room where Suvuk had lain, but McCoy came out of it then, with Sehlk carrying Suvuk, and Jim following them.

Jim went straight to T'Leiar. "Well, Commander?"

"We have the locations of the stockpiles," she said, "and all the basic research data, both hard and soft copy, is here in this shielded part of the installation. However, there is too much of it to be handled by our group. Transporters will handle it—but the *Enterprise* is still not answering hails."

"Well," Jim said, "this station has transporters of its own, Commander."

T'Leiar looked at him with cool approval. "You are suggesting we secure those, then beam up to *Intrepid* with all our people—transferring you to *Enterprise* when it becomes clear what the problem is. If there is a problem."

"Correct. Mr. Spock, what's the status of the computer?"

"It is in a sorry state, Captain," Spock said with satisfaction. "The Commander's parameters for a whole-system virus program were most effective; the system is being subverted even as we speak. Within fifteen minutes there will not be a bit of data left in it. It will make someone an excellent adding machine."

"Mr. Spock, Commander," Jim said, bright-eyed and alert again, "my compliments. Bones," he said to McCoy, who was passing by, "one question. How's Naraht?"

McCoy scowled genially at the Captain. "Boy's got

the worst case of indigestion I've ever seen," he said, "but he'll be all right."

"Good. Mr. Spock, let's find those transporters and get the hell out of here. I want to know what's the matter with my ship!"

They headed for the melted door together. As they went a look of doubt crossed Jim's face—for out in the hall, he could hear their rearguard shooting at something again.

"More company," Ael said.

"And our phaser charges are running low." Jim sighed, then grinned again—that fierce, defiant look. "Well, let's just get out there, do what we can, and hope for the best. . . ."

"Hope, Captain?" Ael said in a soft imitation of T'Leiar's voice. "Hope is illogical."

"So it is. Then let's just go out there and fight like crazy people to shame the Devil."

At that Ael laughed. "Now I understand you very well. Let us shame her by all means. . . ."

They went out together into the phaser fire and the smoke.

Seventeen

In the tight hot dark of the 'tween-decks crawlway, three shadowy forms lay one behind the other, holding very still. One of them had his ear pressed to the duct's plating. His open eye, moving as he listened, gleamed momentarily in the dull glow of a circuit-conduit's telltale.

"What do you hear?" Chekov said softly behind him.

"Disruptor fire," Khiy said. "But it sounds to be some ways off."

"Thank God for that," Sulu said from the rear. "That last little episode was a bit too close for my taste."

"Easy for you to say," Chekov muttered. "They missed *you*."

"How is it?" Khiy said, starting to inch forward again.

Chekov started to move too, and involuntarily gave

Khiy his answer in a word that hadn't been taught him at Starfleet Academy.

"Hang on, Pavel," Sulu said. "We'll get you to Sickbay as soon as we find some more people."

"And retake the Bridge," Chekov said dismally. But he hitched himself along at a good rate. "Where next?"

Sulu had been considering that for a good half hour now, as they wormed their way along between decks, heading toward the turbolift core of the *Enterprise*'s primary hull. The access to the Bridge would be fairly simple from the lift core—always granting that the lifts didn't come on again at the wrong moment and kill them all. But besides that sticky question, he didn't care for the odds. Three of them might not be enough to break through the resistance they would surely meet when they had to come out into the real corridors and access the core. Tafv would not be fool enough to leave that route unguarded. *Hikaru my boy,* he had said to himself some ways back in this seemingly infinite tunnel, *there has to be another way. There's always a loophole, a shortcut, if you can just see it. . . .*

"Pavel," he said, "I lost count. Where the hell are we?"

"Between three and four," Chekov said. "Somewhere between Administrative and Library Science, if you're looking up at three."

Hikaru closed his eyes to look at the ship in his head, going around the circle of the disk on his mental diagram. "Then below us on four, nacelleward, are the Chapel, and Dining Three and Four, and the Rec deck. . . ."

Chekov pushed himself up on his elbows a little, an alert movement. "I will bet you there are a lot of people down there—" He shook his head. "Hikaru, if we take the duct from here, that's a three-story drop to the deck!"

"Sure is. But even if we can't jump down that far, we can throw them some guns so that they can break out of there. . . . And I bet we'd get down somehow."

"Is this wise?" Khiy said softly from up ahead. "Mr. Scott did tell us not to do anything stupid. . . ."

"It's not *too* stupid," Chekov said. "And numbers would be a help. We can't afford to screw up an attempt on the Bridge."

" 'Screw up'?"

Chekov said another word not usually considered part of the language of officers and gentlemen, one that the translator would nevertheless render more accurately than idiom. "Oh," Khiy said, and laughed, though so softly as not to be heard by any listener. "Yes, I agree. So where shall we go?"

"Back the way we came, and to the right."

"You are jesting," Khiy said. "In *this* space?"

"It's no joke, brother," Sulu said. "Let's move it."

It took them fifteen minutes, and besides becoming acutely aware of every bruise and aching joint he already owned, and of new ones that the painful process of turning was adding to the collection, Hikaru was acutely aware of the minutes crawling over and past him like bugs. Time, time, there was too little of it for anything: who knew what was going on down at the station, whether the Captain and the landing party and the crew of the *Intrepid* were still even alive? There was no news from them—and until the situation aboard *Enterprise* was resolved, no way to get news to them either. *Damn, damn,* Hikaru thought, bending himself once more into an impossible shape, *we've got to do something, and fast, and everything's taking too much time. . . .*

He finished turning first. Chekov was having even more trouble, being bigger than Hikaru, and poor Khiy, the largest of them, was in torment; but there was nothing Hikaru could do for either one. "Pavel," he said, "the clock's running. I've got to take some of those guns and go ahead."

"Go on," Pavel said. "Hurry. We'll catch up. Khiy, try it again, you're close, but this time don't put your boot in my eye!"

Hikaru headed back the way they had come, crawling on raw hands and elbows, pushing four or five phaser rifles ahead of him and trying to ignore the renewed pain of all the phasers and grenades hung about them as they dug into his ribs and belly. He had never been fond of tight enclosed spaces; they were becoming positively hateful to him now, and he suspected he was going to have to have a long talk with Dr. McCoy at the end of all this. If there was an end to it that would leave any of them talking.

He bit his lip, watching for the turning he wanted as he went. The prospect of death had faced him often enough before; but it had always seemed oddly tolerable with his helm console in front of him and his friends and superior officers around. *Suppose something should hit us right now,* he thought miserably. *For all our trying, we die right here, crawling through a hole in the dark—or in a hundred other stupid ways, all over the ship. No battle, no valor, everything wasted, and no one will ever know what happened. . . .*

There was a peculiar horror in the thought. Theoretically Hikaru knew perfectly well that courage was courage whether anyone saw it or not; it was of value, and the Universe lived a little longer because of it. Well, there was no proof of that last part, though it was still what he *knew*. But theory and that calmer knowledge, so often his in meditation, were a long way from him now. What he mostly felt could have been summed up in a single thought: *If I have to die, let me do it with my friends, and in the light!*

That turning— Hikaru wriggled around the corner, pushing hard, hurrying. He was close. There was sound here, too; not disruptor fire, but rather the low murmur and rumor of many voices, reflecting vaguely through the ducts. *A lot of people,* he thought, and at the prospect of being about to do something besides crawl, he forgot his horror. He hurried faster.

The voices had a sound he had never heard aboard *Enterprise* before—the sharp rasp of many, many people being angry all at once, at the same thing. It infected him; grinning, he practically shot the last twenty or thirty meters down the duct and came up hard against the grille at its end. Oh, the lovely light, the pale gray walls of the Rec Room, seen from right by its ceiling; and the big windows of the Observation Deck above, and through them, the stars. . . .

He pounded on the grille. It wouldn't give, and he didn't think any of the hundred or so people milling around down there could hear him. *Oh well,* he thought with nearly cheerful desperation. He backed away down the duct, picked up one of the phaser rifles, and blasted the grille away.

He didn't bother waiting for the smoke to clear, or the floor and walls of the duct to cool down—just scrambled forward again. And nearly got shot for his pains; just before he reached the spot where the grille had been, phaser fire came lancing up at him and hit the roof of the duct. He convulsively covered his head and eyes, but there was nothing to be done about the burns he took on the back of his scalp and the backs of his hands. *"No, you idiots, don't shoot,"* he yelled, for the moment forgetting courtesy and discipline and everything else, *"it's me, it's Hikaru Sulu!!"*

There was a moment's silence from outside. "Move forward very very slowly," said a stern voice, "and let's see."

Very slowly indeed he poked his head out and looked down. There stood Harb Tanzer, at the head of those hundred people, aiming a phaser at the duct. He was the only one of them armed with anything deadlier than a pool cue or a bowling ball; but Romulans and *Enterprise* people alike, they all looked quite ready to do murder. Until the *Enterprise* folk recognized him. Then there was cheering.

"Oh God, I could have killed you!" Harb said, tossing someone else the phaser. "Come down from there, man. Hwavirë, how long are those tentacles of yours? If you stand on something, can you reach? Get that table over here and put that other one on top of it—"

It turned out to be rather more difficult than that. At the end Hikaru was simply glad that he knew how to fall properly. He added several bruises to his collection, but even so couldn't care much about them when he found himself lying on a heap of his friends, and still hugged tight in the tentacles of one of his Sulamid junior navigators, Ensign Hwavirë. "Didn't know you cared, Hwa," he said. "Thought we were just good friends."

"Don't tempt," Hwavirë said, with a bubbling laugh, as he put Hikaru back on his feet. "Not bad looking for hominid." And then they got to repeat the performance twice more, once each for Chekov and Khiy, with mad cheers from the Romulans for the latter.

"Get them coffee," Harb said. "What's your name—

Khiy? Khiy, do you drink coffee? Never mind, we'll find out. Satha, get the first-aid kit for Hikaru's burns. You three, tell us what's happening. Hurry."

They did, interrupting one another constantly. "Mr. Scott and Mz. Uhura can't hold down the auxiliary Bridge forever," Hikaru said at last. "If we can make it to the Bridge, they can transfer control to us there before Tafv and his people get at it. The Romulans stuck on the Bridge are with us, they'll lend a hand from inside if they can. But we have to get there first. . . ."

"They're all around us, Hikaru," said Roz Bates, a tall broad lady from Engineering. "Trying to break out seemed a little dumb before, when none of us were armed. Now, of course, the odds are a little more in our favor. But still—"

"Crawlways," Mr. Tanzer muttered. "Incredible waste of time. If only we had the transporters—"

Chekov shook his head. "They're all shut down, sir. . . ."

Harb sat there, staring into the distance for a few seconds. "Yes, they are." And then suddenly his eyes widened. "No, they're *not*. . . ."

"Sir?"

"They're not!" He got up and left the group, heading across the room and stopping to stare down at the 4D chessboard. "Roz, get the tools out of my office, would you? Moira!"

"What's the problem, Harb?" the Games Department computer said from out of the middle of the air.

"Moira, what's the present maximum range for piece control in the chesscubic?"

"Ten meters, Harb. But no transits so large are needed."

"I know," Mr. Tanzer said. "We traded off distance for small-scale precision when we programmed the system. I want to arrange a different tradeoff."

"Mr. Tanzer," Hikaru said, caught between dismay and delight, "are you suggesting that one of us beam out of here via the *table* transporter? There's not enough power—"

"Maybe so, maybe not. Let's find out. Moira, think about it. Maximum transportable mass, over maximum distance, after *in situ* alteration, no new parts. All possible solutions."

"Thinking, Harb."

Harb bent over the games table, shutting down various of its circuits. "Besides, even if the table can't handle a whole person's mass—thanks, Roz, pop that other cover off, will you?—even so, there's nothing to stop us from beaming smaller masses out."

Chekov, beside Sulu, began to smile. "Take a grenade," he said, "prime it, and beam it out into the middle of a crowd of Rom—I mean, a crowd of Tafv's people—"

"Mr. Chekov," Harb said, "I always knew you were a bright fellow. Not that solid, Roz, the next one. Don't joggle that dilithium crystal, either. Moira, what's taking you so long?"

"You always yell at me when I interrupt. Maximum mass with maximum distance, fifty kilos, eighteen feet. Maximum mass with minimum distance, eighty kilos, two feet. Minimum mass with maximum distance, zero to fifty grams, five hundred meters."

"Try something a little heavier."

"One kilogram, two hundred meters."

"That's more like it. Who's got a tricorder? Harry? Good man. Start scanning. We won't be able to tell which Romulans are ours, but—"

"Yes you will, Mr. Tanzer," Khiy said between gulps of coffee, and held out his arm.

"My stars and garters," Harb said. "Mr. Sulu, your assessment of my idiocy is accepted with thanks. Harry, scan for cesium-rubidium in the Romulans in the area. Pinpoint groups without it and note the bearings for me. Decimal places on those bearings, too! I don't want to hurt the ship more than necessary; the Captain'll have my hide when he gets back, and Dr. McCoy'll rub salt where it used to be. Who're the best shots in here? Who's got a good arm? Don't give me that, Loni, I saw you with those darts last week. Have a grenade. Have several. Get off it, people; we've got work to do!"

Maybe five minutes later, Harry Matshushita had every one of Tafv's parties on the nacelleward half of the primary hull pinpointed—most particularly two parties moving along deck seven, converging on the Auxiliary Bridge in a pincers movement. "They're first," Harb said, looking rather sorrowfully at the sonic grenade he held in one hand. "Ready, Roz?"

"Just about."

"Good. Ladies and gentlemen and others—one word before we start."

Hikaru looked up, with the others, from the readying of weapons.

"Don't get to liking this too much," he said. "Any other way of freeing this ship would be preferable—and should we find ourselves able within the scope of our oaths to allow our enemies mercy, I will expect it of you. Otherwise—protect the ship and your shipmates. And our guests." His eyes flicked from place to place in the crowd, picking out the Romulans. Hikaru noticed that there was suddenly no more clumping of type with type—just people defending the same ship, and all wearing the same rather frightened expression of resolve.

"Good," Harb said. "Roz, we'll take care of those deck seven groups first, and then clear our own path to the lift core, and anything else this transporter can reach. I don't care to use the 'com system as yet, but I bet our shipmates will look out to see what's happening when they hear all the noise. Harry, give Roz new bearings for the Auxiliary Bridge, and project them a bit forward to allow for movement."

"Done, sir."

"Here; then," Harb said, and pulled the patch on the sonic grenade, and laid it on the game table.

It sparkled with Transporter effect, while all around Hikaru people were counting softly. He couldn't remember a time when dematerialization had seemed to take longer—

—and then it was gone. And was that the slightest shudder in the ship, a booming of the air in the ducts?

"Bearings for the second group," Harb said. "Roz, Harry, don't give them time to react—"

"Ready—"

Harb laid down another grenade. It beamed out. Another shudder—

Harry paused to check his tricorder. "There's nothing alive in that corridor now, sir," he said softly. "Nothing *very* alive, anyway. A few weak life readings; no movement at all."

"Next," Harb said. Sulu noticed that he did not say "good," though Harb *always* said "good." "The bunch on deck four—"

All told, it took them about twenty minutes to decimate three-fourths of the force of seventy-three that had invaded the *Enterprise*. Some of the Romulans were out of the table transporter's reach, in the forward half of the primary hull; but very few, enough for them to handle.

Their own corridor came last. Hikaru watched Harb keep checking, hoping that the Romulans besieging them would go away. But they didn't. Harb put the last grenade down, took the controls from Roz, got a bearing from Harry, and beamed the shiny little egg out himself. All over the Rec deck, things bounced and fell off tables and broke, and people grabbed one another for support.

"That's done it," Harb said, deadly quiet. "Weapons at the ready. Let's go."

They went to the main doors all together. Harb released the emergency lock and led them out into the hallway.

There was very little left out there to offer mercy to.

"We'll separate," Harb said. "Mr. Sulu, Mr. Chekov, you'll be needed on the Bridge; take about ten people with you for security's sake. About twenty of you, come with me down to Auxiliary, we'll see what the story is down there and have them release the lifts. Ten of you to the main transporters on six; ten of you to Sickbay—make yourselves available to Doctors Chapel and M'Benga. The rest of you head out and see what's to be done about the forward half of the hull. Go."

"Yes, sir," they all said, and headed off in their various directions. Hikaru and Chekov and Khiy headed off toward the lift together. It took about ten minutes, but at that point Khiy cocked his head. "I hear something—"

Sulu and Chekov listened for all they were worth, but didn't hear a thing, at least not until the lift was about two seconds from arriving. The doors whooshed open for them, the obedient, wonderful doors that Hikaru had wondered whether he would ever see working again. They stepped in together, turned to look back the way they'd come—and wished they hadn't.

"Bridge," Hikaru said softly, and the doors shut.

The three of them pressed up hard against the walls of the lift before it reached the Bridge, just in case anyone should fire at them from inside. It was a good thing that they had taken the precaution; several disruptor bolts hit the back of the lift as its doors opened. "No, no, Eriufv, it's us!" Khiy yelled at the Bridge's occupants.

Moments later they were all being pounded and hugged. Hikaru found himself being hugged by Eriufv —who was very pretty—and considered that there were certainly worse things that could happen to him. He hugged her back, but made it very quick. "We don't have time," he said to the group on the Bridge as he stepped down to the center seat, and thought simultaneously (as always) how marvelous this was, and that he'd rather be anywhere else. "Eri, you held the fort real well—and now we have to get busy attacking. First, though, we need to talk to Mr. Scott." She nodded, sat down at Uhura's station and started flicking switches as if she had been there all her life. "Auxiliary Control, this is the Bridge—"

"Auxiliary," said that wonderful Highland voice. *"Scott here."*

"We made it, Mr. Scott."

"Aye, so Mr. Tanzer tells me. Transferring control now."

"Noted," Hikaru said, as all around, the "executive" lights came on at the various stations. "Transfer complete."

"Good lad. Uhura and I are on the way up. Call the Captain and find out what the devil's goin' on down

there. Oh, and Mr. Sulu—tell him we found Tafv down here. Just barely alive. He's on his way to Sickbay."

Eriufv started up out of Uhura's seat, her eyes glittering with rage. "I will go down there and kill him myself—"

"As you were, Eri," Hikaru said, and said it so forcefully that Eriufv sat back down in the chair as if she had been pushed there.

"He'll have to die anyway," Eri said, more quietly, though her eyes were still angry. "There's no punishment but death for treachery."

"That's the Commander's prerogative, and maybe the Captain's," Hikaru said, "but not ours. I need you here. Anything else, Mr. Scott?"

"No, lad. Call the Captain, and prepare me a Damage Control report; I want to see it when Uhura and I get up there. Out."

"Pavel, take care of the report," Hikaru said. "And while you're at it, activate Intruder Control and flood the sections where there are still Romulans. Some of our people will take a nap, but it can't be helped. Then get somebody from Security and have them go in with masks and get the Romulans out."

"Right, Mr. Sulu."

"Eriufv, ship to surface. *Enterprise* to landing party, please respond!"

"Spock here," said another very welcome voice. *"Report, Mr. Sulu."*

"There was an armed uprising aboard ship, Mr. Spock. Subcommander Tafv led some seventy Romulans from *Bloodwing* over here in an attempt on the Auxiliary Bridge and other key portions of the ship: motivation presently unknown. He seems to have timed his incursion simultaneously with your beam-out, when the shields were down."

"Logical," Spock said. *"That was the only time we were vulnerable. Continue."*

"There was sabotage to systems, now under repair, and there have been numerous casualties. But elapsed time from first incursion to ship secure"—he glanced at the chrono and could not believe his eyes. The ten years he had aged had only taken—"seventy-eight minutes, Mr. Spock."

"Understood." There was the slightest grim humor to that. *"We also have been busy, Mr. Sulu. Drop the shields and beam us all up; we have a great deal of large-scale transporting to do and our position here is untenable to say the least."*

"Acknow—" And Sulu looked at the forward screen, and stopped at the sight of something Chekov, now staring in horror down Spock's hooded viewer, had transferred there. "Mr. Spock," Hikaru said, "I'm afraid I can't do that. Scan shows three more Romulan ships coming in fast: firing at us now. IDs read ChR *Lahai*, ChR *Helve*—and ChR *Battlequeen*."

Eighteen

"Tafv did what!"

Ael stared at Jim and Spock, and her heart hammered in her gut as if she had been wounded again. Suddenly the phaserfire all around, the sound of explosions, meant nothing to her at all. "But, but he—"

"They don't know exactly why he did it," Jim said, looking as angry as Ael did. "He's in Sickbay, unconscious from injuries. The people he brought with him are almost all dead. But Ael, we don't have time for it now! We've got other problems."

"Battlequeen is up there, Commander," Spock said, "with two other ships, and they are firing at *Enterprise.* Your friend LLunih may have found the help he was looking for despite our best efforts."

It was easy for them to say that they had no time for other problems. Ael's rage at her own blindness and folly was terrible. The one spot she had reckoned her strongest, the one person she could trust above all others, suddenly betraying her— And her honor was truly in rags now, she was disgraced before her own heart and the Elements forever— Bitter pragmatism reasserted itself, though, the old habit ingrained by so many other defeats. "How close are we to the transporters?"

"About a hundred meters," Spock said. But they might as well have been a hundred light-years away, for this corridor was the most fiercely held of any they had come down yet. The Rihannsu at the far end of it doubtless knew that if they could only hang on a little longer, *Battlequeen*'s people would arrive in force— and there would be an end to fighting, and a beginning to an interesting evening of tortures.

"Captain," she said, "we cannot hope to break out of here! We are almost out of weapons, those few we still have are almost out of charge, we are almost all wounded, even the poor rock can barely move—"

"Hope," Jim said, still looking around him for possible options, "*is* illogical. . . . Still, it has its uses. Spock?"

"The Commander's summation, while emotionally delivered, is quite correct," Spock said. "We are pinned, and scan shows another group of Rihannsu working around to join those presently attacking our rear. They do not have to do much to us, Captain. They can easily contain any attempt we might make to break out of this area."

"Noted. However, Mr. Spock—if it becomes plain that this is a nonsurvival situation—we will not be taken without a fight."

"Yes, sir."

And having decided that, they began to look around them for ways out again. Ael shook her head slowly, feeling shamed by their courage and privileged to have seen it. "Gentlemen—"

Jim's communicator beeped. "Kirk here."

"Captain," Mr. Scott's voice said, *"we've got a problem. . . ."*

"The shields, I would imagine."

"They're holding, sir. Barely. Helve and Lahai are whittling away at them—Battlequeen's not in range yet. Sir, that ship looks like one of the new-model Klingon destroyers. We're going to be in deep trouble if it gets here . . . and I dinna see any way to stop it."

"Mr. Scott," Jim said, "under no circumstances are you to allow my ship to be taken." His eyes flickered to Ael, asking her silently about her crew. She simply nodded. "The Commander concurs as regards *Bloodwing* personnel aboard the *Enterprise;* you had better let them know. And should things come to that pass, blow *Intrepid*, and the station too."

"Understood," Scotty said. *"What the devil—"*

"What's wrong, Scotty? That hasn't gone wrong already, anyway."

"Ach," Scotty said, sounding disgusted, *"it's that* Bloodwing, *Captain;* she's *firin' at us now, point-blank!"*

Ael shook her head miserably and leaned it against the fire-blackened wall, sick at heart. *"Something odd about that, Mr. Scott,"* she heard Mr. Chekov say in the background.

"What then, lad?"

"Her phasers are firing at minimum intensity, Mr. Scott," Chekov said, his voice sounding very odd—almost jubilant. *"No effect on our screens—"*

"Give me a power consumption curve on her."

"Normal, Mr. Scott! No damage to Bloodwing, *no engine trouble and she doesn't have her shields up—"*

"Scotty," Jim said urgently, "hail her!"

"Uhura—"

In the background they could hear Uhura opening a frequency, challenging *Bloodwing*. "On screen, Mr. Scott—"

"*Enterprise*," came a familiar voice—Aidoann, frantic, but thinking as usual. The sickness about Ael's heart came undone, and she sat up straight. "*Mr. Scott, where's the Commander?*"

"Scotty," Jim said, "patch me through! Aidoann, this is Kirk, the Commander's with us and well—"

"*Captain,*" Aidoann said, "*you must get out of there! We can't keep up this pretense much longer, the other ships will be within range to read our status on sensors—*"

"Energize, wide scan!" Ael cried. "You can take us in three groups, four at the most! Beam us over to *Intrepid!* Captain, where? Their Rec room?"

"Yes—! Spock, warn everybody—Scotty, give *Bloodwing* our coordinates, take everybody with a translator installed, the Vulcans have them too! Hurry it—"

The phaser fire broke out close behind them. People threw themselves in all directions, firing back—

—and the world dissolved in a storm of crimson dazzle, the form of fire that Ael decided right then she would always like best—

O, by my Element!! she thought, as *Bloodwing*'s transporter let go of her and dropped her six feet to the carpeted floor. The carpet was no help; she heard various *Enterprise* people complaining about the drop, though the Vulcans all somehow seemed to come down on their feet. "Move it," Jim was shouting, "get off the coordinates, there're two more groups coming—!"

People scrambled desperately for the walls. Ael ran

with the rest, pausing only long enough to scoop up Dr. McCoy in the process and drag him along with her; he had been trying to stand and failing. Now he was testing his left leg for breaks and saying a great many things that her translator flatly refused to render. She dropped him more or less against the wall, looking frantically around her to see how her people were doing. In midair another great group of people materialized and, slam!, fell to the floor. "Never complain about our transporters again," McCoy was growling behind her, "*yours* are even worse!"

"Physician," Jim said, kindly but hastily, as he came up behind Ael, "stuff thyself. Better still, get down to the Sickbay with Dr. Seiak and start healing some of these people." He paused, watching the third group materialize and go *slam!*; then lifted his communicator again. "Scotty, is that it?"

"It is, Captain," Aidoann said. *"We've got to put our screens up; and they're getting close enough to hear our 'com.* Enterprise, *we're with you!"*—and she closed her channel down.

Ael began holding her breath.

"We've got a hole card, Mr. Scott," Jim said, as jubilant as Chekov had been. "We're going to get this creature going—"

"But she's cold! It'll take fifteen minutes, Captain—"

"Hold as you can, Scotty. If the situation becomes unsaveable, my earlier orders stand. No more communication, or you'll give away the fact that there's someone on this ship."

"Aye. Good luck, sir—"

"Same to you, Scotty. Out."

Sehlk and T'Leiar had found Jim. "Sir, we have a problem—"

"Where's Captain Suvuk?"

"Still out, in Sickbay. Captain—"

"I know. Cold engines."

"It would not be a problem," Spock said from behind Jim, "if we had some 'hot' antimatter to seed the reaction."

"Too late for a jumpstart," Jim said. "*Enterprise* and *Bloodwing* both have their screens up, and they can't drop them—"

—and Ael let out the breath she had been holding at the sound and sight of a final shimmer of *Bloodwing* Transporter effect in the middle of the room. The forms solidified: Tr'Keirianh and t'Viaen from her engine room, and between them a magnetic bottle in an antigrav mount. Her two crewfolk fell and got up again, complaining softly. The bottle in the mount just hovered there.

"Captain," Ael said, "you were saying you needed some antimatter?"

He *stared* at her.

"I ordered it readied after the question of cold engines came up in the briefing," she said. "Unfortunately things got so busy—"

"Lady," he said, once again with that peculiar courtesy—and then stopped, and shook his head. "Never mind. Mr. Spock, Mr. Sehlk, come along. Sehlk, we're going to do something illogical and very effective to T'Leiar's engines. . . ."

The Bridge of the *Intrepid* was if possible even lovelier than that of the *Enterprise*—bigger, more open and modern. And at the moment it was rather livelier, with T'Leiar holding down the center seat, and people and communications crackling in all directions. It amused Ael that while down in the station, under the worst possible circumstances, the Vulcans had seemed so very marvelous—and now, back on their own ship and theoretically in worse danger than before, they were all immersing themselves in an (apparent) calm that was utterly prosaic by comparison. *Territoriality,* Ael thought, *as strong as a Rihannsu's. They are a lot more fun when they're in trouble. Look at T'Leiar, she was like a mad thrai when she was fighting; now there's nothing left but a businesswoman—*

"Transporter room," T'Leiar was saying, "report! Is the transportation of the genetic material complete?"

"The last load is coming aboard now, Commander."

"Are you quite certain everything's there?"

"Commander," said the serene Vulcan woman on the other end of the conversation, *"we have beamed up every piece of archival copy, of any sort, in the entire station. Tapes, paper, film, metal—nothing was missed. Number four cargo hold was filled entirely with the papers and tapes alone. The genetic material took up six and nearly all of seven. . . ."*

"Very well. Engineering," T'Leiar said. "Captain Kirk?"

"Kirk here. Five more minutes, T'Leiar—the warp engines are in restart cycle now, and Spock and Sehlk are in decontamination. Sihek says you can have impulse, though, if you want it."

"Excellent. Si'jsk, take us out at maximum impulse. Advise *Enterprise* and *Bloodwing.*"

"T'Leiar," said Jim from Engineering, *"have them lay in courses for eta Trianguli—but have them depart this area in three different directions."*

"Sir," T'Leiar said politely, "there are only two of them."

"Noted, Commander, but I want you to do it too. . . ."

"That is what I thought you meant, Captain. But ambiguity might—"

"*Yes, I suppose it might. Is Commander t'Rllaillieu there?*"

"Here, Jim," Ael said.

"*I forgot to say thank you.*"

"For what?"

"*The antimatter.*"

"No matter," Ael said. "Perhaps I'll borrow a cup of it from *you* some day."

Jim chuckled. "*Oh, oh. Sorry, T'Leiar, Terran error creeps into a calculation again. No warp engines in five minutes.*"

"No, Captain?"

"*No, warp capacity* now. *And here come Spock and Sehlk early.*"

"Noted, sir. Mz. T'Kiha, how far are we from this system's primary?"

"Three hundred million kilometers, madam. Well outside the warpflight boundary."

"That's well. Warp two immediately, accelerate to warp six as soon as feasible. Advise *Enterprise* and *Bloodwing*. Mr. Setek, arm photon torpedoes and report when phasers are ready."

"Photon torpedoes charging now. Phasers ready—"

"Good. Pursuit, T'Kiha?"

"*Lahai* and *Helve* are in pursuit, but not keeping pace," said the helm officer. "Slipping behind. Also, *Enterprise* reports dropping its last jamming buoy."

"Excellent. What is *Battlequeen*'s status?"

"Gaining on us, madam. Warp six and accelerating rapidly."

T'Leiar's face, for all its immobility, indicated that she did not consider *that* excellent. "Evasive."

"Commencing."

Ael sat down at a side station. It was good evasive action, but not as inspired as Mr. Sulu's—and *Battlequeen* was still chasing them. "Mz. T'Leiar, may I suggest something?"

The Bridge doors hissed open. "You snake," Jim said, "what have you got in mind this time?"

"Why, only this—" She saw Jim wince, and laughed, considering that they were still living with the results of the last time she had said those words—and might yet die of them. "Jim, there's *Battlequeen* coming—"

"So I see," Jim said, annoyed. It was hard to miss that ship. "Even with *Intrepid's* new engine refit, I don't think we can outrun one of those things. And I know *Enterprise* can't. So?"

"Well." Ael reached into her pocket and pulled out a logic solid.

"You want us to fake a Romulan ID?" Jim said, half teasing, half annoyed. "Ael, this is no time—"

"Of course it isn't, you fool." Heads turned around the Bridge, and Ael ignored them. "Before Spock started infecting the Levaeri computers, I was looking through the system and stumbled on something interesting." She juggled the solid lightly in one hand. "The Sunseed program."

He stared at her blankly.

"Sunseed!" Ael said. "They had to have it to catch all those little Vulcan ships, Jim." She held it up in front of his face. "Wouldn't you like to start your very own ion storm—and leave those three ships to founder in it? Here's the program."

"Oh my *God*," Jim said. "Sehlk!"

The doors hissed open. "Will I do, Captain?" said a mellow voice—and Captain Suvuk walked in. He looked wasted and tired, and the plast that McCoy and Sihek had put on him did little more than cover the worst of his facial wounds; the thought of what injuries lay hidden under the uniform was terrifying. But the man was all power and certainty, though he staggered, and had to support himself on the back of his center seat as he stepped down to them.

"Sir—" Jim said.

"I heard," Suvuk said. "I have been listening from Sickbay. Commander," he said to Ael, "there would be a certain irony in turning against our pursuers the weapon they used on us. Am I correct in hypothesizing that we are going to need a star to make this work?"

"Yes, sir." She and Jim followed Suvuk up to the communications station. "We would be stimulating the star's corona not only with phasers and photon torpedoes, but our own warpfield. I understand that though it works well enough with one ship, it would do better yet with two, or three—"

"Two, I think, Commander," said Suvuk. "I doubt *Bloodwing* could match the"—he paused to put the solid down on the comm station's reading plate—"the warp eleven speeds that this requires. And we have little time to implement; the fewer ships we must coordinate in this maneuver, the better. I see that the parameters and frequencies for the phasers are adaptable to our standards. T'Leiar, pass this information on to *Enterprise*—"

"Already done, sir."

Ael blinked. "Intrepid," Scotty's voice said, *"this is* Enterprise—"

"I'm here, Scotty," Jim said. "Don't stop for discussion. Do it!"

"Aye, sir." And Scotty switched off.

"Timings, sir—"

"I am adding them now," Suvuk said. The Bridge doors opened and Spock came hurriedly in, followed by

Sehlk. "Sir, what are we—" they both said, practically in unison, to Jim and Suvuk respectively.

"What a fascinating program," Suvuk said mildly. "Mr. Sehlk, pass these phaser settings and photon torpedo dispersal patterns on to the weapons officer at once. Do you see the ingenuity of it, madam, gentlemen? The ionization effect propagates from the star's coronal discharges, but in a spiral pattern like a pulsar's series of 'rotating' wavefronts. Of course we shall have to get quite close to that star, inside the warp boundary in fact; but paradoxically the stimulation of the corona will keep the stellar chromosphere from being over-stimulated, a most elegant—"

"Sir," Sehlk said, in a voice that sounded much more like Jim's than like Spock's; and Suvuk turned, looking calmly at his First Officer with an expression more like Spock's than like Jim's. Ael raised one hand to hide her mouth. *Enterprise reports ready.*"

"Mr. Sehlk, a word with my ship, if I may?"

Sehlk nodded at the 'com console, and the Vulcan communications officer looked up at Jim. *"Scott here,"* said that oddly-accented voice.

"Just this, Scotty. Be careful not to set up a backlash effect—this is *not* the time to go back in time twenty-four hours!"

"Aye, indeed, Captain," Scotty said, as close to laughter as Ael had heard him in some time. *"Good luck to you. And to* Intrepid.*"*

"The same from them," Jim said, looking at Suvuk's calm face. "Out."

"Battlequeen is closing with us, Captain," said Sehlk. "One light-minute and closing."

"Implement the ion-storm maneuver, then," said Suvuk.

The ship's great warp engines began to roar. Ael,

glancing at Jim, noticed that he had found himself an empty station and had closed the anti-roll arms down over his thighs: Spock was doing so on the other side of the room. Ael sat down at one of the security stations and did the same. Suvuk, hanging on to things all the way down, found his way to the center seat.

"Computer lock on the star," Suvuk said. "Shut down ship's sensors for the closest part of the pass. Screen off."

It was just as well, for they were already closer to the Levaeri primary than Ael had ever wanted to be to any star; she could see its corona already beginning to flare and twist wildly at their approach. Unfortunately, there was now no telling except by report how *Bloodwing* was doing, or how close *Battlequeen* was getting. . . .

Ael began to sweat. The thought of Lyillu blowing them all up was bad, but the thought of him getting hold of them and taking them back to ch'Rihan was worse still. *O, Elements,* she thought, *if it has to be one or the other, let him blow us up!* Then she rebuked herself; perhaps the *Enterprise* people would prefer to survive, on the grounds that while there was life there was hope. *They may have something there,* she thought. *I have never seen such a lot of survivors. . . .*

The Bridge doors hissed open again, and there was Doctor McCoy, hobbling in, with his left leg in a light pressure cast. He walked slowly over to where Jim was sitting, braced himself firmly against the rail, and said, "Broken fibula. I told you this'd happen that some day."

"Doctor," Ael said, laughing at him, "if you have been predicting such an occurrence for so long, why are you surprised that it happened?"

"As for *you*," McCoy said, "with this damn fool idea of yours, let me tell you, young lady. . . ."

Ael said nothing, but the look Jim traded with her told her that she had been admitted to a very exclusive group: those people McCoy would rant at. She let him rant, and nodded contritely in all the right places, and otherwise concentrated on what was going on.

"One hundred million kilometers from the star," Sehlk said. "Ninety million . . . sixty . . . thirty . . ." *At this speed,* Ael thought, amazed, *if I blink I'll miss it.* . . . And indeed, a second later, everything seemed to happen at once. *Enterprise* and *Intrepid* dove into the star's corona together; *Intrepid* shook hugely as she first hit the star's bowshock at multiples of the speed of light, then created another of her own, trailing jointly behind her and *Enterprise.* The ship lurched again, and again, as photon torpedoes and phasers fired. Then a third terrible lurch of heaviness, and stomach-turning lightness, and normal weight again, as the artificial gravity wavered, the ship malfunctioned in trying to compensate for the star's terrible mass, and slowly went back to normal again.

"Report," Suvuk said, as calmly as if he did this every day.

"Enterprise reports intact, Captain," said Sehlk. "Maneuver complete. *Helve* and *Lahai* are far behind, not even in the area. *Battlequeen* is hitting the bow-shock of the ion storm now—"

"Force reading, please."

"Force twelve and escalating."

"Evidently you were right, Commander," Suvuk said to Ael. "It is more effective with two starships. They are getting rather worse than they gave us as a distraction."

"Communication from *Bloodwing,* Commander t'-Rllaillieu," said the comm officer. "They report they are cutting across our hyperbola to meet us, ahead of the ion storm. Rendezvous in approximately four minutes—"

"Thank you," Ael said.

"*Battlequeen* is slowing somewhat, Captain," said Sehlk. "Possibility that her navigations are going out on her due to the extreme intensity of the storm—"

"Intrepid, *this is* Enterprise," said Scotty's voice.

"This is *Intrepid,*" Jim said, at a nod from the Vulcan comm officer. "How's she riding, Scotty?"

"*Smooth enough so far,*" Scotty said, "*but we'd best pour it on a bit. That lad behind us isn't taking no for an answer; he's come through the far side of the bowshock and he's accelerating again. Maintaining warp eleven cruise speed on the eta Trianguli course.*"

"Noted, *Enterprise,* we will match you," Suvuk said. "Screen on, Sehlk. Deflector shields up; phasers ready. Commander, can *Bloodwing* maintain a warp eleven cruise?"

"Not for more than a few minutes, Captain," she said. Her hands had been sweating now for several minutes over just that issue.

"Very well. *Enterprise, Bloodwing* cannot match warp eleven. I suggest we maneuver close enough together to allow a joint warpfield, and take her into it."

"*Captain Suvuk,*" Scotty said, sounding very distressed, "*wi' all due respects, that's extraordinarily dangerous for two ships of the same model, let alone ones with different engine specs—*"

"—which we now have," Suvuk said. "Granted, Mr. Scott, but we cannot leave *Bloodwing* behind, either. Do you wish to speak to your Captain?"

"*Not now,*" Scotty said, "*but I will later. . . . Implementing, sir. Scott out.*"

Suvuk looked at Jim with calm approval. "Sir, have

you ever noticed that while we run our ships, our engineers own them? . . ."

Ael watched the slow smile cross Jim's face. He said nothing, only turned back to the screen.

"Rear view," Sehlk said. And there was *Enterprise,* great and shining, all white fire and stark black shadows from the Levaeri primary, and growing dimmer as they fled the system. She was getting quite close . . . pulling up alongside the *Intrepid* now, the two of them streaking along much closer together than any two ships traveling at warpspeed had any right to be. "Coming up on *Bloodwing*'s position." Sehlk said. "She is accelerating to warp eleven to meet us. —Warpfield match with *Enterprise*—"

Intrepid lurched again, a violent motion that made the earlier shaking seem very mild. "Warpfield match with *Bloodwing,*" Sehlk said—and this time even a few of the Vulcans went flying about the Bridge.

Not Suvuk; he might as well have been glued into his center seat. "Match complete," he said. "Mz. T'Khia, head for the Zone, eta Trianguli course—"

"Battlequeen gaining on us again, Captain," Sehlk said. "Warp twelve . . . warp thirteen . . ."

"We cannot long maintain our lead," Suvuk said, looking over at Jim and Ael, "not while they pursue at warp thirteen."

"Fourteen now," said Sehlk. Spock looked across the Bridge at Jim and shook his head, ever so slightly.

"Recommendations, Captain? Commander?" Suvuk said.

"Not to be taken, sir," Jim said.

"Commander?"

"I agree."

"My ship has such orders already," Jim said.

Suvuk nodded.

293

"Battlequeen is once more at one light-minute," Sehlk said. "One-half light-minute—"

"Captain," Suvuk said, "by the way—though thanks are said by some to be illogical—thank you for another three hours of life."

Jim bowed where he sat, straightened again. "My only regret is that I could not return you to your ship before this," Suvuk said quietly. "Or you to yours, Commander."

"The fortunes of war, sir," she said.

"If fortune exists," Suvuk said. "And if this is war. At any rate, I thank you also, Commander. It has been an unexpected—gratification—to discover that our cousins may also be our brothers."

Ael bowed her head too.

"One-tenth light-minute," Sehlk said into the great quiet of the Bridge.

"Enterprise," Jim said.

"Aye," Scotty's voice came back—and that was all he said.

"Bloodwing," Ael said.

"Commander—"

"Wait for it," Ael said softly. "We shall meet shortly."

"Four light-seconds," said Sehlk.

Ael saw Jim look across the Bridge at Spock, a long glance: then another one, up at McCoy. And then at the screen, toward the empty space ahead of them, toward the border of the Zone, that they would never reach.

"One light-second," Sehlk said. "She's firing—"

The ship rocked. And rocked again, but not with the same sort of response. Someone was firing phasers near their warpfield, distorting it from the leading side.

"Contacts—" Sehlk cried. "ID's—"

But Ael sat up in her seat with a cry. There was no identifying them by shape, those white streaks that fled past them, lancing the starry night with fire; but she knew what they were. *"Constellation,"* Mr. Sehlk said, "and behind it, *Inaieu—"*

Ael turned and stared at Jim in astonishment. He was still staring at the screen, as if turning might change what had been. "They're firing," said Sehlk. *"Battlequeen* is turning to engage *Constellation*. Firing at her—"

He flicked a switch, reversed the screen. Behind them a sudden great flare and violence of light appeared, spreading outward and outward. Very slowly, Sehlk sat down at his station.

"Inaieu fired at *Battlequeen* point blank *en passant*," he said. *"Battlequeen* is destroyed."

"What about *Inaieu?"* Jim said, not looking away from the screen.

"Intrepid," said the 'com. *"This is* Inaieu. *Suvuk, you old villain, where have you been? Shirking again?"*

"Without a doubt, Nhauris," said Suvuk. "Just as at Organia."

"Nhauris," Jim said, "nice job."

"I keep my appointments," the Denebian said, and laughed her bubbly laugh. *"Let's get across the Zone, gentlemen, before more of the Romulans notice that the silver is missing.* Inaieu *out."*

"Reduce speed, T'Khia," said Suvuk, "and set a course."

"Aye, sir."

Ael got free of her seat and went over to Jim, unable to stand it anymore. He looked away from the screen and regarded her with a truly insufferable smile.

"How did you do that?" she cried. "You called it to the minute, to the second, in all these light-years of space? How!"

He did not answer her but McCoy, who was looking at him in an astonishment as great as hers, but quieter. "You did tell me," Jim said mildly, "that I should have more confidence in my game. . . ."

Nineteen

"*Captain's log,* stardate 2816.3:

"According to our patrol orders, we are continuing Neutral Zone patrol until such time as the starships *Potemkin* and *Hood* arrive to relieve the task force.

"The Zone has been unusually quiet since we left Romulan space. Captain Rihaul has speculated that this has to do with our possession not only of the pirated Vulcan genetic material (which the Romulans may fear we will use against them) but the Sunseed ion-storm generation program, very obviously worked out in their own programming languages and protocols, on their media, and with much documentation concerning the Romulan High Command's complicity with the Senate and Praetorate in the alteration of the weather hereabouts. We suspect we will not be hearing much out of the Zone for a while, as the Empire becomes busy shaking itself up.

"I am entering requests for special commendations for the following personnel: First Officer Spock, Lt. Cmdr. Harb Tanzer, Lt. Cmdr. Nyota Uhura, Lt. Hikaru Sulu, Lt. Pavel Chekov. There are many, many others on the general commendations list (see attached).

"Meanwhile, the crew of *Bloodwing* (formerly ChR *Bloodwing)* are preparing to depart. If it were possible to request a commendation for their Commander, Ael t'Rllaillieu, I would do so. She has at all times exhibited an integrity and courage which give the lie to many of our cherished old myths about Romulans."

. . . And there he stopped, apparently unsure what to say next, or whether to say anything. He clicked the viewer off. "Ael," Jim said, "where *are* you headed?"

She turned to him from studying the medical scanner over one of the beds in Sickbay, where they had been taking care of the worst injured of her people with McCoy. "There is a lot of space," she said, "that neither Federation nor Empire owns; a lot of planets where a trim ship can make its own way, hiring out as a mercenary ship, a free trader . . . perhaps a pirate. . . ."

"Ael! . . ."

"Oh come," she said. "You know me better than that by now. Or you should."

He swung back and forth gently in the chair. "Space hereabouts will not be safe for us," Ael said, looking up at the scanner again. "We have exposed the mind-researches and Sunseed, and destroyed a great deal of supposedly indestructible Romulan material. Very embarrassing. They will not dare to strike at you in revenge—even if they find themselves able to get at you. Rihannsu have no luck with *Enterprise*, that's certain. . . ."

"The Vulcans would be glad to have you," Jim said. "If Spock's and Suvuk's word weren't enough—and I assure you they are—you've done more for that species—"

"I did not do it for them," Ael said. "I did it for my Empire, and my oaths. I will not take coincidental thanks, or gratitude that is offered me for the wrong reasons."

Her eyes rested on the door to the other room, where McCoy was working. "What about him?" Jim said quietly.

"He will not live," Ael said, her back turned. "My doing."

Jim looked at the table. "You can't blame yourself—"

"It is not a question of blame." Her voice was calm enough, but oh, the bitterness buried in it. "It's merely the way the universe is, the way the Elements are. Become careless with fire, and sure enough, fire will burn you. Do treachery, and treachery will be done you. Kill, and be punished with death. All these I've done. Now I pay the price, in my own flesh and blood. And more: for I'll die far from home, unless I dare the ban in my old age, and walk on ch'Ríhan again, to be killed by the first person who recognizes me. And there will be no child or friend to hang up the name-flag for me before I die; no family, no one but my faithful crew who go into exile with me. Family . . . but not the same. Never the same." She looked at him, almost in pity now. "And I would do it again, all of it. You still don't understand. . . ."

Jim looked up at her sorrowfully, again unable to find anything useful to say. "When will you be leaving?" he said at last.

"Ten or fifteen minutes."

"I'll meet you in the Transporter Room."

Jim went out.

It was a relief, like a weight lifted, when he was gone. But the worse weight came right down on her as McCoy came out of the next room, and looked at her, and shook his head slightly.

"His brainstem and spine were severely damaged," McCoy said. "Nonregenerable. He'll die if he's taken off support."

"And if he is not?"

"A few days of pain. A few hours, if he's lucky."

"But the same result."

"Yes." McCoy's voice was quiet, and very sad.

Ael bowed her head and went in.

There he lay, looking waxen already; and the pulled-up blanket only accentuated the place where his right arm had been. She stood by the bed a long time before speaking.

She could not see him as he was, close to death. All she could see was ten years ago, twenty years, forty: a child waving a toy sword and saying he would be like his mother. So he had been; and this was where the likeness had led him.

"You saw my writings," Tafv said, a thread of voice, thinned to breaking.

Ael nodded. His room's computer had been full of them. Years he had been planning this revenge for his beloved cousin. Oaths did not stand in his way when his opportunity arose, any more than they had stood in Ael's way when she saw her chance to betray Levaeri V, and *Cuirass*, and all the others. He had been preparing for that opportunity for a long time, suborning the newer members of her crew with money and the promise of power; and the delivery of *Enterprise* into his hands had seemed to Tafv to be a gift from the Elements. What he would have done with it, and with her, that Ael knew from his writings too. He would have become rich, and famous, and powerful in Command. She would have been swiftly a prisoner, and then a corpse. He had never forgiven her for falling silent before the Senate, for ceasing to try to save his cousin, the young Commander, though the attempt might have killed her, and Ael too.

"I did what I had to," he said. "I would do it again. It was *mnhei'sahe*."

"I understand," she said.

"Now you must also do what *mnhei'sahe* requires," he said. And the effort exhausted him, so that he lay gasping.

She stood a long time before she could agree. And then she did what she had to; for treachery had no payment but death.

When she went out again, McCoy stood aside for her, not moving, not speaking. She paused long enough to trade a long glance with him.

"Thank you," she said, and left.

And then there was only one more barrier: the Transporter Room, where Jim waited. At least there was no one else there.

"Spock asked me to make his farewells for him," Jim said.

"He is a prize, that one," she said. "All the Elements

walk beside you in him. Take all care of him—and thank him well for me."

"I will."

She turned toward the platform. Jim made a small abortive motion that somehow made Ael stop.

"You never did tell me what 'Jim' meant," he said.

Ael looked at the closed door, and at the intercom to see that it was off, and she told him.

He started to laugh—very hard, as might have been expected—and to her own great surprise, Ael started to laugh with him. "Oh," Jim said after several minutes, "Oh, oh, no wonder. . . ."

"Yes."

He stood there with his arms folded—a gesture left over from the way he had been hugging himself while he laughed; seemingly to keep from hurting his stomach, or because it already hurt. This man . . .

"Now let me tell you what 'Ael' means," she said, glancing again at the closed door. She told him. She told him what the second name meant, and the third. And then—very quietly—the fourth.

He looked at her and said nothing at all. It seemed to be his day for it.

Ael stepped up onto the Transporter platform, and waited for him to step around to the controls. The singing whine scaled up and up in the little room. And bright fire began to dissolve them; the overdone little room in the great white ship, and the man who had no fourth name to give her in return.

But no, she thought. *He* has *a fourth. And he gave me not just the name—but what it names.* Her . . . *whole and entire.*

To her relief, and her anguish, the Transporter effect took her away before she could move to match him, daring for daring, with an equal gift.

Twenty

Jim stood there quietly for a good fifteen minutes, considering the words he had been told, especially the fourth one—considering the nature of the sword that had cut him. *Entirely appropriate,* he thought, remembering Ael in Spock's quarters. After all, a sword was a thing of air and fire; and it was almost universally true that, with the best swords, you might not even know you'd been cut until you began to bleed. . . .

He left the Transporter Room, heading for the Bridge: something familiar, something his, something he could control.

Something he had not lost.

It was two months' work, getting back to Earth this time, and then several days of dull and depressing debriefing on the Levaeri incident.

He put up with it all; it was part of the price of

captaincy, after all. But his mind was elsewhere, especially on the last day.

By luck, or something else, the debriefing that day was at Fleet San Francisco, and the *Enterprise* was right overhead in synchronous orbit. He got out of the offices around five, went out into the fog, and called Spock; then once aboard, went down to his quarters to pick up the small object he was after, and take it right back to the Transporter Room.

The transporter chief had left—which suited Jim well. He paused only long enough to bring up a visual of Earth on the screen and note with satisfaction that the terminator had crept barely past the California coast; Seattle and San Francisco and Los Angeles were tiny golden spatters against a velvet darkness ever so faintly silvered with moonlight. *Perfect,* he thought, killing the screen. Jim set the transporter for the coordinates he wanted, checked his belt for his communicator, and set the console for delayed-energize.

When the shimmer died he looked around him a bit warily—he hadn't been to these coordinates in years, and there was no telling how much the place might have changed. But he was pleasantly surprised to see that it was no different at all. Jim was surrounded by high hills, soft rounded shapes covered with scrub oak and manzanita, wild olive and piñon pine, and here and there a palm. The cooling air was sweet with sage and with the wet green smell of the creek in the gully to his right. It ran where it had run, where it should run, whispering around what seemed the same old stones. Jim smiled. Sometimes, just sometimes, things stayed the way they were supposed to.

He began to walk along the top of the gully, upstream, toward the creek's source. A long time it was since he had last been here at Sespe. Once it had been a condor preserve, hundreds of years ago when the great birds were in danger of becoming extinct. Now that they flourished, Sespe was just another part of the North American Departmental Wilderness that surrounded it—a trackless, houseless place, accessible only on foot, or by transporter. Indeed Jim could have beamed directly to the place where he was headed but he wouldn't have had time to get in the mood for what he had in mind. He started off into the great silence, moving as softly as he could; for there was no sound anywhere but the bare breathing of the wind, and his footsteps seemed too loud for the twilit sanctity of this place.

He passed other streambeds in the gathering dusk. They were dry, as well they might have been this time of year. But the watercourse Jim followed as he trudged up the hill was not affected by the weather. Breathing a bit harder than usual with the steady exertion, Jim kept climbing, making his way around the shoulder of one hill, crossing the stream with a splash and a shock of cold when he found this side blocked with an old rockfall. Another twist in the watercourse, and then one more—

Jim stopped. It was exactly the same, *exactly*. From the side of a high, dark hill, water sprang, slowing down as if from a smitten rock; and above the spring-source, growing straight out of the sheer hillside and then curving upward, there was the tree. It had apparently known some hard times since Jim had seen it last. It was lightning-blasted, this old twisted olive, so that branches were missing at the top; and the clawmarks of black bears, their calling cards for one another, were scored deep and ragged down its trunk. But the tree survived. Its roots were still sunk deep in the heart of the hill, and the sharp aromatic scent of its ripening fruit hung on the still air. Jim looked up at the tree with silent approval and began to climb the hill toward it.

Reaching it took some doing—the stones of the hillside were loose—but Jim perservered. Finally he reached the great horizontal truck, swung himself up onto it and stepped out to where the tree's branches began to curve outward. One strong branch thick with olives reached out over the spring; the smell of splashing water and of new fruit mingled, a cool spicy scent of life. *Here*, Jim thought, *right here*. He took out the small bundle he had brought with him from the ship, untied the cord around it, and shook out the little pennon—a strip of supple woven polymer that would hang here and last through years of wind and rain, unchanged. Fasteners—Jim felt in his pocket for them, threaded the polymer strips through the eyelets in the pennon, then reached out to hold them shut around the tree branch one at a time, melting them shut with bursts from his phaser on its lowest notch.

Then down the tree again, and back to his vantage point by the streambed. The pennon hung down, swinging very slightly in a breath of breeze that came down over the hillside—the pennon's scarlet muted in this darkness to an ember-gray, the black characters on it hardly visible except as blurs of shadow. Jim looked up at the sky. Not much of it was visible, hemmed about as he was by hills; but the brightest stars were out already, and others followed. The summer Triangle, Deneb and Vega and Altair, lay westering low. Jim smiled slightly at Deneb, then let his eyes drift on northward through the base of the Triangle, following the faint band of the Milky Way and the Galactic Equator through Cygnus into Lacerta, Cassiopeia, Andromeda. There was beta Andromedae; then a bit southward . . . Jim stood and waited for his eyes to get used to the gathering darkness. He knew he wouldn't be able to see the star he was looking toward, anyway. But right now, sight, or eyesight anyway, wasn't an issue. He waited.

And when he felt the moment was right, he drew himself straight and spoke her name the necessary five times—the fourth name by which only one closer than kin might know her, the name by which one was known to the Elements and Their rulers. One time each he spoke that name for the earth, the air, the fire, the water; and once for the Archelement which encompassed them all, that It might hear and grant the weary soul a home in this place when at last that soul flew. The fifth time he said that name, the wind died. A listening stillness fell over everything. Jim didn't move.

That was when the great dark shape came sailing over the hilltop, low; planing down over the stream on twelve-foot pinions, black-feathered, showing the wide white coverts under the wings; a dark visitation of silence, grace, freedom, flight, indifference. Riding its thermal, the condor swept over Jim's head, a shadow between him and the stars. It tilted its head as it passed—a glance, no more, a silhouette motion and a look from invisible eyes. Then it leaned to its port side, banked away on the thermal, was over the next hill, was gone.

The sigil-beast of my House, she had said.

A big, ugly scavenger . . . but nothing can match it when it flies. . . .

Jim stared after it, and let out a small breath of bemusement, uncertainty, wonder. *How about that*, he thought. The night breeze began to blow again; bound to the olive branch, the name-flag stirred.

Jim pulled out his communicator. "Kirk to *Enterprise*."

"Spock here."

"Mr. Spock, have someone get down to the Transporter Room and beam me up."

"Yes, Captain." There was a pause. Jim got the feeling that Spock was glancing around the Bridge to make sure no one was listening, for when he spoke again, his voice was private and low. *"Jim—are you all right?"*

"I'm fine." Jim looked down the watercourse, the way the dark apparition had gone, and for the first time in days, actually felt relieved. The feeling was very belated. He didn't care; he embraced it. "Mr. Spock . . . you don't suppose there might be some spot in the Galaxy where we're needed right now, do you?"

"Captain," the calm voice came back, *"our new patrol-information dispatches just received from Starfleet this past hour include news of two armed rebellions, a plague, and a mail strike; various natural disasters attributed to acts of Deity, and unnatural ones attributed to inflation, accident and the breakdown of diplomacy; seventeen mysterious disappearances of persons, places or things, both with and without associated distress calls; eight newly discovered species of humanity, three of which have declared their intention to annex Starfleet and the Federation, and one of which has announced that it will let us alone if we pay it tribute. And probably most serious of all, a tribble predator has gotten loose from the zoo in a major city on Arcturus VI, and for lack of its natural prey has started eating peoples' cats."*

Jim paused. "Well, Mr. Spock," he said, very seriously, it's going to take us at least a week to get all that cleared up. I think we'd better get out there and get started, don't you?"

"Undoubtedly, Captain. Energizing."

The world faded into the golden shimmering of the Transporter effect.

The pennon stirred again, saying one dark word, a name, to the wind, in the strong Rihannsu calligraphy.

Starlight glinted on the swift water. And one small star slowly subtracted itself from that light, soaring more and more swiftly outward, past the setting sickle Moon and into the ancient night.